TO
KILL
FOR

PHILLIP HUNTER has a degree in English Literature from Middlesex University and an MA in Screenwriting from the London Institute. He was also part of the team that sequenced the human genome.

By the same author

To Die For

TO KILL FOR

PHILLIP **HUNTER**

HEAD
of ZEUS

First published in the UK in 2014 by Head of Zeus Ltd

9 7 5 3 1 2 4 6 8

A catalogue record for this book is available from the British Library.

ISBN (TPBO) 9781781853382
ISBN (eBook) 9781781853405

Typeset by Palimpsest Book Production Limited,
Falkirk, Stirlingshire

Printed and bound in Germany
by GGP Media GmbH, Pössneck

Head of Zeus Ltd
Clerkenwell House 45-47
Clerkenwell Green
London EC1R 0HT

WWW.HEADOFZEUS.COM

To my mum, Betsy, and my sister, Louise, for their
endless love and support

ONE

We burned her on the Thursday. It was one of those dull March days. There was no sky, just wall to wall grey, no colour anywhere, no sun, no wind. It wasn't warm. It wasn't cold. It wasn't anything. It couldn't even be bothered to rain.

It didn't matter.

We crawled along the Eastern Avenue and Blake Hall Road and past the Flats, and I watched people trudge by with their heads down and their hands in their pockets, pushing their children and pulling their shopping and dragging their lives about. The whole world was in mourning. I saw an old Sikh bloke by the side of the road. He watched us go by and bowed his head.

I could have carried the coffin in one arm, it was so small. Instead, four of us walked with it; me and Browne and Eddie and some bloke the funeral house laid on. Browne couldn't walk straight.

The service was a rushed job and I had the feeling the vicar, or whatever he was, wanted to get to a wedding or christening or something, anything that was far away from a lump like me and an old drunk Scot and a black gangster

1

and a small dead girl in a small brown coffin who'd never had a fucking chance. He gave us the usual such-a-tragedy spiel and mumbled a prayer or two. When he told us that she was safe now and in God's arms I wanted to grab him by his clean white collar and drag him down to where she'd held her dead, blood-soaked sister and to where she'd been used as bait for a robber who'd liked kids, and I wanted to ask him where his fucking god was then. Eddie put a hand on my arm. He said, 'Take it easy, Joe.'

Maybe he was thinking the same thing I was. Probably not.

Browne wept through the whole thing. I couldn't blame him for being drunk. He'd liked the girl. He'd thought he could help her. He'd thought he could help me. He couldn't even help himself.

Cole came to the funeral. Some of his men were around, out of the way. They were tooled up and edgy, but Cole seemed okay. He and Eddie nodded to each other. Browne avoided him.

We went to a pub afterwards, me and Browne and Eddie. A couple of East European women came in. They told us they'd worked for Marriot and they were glad he was dead and they were sorry about the girl, even though they'd never known her name. Eddie bought them a drink and they cried a bit. While we were there, other people in the pub quieted their talking and avoided eye contact and dribbled out. A thug, an old drunk Scot, a black criminal and two prostitutes sitting in a bar. It sounded like the start of a joke.

Browne was still pissed but downed a few glasses of

Scotch and managed to get pissed all over again and bawled some more, which left Eddie as the one to do the talking, even though he'd hardly known her either. He tried, though, and said things like 'She had you two at least' and 'He paid for it, Joe. Marriot. And Beckett too,' and stuff like that and all the time I sat there knowing I might've been the one who'd fired the round that killed her. It had been a blazing fight and my head wasn't right and I'd let loose my old Makarov semi-auto and shot the place to shit. So, yes, I could have been the one.

Then Eddie bought another round and raised his glass and said, 'Here's to Kid.'

And we all raised our glasses to a tiny dead African girl who was so thin I was scared of crushing her to death when I held her, and who looked at me wide-eyed and open-mouthed, like she was looking at something frightening, and who was named Kindness and who we called Kid.

TWO

I was staying at Browne's. I was still weak and I'd fucked up my arm again when I'd charged into Marriot's club and flattened the place and ripped through his men and killed the cunt as he'd tried to crawl away from me, blood trailing from his gut. So I needed to mend it, my arm.

Browne fussed over me like an old woman. In his eyes, I'd tried to save Kid. I can't say if that's true. Maybe it was more like she'd saved me. I don't know. I didn't tell him that I might've been the one who'd killed her.

I remembered that night in fragments, as if my memory had fallen to the ground and smashed, and when I looked down at it I saw only broken reflections of myself.

It was getting harder to remember things clearly, to put them in some kind of order. Events, people, time kept getting mixed up in my head so that the past and present were jumbled together. Brenda, Kid, that Argentinean conscript on the foggy mount; all these things would come to me still, and I'd be back there, with them.

What I remembered was that Marriot and Paget had used a thief called Beckett to rip off Cole. They were taking Cole's turf away from him bit by bit. I was the mug they chose to pin it on. And then Marriot had double-crossed Beckett and kept all the money for himself. That's where Kid came in. Beckett liked children, and Marriot had used Kid to get inside his place and let in the killers.

And then I went in looking for Beckett and she was there, curled up in a cupboard, nothing more than a bundle of bones and loose clothes and a .32 pointing at me.

But, of course, it went back further than that, way back into my own past, back to Brenda, and the past became the present.

So, Browne fussed over me and, in between being unconscious, kept checking my shoulder and my arm.

'This time let the bloody thing heal,' he'd say.

Cole sent some doctor round to help fix me up. The doctor was a specialist at something or other. Cole was trying to pay me back for fixing Marriot and getting his money back; money that I'd helped steal in the first place. Anyway, Browne didn't like it, this doctor turning up. Maybe Browne thought I was his patient, or maybe his ego was hurt. He cheered up when I told the other doctor to fuck off. I didn't want a gaggle of them round me all the time.

The law had to be bought off, or shut up anyhow. Nobody wanted them involved, least of all me. I'd murdered Marriot, after all. If you can call it murder, which I didn't. Anyway, Cole and Dunham had clout and they fixed the law. There was an understanding between the two of them. They were friends now, like Stalin and Hitler. They fixed it so that the blame went onto the Albanians who, like Eddie had said, were getting too big for their Albanian boots. There was a lot of stuff on the news about clampdowns on foreign gangs and the Albanians got mentioned. It suited Cole and Dunham that everyone thought they were to blame. The Albanians had brought Kid into the country in the first place, and they'd worked with Marriot, and if Cole and Dunham managed to wipe them out of existence, I, for one, wouldn't mind. So it was all neat and tidy and everybody was happy because the Albanians had been officially declared the bad guys and one thing people like is to know who the bad guys are.

Paget was still out there, of course. He was another matter. I had to get him, for my reputation if nothing else. He'd been Marriot's enforcer, his killer, his pit bull. Six years ago, Brenda had grassed Marriot to the law. He'd found out and Paget had sliced her up. I learned all that too late. Six years too late. I'd buried her death in a frozen part, hoping I'd never have to see it again. Instead, it was before me, thawing, festering in the heat of recent events.

So, I knew now what had happened, and I knew that others knew. If I let it go, I'd lose face. I tried to tell myself that destroying Paget was just business, but I don't think I believed that.

With Marriot and the others it had been different. I'd killed them because I'd had to. Marriot wanted revenge on me for what Brenda had done to him, and I'd had to hit him before he hit me. Then, too, there was the money. He'd used me to get Cole's robbery takings and I'd had to get it back because I'd been on the job and I had my reputation to keep clean. Yes, had to keep that reputation clean. It was all I had.

With Paget, it was something else. Paget was on the run and Cole was after him. I'd got Cole's money back, but Paget still had a million quid's worth of Cole's heroin. I didn't need to go looking for him; I could let Cole do that. But I wanted him, and I knew when I had him I'd tear him slowly apart. I'd murder him by inches, and murder it would be. I couldn't lie to myself about that.

THREE

Brenda.

It started with her. It would end with her, one way or the other.

Brenda.

I tried to remember her sometimes, tried to recall the best things about her. Mostly, I failed.

But there were other times when I tried not to think of her at all, other things I tried not to remember. Then, she came to me. In the darkness, she came. In the moments of madness, when my head hurt and my eyes stopped seeing what was real, she'd come and her face would be full of blood.

And yet, for a while it had seemed so ordinary between us. It had seemed just like I see it on TV, or in pubs on a Saturday night, two people, their eyes locked on each other, smiling, laughing, talking quietly as if there was nobody else in the whole world.

Well, maybe it had never been like that, but it had been almost like that. Sometimes. And those were the times I tried to remember. But, somehow, the sweetness always soured.

One time, we went to the market. I forget which one, probably Petticoat Lane or Brick Lane or one of those poncy ones with expensive gear for tourists. Maybe it was Portobello Market. They'd changed a lot since I was a kid, these markets. Back then you bought cheap boots for a tenner. Now you bought cheap rip-offs for a hundred quid.

So, we went, me and Brenda. It was a Monday and we both had the day off. This was only a couple of weeks or so after we'd started going out. I'd picked her up at her flat. She'd invited me in and made me a cup of tea. She'd made an effort, make-up and perfume and all.

She brought the tea in and handed it to me and I told her she looked nice. She smiled, that broad open smile, her eyes sparkling for a moment. She looked young when she did that.

But, then, the smile would fade and a sadness would creep into her eyes. I would think that it was me who'd caused that. I'd think that I wasn't what she was looking for. I wasn't the romantic type. I didn't know what to say, how to act. So, I'd always be expecting her to tell me it was over.

But just when I'd think that, she'd smile at me and take my arm and push herself close to me and I'd start to think that maybe I had a chance after all.

The market was busy. It was summer and hot and there were tourists and locals squeezed along the road, between stalls that sold cloth and handbags and leather jackets that smelled warm in the warm air. Brenda tottered along on her high heels, picking things up and showing them to me and saying stuff like, 'What do you think, Joe? Does it make me look sexy?'

I could never tell if she was making fun of me. I didn't much care if she was. She had that spark in her eyes. She was enjoying herself. That was all I cared about.

At one stall she tried on a pair of shoes and asked how much they were. The bloke said he'd let her have them for fifty. She put them back.

'I'll think about it,' she said.

Finally she bought some make-up stuff, beauty cream, that kind of thing.

But then something happened to her. She froze, and I looked at her and saw that her gaze was on something in the distance. I looked, but could only see a crowd of people.

I asked her what was wrong, but she only said it was too busy for her. She didn't like so many people, she said.

She dumped the creams in the plastic bag the woman had given her. Then she took my arm and said she was hungry. I was hungry too. I'd been hungry for a couple of hours.

She dragged me to a greasy spoon, well away from the market. We had burgers and chips. She ate in silence and that spark was gone from her eyes. I wondered about that.

When we were having coffee, she opened the bag of stuff she'd bought and fished through it all and then put the bag down on the floor.

'Shit,' she muttered.

I asked her what was wrong.

'Oh, it's nothing.'

'What?'

She sighed.

'I'm annoyed with myself. With this lot, this junk.'

'Why'd you buy it?'

'I dunno. Retail therapy, I suppose. Only I can't afford to really treat myself. So, I buy this crap, when what I really want is something really nice.'

She looked at me, waiting, so it seemed. Then she went back to drinking her coffee and I went back to drinking mine, thinking there was something she was waiting for me to say, not knowing what it was. I felt a fool around her, sometimes. I felt old and ugly and stupid. Usually, I didn't care about all that. But with her...

'You haven't been out with many women, have you?' she said.

The coffee cup had been halfway to her mouth. Now she'd put it down.

I thought about what she'd asked me. I'd been with women, of course. But 'out' with them?

'No,' I said. 'Not really.'

'You see,' she said, quietly, 'you're supposed to buy something for me.'

And then I went cold, and a kind of fear hit me in the guts. I call it fear, but I'm not sure that's right. I don't know that I have the words for it.

I'd known fear lots of times. You couldn't live like I had and not know it. But it was always a kind of good fear. It was something you could get hold of and fight and use. It pushed you on. It fed you.

Often, it was a fear of dying. In those times, if you tell yourself you probably will die, the fear has no way to get to you. You say, yes, I'll die, so what.

But this time, in the cafe the fear was different. It was a sick kind of fear, a terror, in a way. Mostly, though, I think it was more like sadness.

Or despair.

So, there it was. I'd wondered all along why she'd want to be with me.

I took my wallet out and started to pull some notes from it. Then she put her hand on mine, and I looked at her, not knowing what the fuck I was supposed to do. And I saw on her face I'd made a mistake. There was an odd look to her. It was almost panic.

'Christ,' she said. 'No. No.'

That first night she'd talked to me and asked me if I wanted to get a cup of tea, I'd asked her how much it would cost me. I wasn't used to any other kinds of women. And she was a pro, after all. So I just assumed I was a john to her.

But I'd hurt her that time.

And now I'd hurt her again.

'Shit,' she said. 'I didn't mean that. Oh, Christ.'

She wiped a tear away from the corner of her eye.

'Sorry,' I said, putting the money away.

I felt relief, though. I felt that.

'Is that all you think of me?' she said. 'After the time we've been together, and you just think of me as a whore?'

'No.'

I thought I'd blown it. I thought she'd get up and walk out. Instead, she was quiet for a long time, her gaze on the table top. I didn't say anything. I didn't move. I don't think I breathed, not even wanting to disturb the air in case she remembered I was there. I wanted her to forget I was there. I was offensive to her, I thought. I was a stupid lump, I thought.

But just when it seemed she was getting up the courage to leave, she looked at me and smiled a bit and said, 'I'm sorry, Joe. I'm being unfair. It's just... well, it's that men often buy something for the girl they're with, especially when they've only just started going out. And... and I thought, maybe you don't really like me.'

'I'm here,' I said.

'Yes,' she said, sliding her hand over the table. 'You are here.'

It was odd, I thought, that she was so afraid I wasn't interested in her, that I didn't want to be with her. I was no catch, I knew that, but it seemed important to her that I like her, wanted to be with her. I didn't understand it. Not then. Later, of course, I did.

After a while I told her I had to go out, make a phone call. I ordered her another coffee and told her to wait there. I went to find the geezer who'd had the shoes. He was closing up his stall, as most others were.

'Gone, mate. Sold.'

'Haven't you got another pair?'

'They're originals.'

'Huh?'

'They're from the seventies. Retro. They don't make 'em no more. I can't just go out and buy a few pairs. I can only sell what I get, see.'

'Right.'

I felt a fool, standing there. I didn't know what the fuck

I was doing, running around after a pair of shoes for some bird who'd probably ditch me in a week anyway.

Still, I stayed, looking around the stall for something to buy. The bloke carried on packing his stuff away, glancing at me now and then. Finally, he stopped, looked at me and said, 'You were here with that black bird. Tall thin girl.'

'Yeah.'

'You know, I've got a dress, cotton, would fit her to a T. It's similar to them shoes too.'

So, I bought the cotton dress. It cost me sixty quid. The bloke said that was a bargain.

I gave it to her when I got back. She went all misty eyed and smiled and unwrapped it and held it up and said, 'Oh, Joe. It's beautiful.'

I thought she was trying a bit hard.

'The shoes had gone,' I said.

'This is much better. I've got a secret place where I can put it.'

I must've looked at her a bit odd because she burst out laughing, and whacked me on the arm.

'Not there, fool,' she said.

She put a hand over her mouth, as if she'd done something wrong. Then she got a bit flustered for some reason.

'What secret place?' I said.

'Maybe I'll show you one day.'

After that, things were alright. We had another coffee then we wandered back along the market, which had all shut up by then.

I can't remember much more about that day. But when I do think of it, mostly I remember that moment when I thought I was just another punter to her, just a mug who had to give her money.

So, yes, I'd felt fear a hundred times, a thousand. And I'd learned how to live with it, how to take it out of its hollow and look at it and throw it away. After that, I'd been able to go on, face even heavy calibre Argentinean fire zipping around me, mortars thwumping away, because, when it came down to it, I don't think I'd ever really cared that much about myself.

But, for those few heavy minutes, there in that cafe, I'd been afraid, terrified that she'd up and leave. You don't know how lonely you are until you find someone, anyone. I didn't want to lose her.

I did lose her, of course. And for that Marriot was dead. And for that, I was going to murder Paget.

FOUR

Eddie came round on the Monday. I was sitting watching some old film on TV, and Browne came back from answering the door and said, 'Eddie's here. He's got some other men with him.'

Right then I knew we were all back to business as normal. The mourning was over.

I'd known Eddie for a long time. He'd been a boxer once, sponsored by Vic Dunham, a big name in London, to those in the know. They were close, Eddie and Dunham. I'd heard that Dunham had known Eddie's mum. I'd heard that he'd known her pretty well. I don't know if that was true, but there was something between the two men.

Eddie didn't stay with the fights. He switched trades, went to work for Dunham as his right hand. He had the right stuff for it. He was tough, ruthless. Perhaps not as tough and ruthless as Dunham, but much smarter.

'I told him he couldn't bring them in,' Browne was saying.

He was thinking the same thing as me. What did Eddie want? If he was here, it would be something bad.

Browne was fussing again, probably thinking I couldn't handle them. He was probably right. I was still weak.

Eddie came in and smiled. He sat down on the sofa

next to me. Browne waited and watched us for a moment, unsure now where we all stood. That was how quickly it all changed.

'How about a cuppa?' Eddie said to him.

Browne glanced at me.

'Fine,' I said.

Browne trotted off to the kitchen. Me and Eddie watched the film for a while. It was an old war film. The Nazis were the bad guys now. Browne came back with a couple of mugs of tea. He lingered for a moment then shuffled off.

I had trouble focusing on the film, and my mind kept wandering, going back to Brenda, to Kid, to anything that wasn't here and now.

I didn't want Eddie to know that. I didn't want him to think I was weak. I kept my face pointed towards the area of the TV and tried hard to bring myself back.

It was early afternoon, and getting dark. Sunlight hit the thin sky over London and spread out and carried on weakly through Browne's net curtains and after all that, died a few inches from our feet. Eddie and I watched John Mills kill some more Nazis and we sipped our tea and it was all very cosy and I wondered what Eddie's game was.

'How you feeling?' he said, watching the film.

'Fine.'

'You look half dead.'

'Yeah.'

'Any ideas what you're going to do?'

'No.'

It was hard going, all this chatter. It took all I had. I

could feel things swirling around behind my eyes, but every now and then I'd manage to get a hold.

Eddie tapped his fingers on the mug, watched the film. I don't think he'd noticed how fucked up I was.

'Cole's having trouble finding Paget,' he said finally.

'Uh-huh.'

We were both so fucking casual.

'Vic wants Cole to help sort out the Albanians. Thing is, Cole's got an itch about Paget, won't do anything until he's got that sorted.'

He waited for me to say something to that. When he got tired of waiting, he said, 'You got any ideas?'

'No.'

We sat there for a bit longer, watching the film, watching the day get darker. Finally he gave up with the tea and crumpet act and slid the mug onto the coffee table.

'Alright, Joe, I know you want Paget. I know you're going to try for him.'

I wondered why he cared so much.

'Why would I do that?'

'Vengeance.'

'That's a mug's game.'

He looked at me and smiled.

'Right. So you're not going to try and find him?'

'I'll leave it to Cole.'

'Bollocks.'

I shrugged. What was he going to do? If I'd known where Paget was, I'd have been out killing him. Eddie knew that.

'Well, if you happen to suddenly get any ideas where he is, let me know, alright?'

'Yeah.'

After he'd gone, Browne reappeared and sat down. He had a glass of Scotch.

'Is he going to be trouble?' he said.

'Maybe.'

Browne was right to fuss. I wasn't right. I didn't want him to know that. I didn't need him on my case, lecturing me, prodding me.

'Whyn't you let it go, man?' Browne said.

I didn't answer that. I don't think he expected me to.

We sat together, Browne and me, watching the day die, watching the dim light dim more. The TV blathered away. Neither of us watched it, but neither of us turned it off. It was just something to fill the silence.

Browne mumbled something.

'Huh?'

'I said she was a sweet lass. Too small to...'

Too small? Who was too small? Brenda?

No. Not Brenda.

I heard a sniffling and saw that Browne was wiping his nose. I think he was crying. He tried to hide it from me. He took a gulp of his Scotch.

'I don't understand it,' he said to the air. 'I don't understand any of it.'

I understood it, but I couldn't explain it. How can you tell someone that life is shit? How can you tell someone like Browne, who believed in hope, that believing means nothing?

'She was used,' I said. 'And she died.'

And who was I thinking of when I said that? Brenda? Kid?

I found myself trying to remember that time at the market, me and Brenda walking along, her picking things up, showing them to me.

But when I tried, I stopped seeing Brenda and started seeing the girl, Kid.

She was used. And she died.

And that had been my fault. Hadn't it?

'Joe?' Browne said. 'Are you with me, Joe? Can you open your eyes?'

Somehow, Browne was now standing above me, peering into my face. I pushed him away.

'I'm okay,' I said, knowing it was a lie, knowing, too, that Browne would know it.

There was this time when me and Browne took Kid to a market in West London. I forget where it was, but it must've been somewhere around Notting Hill. We'd gone to pick up some African food so that Browne could cook it up for the girl. He'd wanted to give her something she'd like. This had been only, what, a week or so before?

We walked along, the three of us, like someone's idea of a carnival. Browne on one side, old and thin, his greying wispy hair all over the place; me on the other, a lump, a monster, battered into ugliness. And, between us, the girl, one hand in Browne's, the other in my paw, peering around, afraid to leave us, afraid of everything, but keen to see it all.

'There,' she'd say, pointing to something.

We'd stop and look at it and Browne would hand it to her. It was never anything much, always some trinket or toy – a wooden box, maybe, or a colourful woollen hat or a cheap piece of jewellery. She liked that, the jewellery.

'That is nice,' she would say, handing it back to Browne who, in taking it from her, would gaze at her face for a moment with some expression I couldn't read.

He would've bought it for her. He would've done anything, I think, to please her. How could I ever tell him that I might have killed her? Even if it had been an accident, I think it would've been the end of him.

'Here,' the girl said, pointing to a food stall.

Me and Browne looked and all we could see was a load of roots and vegetables that we didn't know the names of. The girl picked something up and handed it to Browne. It looked more like a tree branch than food.

'Yam,' she said.

'Oh,' Browne said.

I don't think Browne knew what a yam was, but he wanted to buy her something and she wanted to please him and at least she knew what to do with a yam.

'In Nigeria I ate yams,' she told us.

'Then you'll eat them here too,' Browne said.

'She's dead,' a voice said.

I looked up at Browne. How long had he been there? 'Who's dead?'

He shook his head slowly.

'You're in bad shape,' he said.

'Fix me,' I said, trying to remember who was dead.

'Why? So you can go and get yourself broken again?'

'Yeah.'

He looked at me a long time, a kind of pain came into his face, as if he was looking at the body of an old friend, laid out in the coffin.

Then he wiped a hand over his parched mouth.

'You're an idiot,' he said.

'You're drunk.'

'And what of it? How else can I cope with you? With this?'

It was a good question. He went back to his seat, and his Scotch and his silent scolding and disappointment. I understood all that. I would've been the same if I hadn't had so much fury inside me.

I stood slowly and waited for the world to stop turning. I swallowed the bile. Browne watched me, but made no move to help.

'Christ, man, you can't do it.'

'I have to.'

'Have to what? Have to destroy the world? Yourself?'

'Yeah.'

'Wait,' he said, sighing.

He heaved himself up and slumped out of the room. When he came back he had a glass of water. He handed it to me with a couple of pills.

'That'll help your head, for a while. Do you know where you're going? What you're going to do?'

'I'm going to find a man,' I said.

Some funny little man, Brenda had called him. Funny. Yeah.

FIVE

The first thing I did the next day was go see a bloke I knew in Romford. Then I went looking for him, for the funny little man. I knew who he was. His name was Bowker.

He wasn't at the snooker club, and he wasn't at the pub they suggested. I went to his flat. After I'd banged on the door for a few minutes, a small fat lady opened up and stood unsteadily on swollen legs, her breathing raspy. It must've been an effort to get off her sofa and walk five yards to the door. She was all lumps and sags, and she smelled of stale cigarette smoke. When she saw me, she closed her dressing gown, as if she thought I might be tempted to rape her.

'Yeah?'

'I'm looking for Jim Bowker.'

'Yeah? What for?'

'I want him. That's all.'

'I don't know where he is.'

She started to close the door. I put my hand on it and pushed it back.

'Where is he?'

'I told you, I don't know. I never do.'

'Guess.'

She looked at me for a few seconds, pretending to herself that she had a choice.

I found him at a bookies' in Hackney. I waited further up the street in the car that Cole had let me have. I didn't want to go inside the bookies' because these days they all had CCTVs. After half an hour, Bowker came out, lit up a cigarette and started walking slowly in my direction. I got out of the car and crossed the road.

When he saw me, he didn't try to run or call for help. He must've heard what had happened to Marriot. He must've known I'd come for him. Maybe he thought my fight with Marriot was only to do with the Cole thing. But Bowker had set Paget onto me and Paget had tried to kill me and he damned well knew I knew that.

Maybe he just knew that running was pointless. He dropped the cigarette and crushed it out and stared at it. Then he looked up and watched as I neared.

In the daylight, his yellow skin looked paler, his eyes darker, more sunken. He still had his thirty-year-old quiff, but it was too thin to be that black. He was wearing that shabby three-piece suit. He must've had it for twenty years. He was clinging on to some idea of past success, some memory of a decent score when he'd got himself down to Saville Row and blown a load on clobber. The suit was too big for him these days. It looked like his body was shrivelling up beneath it.

I took him by the arm and steered him along the road, between people who moved aside to avoid us. When we got to a pub, I pushed him through to the car park at the back. I had a look around. There was a brick wall along two parts of the car park, but the upper stories of a few buildings overlooked it. At the side, it had access to a residential street, but little traffic went past. It was okay, I wasn't going to do anything serious. All this time, Bowker hadn't said anything, hadn't struggled.

I let him go and crowded him a bit and he pulled away from me and flattened himself against the pub wall. He tried to smile and said, 'I lost.'

I didn't know if he was talking about his betting. I didn't think so.

'You know why I'm here?'

'Paget.'

'Yeah.'

'Had no choice, Joe. You know that. Paget was after you and if he knew I'd seen you and not told him, he would've sliced me up. I had to call him.'

So, there it was. He thought I wanted him because he'd told Paget where to find me. Paget almost got me that time. Bowker thought he could sob his way out of that. He didn't know I knew about Brenda. If he'd known that, he would've run like a bastard.

'I want him,' I said.

'Can't help you. I don't know where he's gone, do I?'

'You can contact him.'

'How?'

'You called him up when you set him onto me.'

'I called him at Marriot's place.'

'You must have had another number.'

He took too long to answer me, and he knew it.

'I got a mobile number.'

'Call it. Tell him I want to meet you tonight, 2 a.m., in the car park, back of the cinema, Lee Valley leisure centre.'

'What?'

'Do it. Tell him I'm looking for him. Tell him I'm meeting you because I think you might know where he is.'

'But...'

'Do it.'

'He'll come for you.'

'That's right.'

'Fuck.'

He was in a spot. If he set up Paget, he was dead. If he set up me, he was dead.

'Fuck,' he said again. 'I can't do that. Cross Paget? Fuck that.'

'You crossed me.'

'I had to.'

'Right. And now you have to cross him.'

'Christ, Joe. He'll skin me.'

'He won't live long enough.'

'You think he'll come alone? He'll come with a fucking army.'

'Do it.'

'I ain't got a phone.'

I took a mobile from my jacket pocket and gave it to him. He looked at the phone like he'd never seen one before. Then he looked left and right, trying to find a way out of the jam he was in. He pulled another cigarette from his pack and lit it with shaking hands. He puffed on the fag for a moment, trying to think his way out. He had no chance of that. After he'd done his thinking, he fished a small black book from his jacket pocket and flicked through it. He found the number he wanted and dialled. I leaned in close so I could hear what was said. A voice came over the line. A man answered and Bowker asked for Paget. There was a pause and finally I heard Paget's voice. Bowker told Paget what I'd told him to say. Paget said, 'Really? That's very interesting.'

The line went dead. I took the phone from Bowker. Paget's mobile number was now in the memory. I put a hand on Bowker's chest.

'Now,' I said, 'tell me about Brenda.'

He stopped breathing for an instant. He said, 'Who?'

I put a fist in his diaphragm. It was only a poke, really. I wanted him to be able to talk. He doubled up and puked, his vomit splashing by my feet. He crumpled to the ground. I let him stay there until he could breathe again. Then I prodded him with my foot and told him to get up. He climbed back to his feet. His greasy quiff had fallen over his eyes.

A man came out of the pub. He looked us over.

'What's going on?'

A few people were peering at us through the window. I told the man to fuck off.

'This is my fucking pub, mate.'

I told him to fuck off again. He went back inside.

Bowker was shaking, rubbing his gut. Yellow spittle hung down from his lip and he wiped it off with a trembling hand. He couldn't look at me.

'You remember Brenda,' I said. 'Tall lady, black, worked

for Marriot. She smiled a lot. They found her in an alley, carved up.'

'Please,' he said to the ground.

'Tell me.'

'I didn't know what he was going to do, Joe. Honest.'

'Tell me.'

'I owed a lot to Jimmy Richardson. I mean, Christ, I owed a lot, twelve grand. Richardson wanted my bollocks in a sling. Paget told me he'd straighten it out if I did a small job. I had to do it. What could I do? And Paget said he just wanted a word with her.'

'You believed him?'

'No. No, I didn't. But I thought he was just going to put the frighteners on her. Maybe rough her up a bit. That's all.'

'You knew I was seeing her?'

'Course. Everyone knew. But I never thought you were a grass.'

'So you knew she was grassing Marriot up to the law, and you thought Paget was just going to rough her up?'

He looked up at me, then, and I could see that he knew he was edging closer to his own murder. He held my jacket loosely in his hands. I knocked them off.

'I don't believe you, Bowker. I think you knew what was going to happen to her.'

The pub's owner came out again, this time with a couple of other men, one carrying a snooker cue. I told them all to fuck off. They looked at me and then at Bowker. The owner dithered and said something to the others. He turned to me and said, 'I don't want no trouble.'

They turned slowly and went back inside. I didn't think they'd call the law.

Bowker was sweating now, and his hands kept coming up and holding onto my jacket and tugging it. He was looking up at me and what he saw made him hold on tighter.

I was tired of his hands on me. They were dirty and sweating and gnarled and they'd touched Brenda up. They clung to me and tugged weakly and I didn't want those hands to ever touch me again. I swiped them away and he staggered and I straightened him up.

'You killed Brenda.'

'You can't hurt me, Joe, there are witnesses. They've seen you. You're not that stupid.'

My hand was around his throat before I knew it. He gasped and struggled, but there was nothing in him, no leverage, no strength. I raised him off the ground and pushed my face into his so that I could watch his eyes as he tried to hang onto life. His face was red, his eyes bulging, his mouth twisted. His hands scrambled against my arm. There was a crackling sound coming from him. I wanted to crush his throat. I wanted to destroy him.

I didn't kill him. I should have done, but he was right, there'd been too many witnesses. And I had other things to do. I could kill Bowker later. Maybe it was a greater punishment to let him live, to let him go back to his prison flat, and to a fat wife with swollen legs who didn't care if some thug was out to get her husband, and to his lifelong losing streak.

'You grass me up to Paget about tonight and I'll know, and I'll come back for you.'

I dropped him and left him on the ground, his face in his own vomit.

I'd thought about holding onto him, using him as bait for when Paget showed up, but it was too long to wait and I didn't want him jamming up the works or delaying me. I wasn't thinking straight, I suppose. My head hurt, as it often did these days, a throbbing in the back of my skull that stretched through to my forehead and into the backs of my eyes.

I drove back to Browne's. When he saw me, he said, 'Your head again?'

'Yeah.'

He went to the kitchen and came back with a couple of pills. I wouldn't have bothered, but I had to be alert that night. I knocked them back and they wiped me out and I had to go lie down for a while.

I woke once. At least, I thought I'd woken. The girl was standing by my bed, her arms by her side and her hair hanging down in plaits. She didn't move, but stared with those large eyes. I reached out for her and touched Brenda.

SIX

The Lee Valley Centre had a sports complex; indoor courts and outdoor five-a-side pitches. It was on an industrial estate in Ponders End. At that time of night it was dark and deserted. There were no cameras. It wasn't near any residential areas, not overlooked by offices or anything like that, and the nearest blocks of flats were way over the other side of the train line. It was the best I could do.

It was nearing 2 a.m., there was no cloud cover and the air was thin and biting. I was wearing my heavy coat and a woollen hat and thick leather gloves. I knew from experience how hard it was to operate a hand-held weapon when your fingers were stiff with cold.

I stood at the back of a bank of spectators' benches. From there, I had a good view of the only road into the centre and of the car park at the back of the cinema. The films had finished an hour earlier. I'd checked on that. I'd parked my car on the other side of the cinema, out of sight. I knew I might have made a mistake by not holding onto Bowker and using him as bait. The way I'd planned it, though, I wouldn't need him.

In the distance, a mile away, I could hear the whirr of traffic along the A10. Now and then, a truck would grind along Meridian Way, but there was no reason why anything other than Paget's car would turn into the centre.

I had an old Enfield L42A1 sniper rifle. I was used to the design, so I didn't have to accustom myself to it. I'd picked it up earlier, from that bloke I'd been to see in Romford. They weren't too difficult to come by. This one was an old no. 4 that had been converted, re-barrelled to take 7.62 mil rounds. I'd test-fired it and it had worked fine. I had a full mag, and one in the chamber.

I had a large canvas bag nearby with some extra magazines. I'd put a beanbag on the bench in front of me and rested the rifle on it. It was a clear night, with quarter moonlight, and I hadn't bothered to attach a night sight, though I had one in the bag. It was still and I hadn't had to make adjustments for wind. It wasn't a great distance anyway, only about two hundred yards. I also had the Makarov in my coat pocket.

I was all set.

I waited.

My head was fuzzy, thoughts clouding over and mixing together. I still wasn't thinking clearly and that bothered me. I'd taken some heavy blows to the head in the last week or so. I'd spent a lifetime taking blows to the head, and things had been getting worse for years, but now they were worse than worse. Browne thought I might've had some swelling on the brain, and he kept a close eye on me, always asking me questions, who was the prime minister, what month was it, that sort of thing. I didn't know what pills he was giving me, but they were strong and left me dazed and unable to concentrate properly.

'Poor old Joe,' Brenda used to say, 'heading for the breaker's yard.'

She'd said that a lot. It was a kind of joke of hers; that I was like the ship in that print on her wall – the Fighting Temeraire, that old warrior being dragged to its death.

She'd smiled weakly this time, so that I knew she was trying to make light of it and not quite getting there.

For a moment I had my old SMG in my grip, not the Enfield, and I was holding it with freezing hands while my clothes were damp and heavy with sweat and wet mud. I was holding the SMG, but when I sighted along it, I saw Brenda's face staring back at me with half-closed eyes and mouth open and I knew she was dead.

They were becoming more common, these hallucinations or dreams or whatever the fuck they were. I saw Brenda and Kid, at night, in the shadows. I saw that dead Argentinean conscript staring at me with his teeth bared and the skin about his face tight and sunken. I didn't know if it was the pills Browne was giving me, or if it was something to do with the scarring on my brain. I wouldn't tell Browne, he'd only worry and fuss and I didn't need that shit.

I heard a car change down gear. I shook my head, trying to clear it, and flexed my hands. A black saloon turned off Meridian Way and drove slowly up towards me, and then made a left towards the cinema. It cruised into the car park and moved towards the back door.

I took the leather gloves off, moved forward, took a hold of the Enfield and viewed the car through the scope.

There were two men in the car: the driver plus one in

the passenger seat. The driver was lean and black, the other man was stocky and white with a shaved head. Neither of them was Paget. If I'd been thinking more clearly, I'd have realized he wouldn't come himself. I'd been so hell-bent on cornering him and gutting him that I hadn't given the plan enough thought. It was a stupid fucking mistake.

I looked through the sight and put a round in the car's rear window. The glass splintered around the hole and the car lurched right and sped up, then spun in a one-eighty and came straight back towards me. I put another few rounds in the windscreen and the car lurched again and crunched into the rear wall of the cinema.

The man on the passenger's side kicked the door open and scrambled out. He started running towards the far end of the cinema. I let off a few rounds, but he was moving all over the place and I couldn't get a bead on him. I fired a few times and missed by a mile. The first thing he was going to do when he got clear was call Paget and tell him it had been a set-up. Wherever Paget was, he would get out quick. I'd fucked the whole thing up.

I stashed the gun and beanbag in the canvas grip, slung it over my shoulder and pulled out my Makarov. I walked over to the smashed car. By the time I got there, the driver had opened his door and was stumbling away, a ragged hole in the back of his denim jacket. He was leaking blood. When I got near, he turned sharply. My Makarov was up and ready, but he wasn't armed, and the action of turning made him stagger and he crashed backwards. He yelled out in pain. His white T-shirt was soaked red from the chest down. I'd hit him high, left of his right shoulder. It looked like his collarbone was smashed. Blood was gushing out, but I didn't think he'd die just yet. He tried to get up, and managed to prop himself up on his good arm. He saw the gun.

'Don't,' he said.

'Where's Paget?'

'I don't know.'

He winced in pain.

'Don't fuck about.'

'Paget would fucking kill me.'

'You're dying now.'

He looked down at his bloody shirt and looked up at me with eyes wide. The idea that he might be dying hadn't occurred to him.

'I need an ambulance.'

'Yeah.'

'Fuck.'

His right arm was useless and he tried to get a mobile phone from his pocket with his left hand, but without that to hold him up, he fell back and the phone fell from his grasp. I stooped down and picked it up and pocketed it.

'Get me an ambulance.'

'Where's Paget?'

'Loughton.'

I could be there in ten minutes, maybe fifteen. Not enough time to try and find an address, though.

'Take me there.'

'I'm fucking bleeding to death.'

'You'll live long enough.'

'It hurts.'

'Yeah.'

I grabbed a hold of the front of his shirt and jacket and hoisted him up. I turned him round, keeping the Makarov in the small of his back, and walked him to my car. He stumbled a couple of times and I wondered if we could get to Loughton before he lost too much blood. We got into the car and I started it up and spun the wheels and fishtailed onto Meridian Way.

They hit us from three directions.

The first car came straight at us. I slammed my foot on the brakes. The second had screeched to a stop alongside, boxing us in. I threw the car into reverse and piled into the third. The impact threw me forward. My head smashed the steering wheel column. The Makarov flew from my hand. Next to me, Paget's man had bashed his head into the windscreen and shattered the glass. He fell back, blood lacing his forehead. He sat for a moment, dazed, mouth open with shock. When he saw what was happening, he woke up, fumbled with the door and managed to get it open. He fell out and two men out there grabbed him and hoisted him up and bundled him into the waiting car.

The cars reversed. They burned rubber and straightened up and drove off with squealing tires. The whole thing had taken seconds. I was seeing double after that blow on my head. I groped for the car keys and got the car started, but I stalled it. When I got it started again, I couldn't see the cars and I knew for sure I'd fucked it all up.

I'd recognized the men, though.

SEVEN

Cole lived in Chigwell, in one of those mock Tudor jobs with a lawn the size of a football pitch. It was close to 4 a.m. by the time I got there, but there were lights on in the downstairs rooms. His driveway was full of cars, one of them with a bashed-in front.

I stashed the Makarov. I wasn't at war with Cole and he would've had the advantage on me anyway. There must've been a dozen guns in that house.

There was a brick wall where his property met the pavement, and a large cast iron gate with security number pad. I jumped over the wall and clumped up his driveway, all the time feeling that I wasn't in control of things, all the time feeling that I was a fucking idiot.

I banged on the front door. The door opened and a small bald man peered up at me. He hobbled forward, one leg stiffer than the other as if it had been injured somehow. I pushed him aside and walked in. I could hear men chattering away and laughing. I followed the sound and stepped into a huge lounge, warm and thick with smoke, decked out with expensive reproductions of expensive antique furniture and cheap ornaments and messy abstract paintings that looked cheap and probably cost a fortune.

There were eight or so men sitting around the place. It looked like one of them soirees; a nice evening at the Coles', weapons optional. They turned as one when I entered, drinks and smokes in their hands, and sneers and aggression on their faces, and thin knowing eyes. The laughter dropped away.

At the far end, behind a built-in bar, was Bobby Cole, a short man, heavy and muscular but moving towards fatness with neatly cut dark hair and sharp eyes. But, in spite of all the power and wealth he showed, I thought I saw strain in the way he slumped a bit, and tiredness in the lines under his eyes and in the colour of his skin, which had lost its tanned glow.

He was mixing a drink for some thin dried-up blonde who sat slouched on the barstool before him. He didn't bat an eye when he saw me.

He raised the glass and said, 'Drink?'

'Where is he?'

'You tooled up?'

'No. Where is he?'

The men shuffled a bit and looked at their drinks and pulled on their fags and that sort of thing. Conversation confused them and, besides, they didn't know what my place in things was. Cole could see that and I knew he was going to have to play with me a bit, just to show everyone that he didn't answer to monsters who plunged into his house in the middle of the night. Regardless of what he owed me, he had to show who was boss.

'My wife,' Cole said, raising his chin towards the woman. 'Marjorie.'

The woman looked at me. Her skin was a sort of orange colour, her hair was a yellow, her nails red, her dress short and green. She was drinking some kind of blue stuff. She looked like one of the abstract paintings, only not as expensive. Whatever the blue stuff was it was alcoholic. She was sloshed and trying not to show it. Her eyelids drooped and she slumped on the seat, but every now and then a hand went up to straighten her hair, as if neat hair would make her sober and twenty years younger and happy.

When I'd had my fill of the woman, I turned to Cole and said, 'Paget's man. You took him.'

'The boys kicked him out in Epping Forest.'

They couldn't know where Paget was or they wouldn't have been here. I wondered if that was the reason for the strain I'd seen in Cole. He must've thought he was onto something but it must've turned out to go nowhere.

'He tell you anything?'

Cole added a couple of things to the drink he was mixing. He was taking his time, playing up for his wife and his monkeys. When he'd prepared them enough, he looked at me and said, 'You must really think I'm some kind of cunt.'

The blonde shrank away from him for an instant, but when she saw that he wasn't going to get heavy, she relaxed. She even forced a smile. It was an effort. She didn't want to be here. Cole must have been getting some kick out of it. It occurred to me then that Cole had known all along that I'd show up. All of this – his men, his wife, his fancy drinks at the bar – all of it was for my benefit.

The thing was, Cole was up against the wall. He'd been in over his head with this Albanian mob, taking their smack in exchange for money he didn't have. When he was supposed to get the money, Paget and Marriot ripped it off him. I got it back, so Cole owed me plenty. But someone like Cole couldn't be seen to need anyone, especially someone like me.

So, he was showing everyone that he was in charge, that he still had a hold on things. But he was trying too hard. I could see it, and I had a feeling his men could see it too.

And seeing this performance, I got the feeling that things were worse for him than I'd realized. He still hadn't got his heroin back from Paget and maybe that was causing a problem.

He was still a big name, still had clout, power, but a lot of that was based on his reputation. If people knew he was in trouble, Cole's name wouldn't be so big and others would start to take away his empire. His was an animal world of blood where the most powerful had to fight always for that place, and when he showed any weakness, the pack would attack him. And there were plenty of scavengers waiting to pick the flesh from his corpse.

'You didn't tell me about your plan to meet Paget,' he was saying. 'You go to a meeting armed with a rifle and you don't invite me. I call that bad manners.'

A couple of his men laughed at that. Cole's eyes roamed the room, enjoying the reaction. Then he fixed me with a stare and said, 'You know he owes me a million quid's worth of junk.'

I didn't say anything. What was there to say? I didn't care about his junk, and he knew it. He wanted me to ask how he'd known about my plan to get Paget. He wanted to watch me run around in circles. This was his revenge, small as it was, for not telling him about my plan. I didn't need to ask him, though. There was only one way he could've known.

'You had me under surveillance,' I said. 'Very clever.'

I felt more stupid than ever. He smiled, as much as he could smile.

'You led us straight to Bowker. I squeezed him a bit and he told me about your plan. The boys here did the rest.'

'Now we've sorted out who did what and why, tell me where Paget was hiding out.'

'Won't do you any good.'

'Where?'

'Some pokey old house on a council estate, apparently. Not his style. He wasn't there.'

'Go on.'

'Place was owned by some bird. Turns out she was an old girlfriend of Paget's. Did you know he had an old girlfriend?'

'Does she know where he is?'

'No.'

'Sure?'

'Oh, yes. I'm sure.'

A couple of the men chuckled. I glanced round at them. I noticed that some of the men, the older ones, didn't look amused by all this. They mostly looked away from me, down at the floor or at their drinks or at the lousy fucking abstract paintings. I turned back to Cole.

'Give me the address.'

'You gonna use your charms on her?'

'Give it to me.'

Cole watched me for a while and sipped his drink. He turned to one of the men behind me and said, 'Carl, give it to him.'

Carl, who looked about twelve, was sitting in a chair, legs stretched out before him, ankles crossed. He grinned at the private joke. He fished in his trouser pocket and pulled out a piece of paper. He held it out, still grinning. I walked over and snatched the piece of paper from his hand.

'I'll get him,' Cole said. 'I've flushed him out of one hiding place. He's running out of friends.'

I was about to ask him about the other man in the car, the stocky white bloke who'd got away. I stopped. Cole hadn't mentioned him. Nobody had. I ran through the moment when Cole's crew had hit me. Did they even know there was another bloke? I tested that idea by saying, 'The bloke in the car, who was he?'

Cole shrugged.

Nobody said, 'Which bloke?' They didn't know there'd been a second man. I'd have to find out about him. Behind me, a thin nasally voice said, 'Who gives a fuck about him?'

I turned and looked at the thin voice. Carl was smiling at me, a cocky look on his cocky little face.

'If he'd known any more, he would have told me.'

I noticed then, for an instant, a flash of irritation cross Cole's face. It was the way Carl was taking credit for the job, I thought, that annoyed Cole. The 'would have told me' bit. The fact that Cole was tolerating him was interesting. Anyone else and he would have given him a bollocking. Maybe Cole was holding back because I was there. Maybe Carl was going to get a slap later.

But there was something else wrong with this Carl. He didn't fit into this crew. Cole's other men were pros, but this one was more like a giddy amateur, experiencing it all in a heady rush. He was enjoying this more than anyone and I wondered what a wanker like him was doing working for Cole.

'By the time we'd got rid of him, he was unconscious,' Carl was saying. 'Geezer was more red than black.'

He seemed to want me to congratulate him. I turned back to Cole.

'Eddie Lane came to see me,' I said. 'Tells me you're bent on getting Paget, that you and Dunham had an agreement to fix the Albanians first and now you're fucking it up. Wants me to get you to play ball.'

'Fuck Dunham. And fuck Lane. And fuck you. I don't answer to any of you lot.'

'What's this agreement with him about?'

'It's bollocks. Dunham's losing it, getting old. He's scared of these Albanians – fucking cowboys. He's scared they're gonna start on his turf after they've taken mine. Well, they ain't fucking taken mine yet.'

Headlights lit the room up. A car ground to a halt outside.

'That'll be Steve,' someone said.

'Show him in,' Cole said. 'Take him out back,' he added, glancing at me.

'And the law?' I said. 'You got them squared away?'

'Fixed. We just gave them some info on the Albanians,

blamed them for Marriot's death. Few payments to senior coppers. Hey presto.'

'Easy,' I said.

'Sure. If you've got the power.'

He took a sip of his drink. It was a slow sip, as if he was thinking about things.

'These Albanian cunts,' he said. 'Dunham's idea. We combine forces, take them out and carve up their turf, divide their business. I don't trust Dunham. Anyway, the Albanians can wait.'

'You know what they're into?'

'I don't plan on exploiting the kids and women they've smuggled in, if that's what you mean.'

'If you did, I'd have to come after you too.'

Carl laughed at that. Nobody else did. Cole was quiet for a while, studying me.

'What do you think I am, Joe?' he said. 'I don't do that kind of thing. I know they brought that girl into the country, the one you looked after.'

'Kid,' I said. 'That was her name.'

'Yeah. Kid. I'm not a fucking animal.'

I didn't think Cole was the type to get involved in that kind of thing. But I had to make my point. I said, 'Got any ideas where Paget would go?'

'Have I got any ideas, he asks me.' He looked around the assembled mass and winked to his wife. 'When I get an idea, you'll read about it in the paper.'

Carl got a kick out of that one. Cole enjoyed his wit for a moment, then he looked at me and his eyes went cold, became hooded.

'Marriot and Paget ripped me off. They ripped off my money and they ripped off my junk. I don't let people get away with that. You took out Marriot. Fine. Well that leaves Paget, and he's still got my junk and I'm gonna get it and get him and nobody's getting in my way.'

'I want Paget.'

'You're not listening to me, boy. I don't give a shit what you want. The only reason you're breathing is because you got my money back off Marriot. I owe you for that.'

'I didn't do it for you.'

'Don't get in my fucking way again,' he said.

EIGHT

One time, about three weeks before she was killed, Brenda said, 'Have you got any ambition, Joe?'

We'd been in her flat, sitting at that small Formica table she had, eating Chinese. It was late and she'd finished work. There was some kind of soft classical music on. It wasn't my thing, but I think she thought it added to the atmosphere, so I let it go.

'To do what?'

'I don't know. Anything.'

'Anything else, you mean.'

She smiled and her eyes sparked to life and her face lit up. She looked a hundred years younger.

'You got me,' she said. 'Well, have you?'

'No.'

She nodded and carried on eating for a while.

'I have,' she said. 'Did I tell you? I'm saving up.'

She had told me, but she'd forgotten. I knew she wanted me to ask her about it, so I did.

'I want to be a beautician. I want to own me own place. A beauty parlour. They call them parlours. I wonder why. Isn't that what they called a lounge in posh places?'

I shrugged.

'I like the sound of that,' she was saying. 'What should I call it? I was thinking Brenda's Parlour, but that's got no ring, you know? I can't think of anything that rhymes with parlour. Or Brenda.'

'Big spender,' I said.

She laughed, but she was forcing it. Something was bothering her. She was trying too hard to be bright and happy.

'If you want money,' I said, 'I can let you have some.'

She touched my arm.

'No, Joe. No. I don't want any money.'

'I've got plenty. You might as well do something with it.'

She leaned over and kissed my cheek.

'That's sweet,' she said.

It wasn't sweet. My money wasn't doing anything. I just saved it up for the sake of it. I'd never known what to do with it. I'd never wanted a fast car or an expensive watch or any of that shit.

'It's not much to ask, is it?' she said. 'To be a beautician? That's not much.'

She wasn't telling me, she was telling herself. Or trying to. I don't think she was getting through.

'You wanted to be a carpenter, didn't you?' she said. 'I remember you told me.'

That was true, as far as it went. It was something I'd once enjoyed, when I was young, when I still thought there was a choice. Then, I'd thought I could use my hands to make something. Turned out I could use them better to pull things apart.

'Sometimes I don't think I'm going to make it,' she was

saying. 'You know? I mean, I think, Who are you kidding? Who do you think you are? I mean, look at me, Joe. Just some over the hill black tart. Who the bloody hell would want me to make them beautiful?'

I said, 'You're not so bad.'

When I looked at her, she was resting her fork on her plate and looking off into some middle-ground. She hadn't heard me. She had that look, the one Kid had had sometimes. It made Brenda look like a child, lost, scared, trying not to show it. Kid had been a child, she had been lost and scared and hammered by the world. I suppose Brenda was a child too, in a way. She still had the sort of stupid dreams that children had, like wanting to be a beautician.

I finished eating and went to make a cup of tea. When I came back, she'd given up with the meal and had gone to sit on the sofa. She had the window open, the curtains pulled back. A weak cold breeze wafted into the place and carried a far-off smell of wet air and diesel, and the sound of droning traffic. She was smoking and gazing at the darkness outside. In her hand was a glass of gin. It was a big glass and it was mostly full. I saw the bottle on the floor. I didn't see any tonic.

There was a glaze to her eyes, and I thought she'd been crying. I put the mugs of tea down on the table. She kept her eyes on the window. In a low, distant voice, she said, 'I can't stand it, Joe. Sometimes, I just can't stand it. What they do.'

I knew what she was talking about. Marriot did things with kids.

'Get out, then. I've told you, do something else. Fuck Marriót. He gives you any grief, I'll rip him apart.'

She smiled vaguely, like she was humouring a child. But the smile wore away from her face, and her gaze was back into that middle distance again, between here and nowhere, between what she was and what she knew she could never be. I don't know why she did that to herself. I'd told her enough times that life was a piece of shit. If she'd got used to that, she wouldn't have been endlessly disappointed. But when I would say that to her, she would look at me with her thin smile and it would be like she was sorry for me, like I was the one suffering, and she was here to make everything all right.

So she carried on with her suffering, and with her life, and with me. She was a romantic, I suppose, or an idealist or whatever. You can't do much with people like that.

Whatever she saw there, in that middle-land, she didn't want me in on it. I think she thought she was protecting me. Maybe she was.

It's funny; Brenda thought she could protect me. Kid thought so too. And Browne. None of them could do anything for themselves except be victims, but they all thought they could protect a violent, war-torn monster like me. I say it's funny. It's not. It's about as far from funny as you can get.

'We could go somewhere,' I said. 'We can start again. Somewhere.'

'You don't understand, Joe. I can't explain it. I have to carry on. Not for me, but...'

There were tears coming down her face. She stubbed her

cigarette out and took a long drink from the glass. She shook her head and wiped away the tears. She looked at me and forced a smile.

'I'm being stupid,' she said. 'Come on, let's go and get some fresh air.'

I should have listened to her. Things would've been different. She might've had six years more life, for one thing. We might still be together. Who knows, she might've got her beauty parlour.

Anyway, I should have listened to her. I should have understood what she was telling me. I should have done lots of things. I should have killed Marriot and Paget back then, before they'd killed her, before they'd used Kid, before anything.

I should have done those things.

But I didn't, and people were going to pay for that.

NINE

When I found the place, it was starting to get light, if you could call it light. The sky was heavy and grey, and the dawn was no more than a strip of lighter grey against the black horizon.

It was a post-war terraced house. The roof made of some kind of corrugated concrete. It must've seemed a good idea to someone once, someone who didn't have to live here. There was a high hedge at the front of the small garden, and an overgrown lawn with children's toys littered about. The toys must've been there for years. The plastics had weathered, the bright yellows and reds now weak and faded. Thick grass had grown around them so that it was like a graveyard, a monument to dead childhood.

I pressed the doorbell and waited. After a while, a middle-aged woman opened up and looked out at me. She was wearing an apron and her sleeves were rolled up.

'Are you the police?' she said.

They'd called the law, then. I didn't want to be around when they came. I said, 'No.'

This baffled her. If I wasn't law, what could I be? It didn't make sense.

'Who are you, then?'

'Are you Paget's old girlfriend?'

'Who's Paget?'

We were going round in circles.

'I want to speak to the woman who lives here.'

'Oh.'

She closed the door. A few seconds later, it was opened again by a younger woman, thin and pale and with long lank blonde hair. The woman's lip was split, the blood dried. Her right eye was swollen and had closed some.

'Please,' she said, murmuring the word feebly.

'I want to talk to you.'

'Please.'

It was all she would say. We were back to the circles.

'I'm not with the men who came earlier.'

From inside the house, a woman's voice called out.

'Shut the door, Tina. Let the police sort it out.'

The thin woman started to close the door and I had to put my hand on it and push it back.

'You're Kenny Paget's ex-girlfriend?' She head bobbed up and down a bit. 'Your name's Tina?'

She had no energy, like she'd just woken up. It was shock, I thought. I wondered if she was concussed. Nobody had said anything about calling an ambulance.

She had a long thin face and high cheekbones and large eyes, and her long lashes gave her eyes a soft look. I guessed her age to be around the mid-forties, but she might've been a used-up mid-thirties. She wore a beige dressing gown and blue nightgown.

'The men who were here earlier, they wanted to know where Paget was. Is that right?'

Another woman appeared then. This Tina must have called on a friend for help after Cole's men had been, and that friend had called on another and they'd come over like a relief column. This one was short and stocky. She had a defiant look, but her mouth was closed tightly and I could see fear in her eyes. I guessed she'd been the one who'd called out just now. She took one look at me and said, 'Fuck off.'

I didn't want to get heavy. I wanted information, and if I had to deal with a lot of hysterical women, I'd never get anywhere. At the same time, the law was on its way and I didn't have time to piss about. I pushed my way into the house and closed the door. The hall was narrow, the ceiling low. I barely fit. Tina moved back a few paces, looking straight into my chest. She didn't try to run, she didn't reach for the phone on the wall or a weapon. She didn't do much, except move backwards, her toes dragging on the carpet. The short woman lunged at me and pushed, trying to get me back.

'Fuck off,' she kept saying.

It was a token effort, and we all knew it. She smelled of alcohol and when I knocked her aside she lost her balance and stumbled. I took hold of Tina and steered her through to a small back lounge. Here, too, there were some children's toys and I saw photos of children, old faded photos and newer ones. I guessed that the woman's children had grown up and had children of their own and that those toys in the front belonged to her grandchildren. Maybe she looked after the kids in the day. On top of the TV set was a framed photo of a bride and groom: Tina with another man. Both looked middle-aged in the picture.

I said, 'Where's your husband?'

'My... who?'

I put her in a chair and she looked up at me with drowsy eyes. She said, 'Who are you?'

Her speech was slurred and her eyelids were falling down. I leaned forward and slapped her lightly on the cheek. The short one tried to grab hold of my arm.

'Leave her alone.'

I pushed her off. Tina opened her eyes a little, but not much. The short one was about to attack me again when Apron stopped her.

'Something's wrong,' Apron said.

I walked into the bathroom and opened the cabinet. There was a load of medication, mostly antidepressants, benzodiazepines, that sort of thing. There was nothing in there that belonged to a man; no shaving foam, no razors, except a pink woman's one. I saw a small white plastic bottle by the side of the sink next to a glass of water. The bottle was empty, but it had contained diazepam, in ten-milligram tablets. It had been prescribed to Christina Murray only a week earlier. It had contained thirty tablets.

I took the empty bottle into the lounge. Apron and the short woman were sitting around, looking at Tina who was slumped in the seat, her head down. I grabbed hold of her and hoisted her up. I pinched her cheek, slapping her a little. It didn't matter to me what she did to herself, but I wanted information. I held up the bottle. I said, 'How many did you take?'

Her eyes were barely open, and wouldn't focus. Her head lolled to one side. I dropped her back onto the seat. I looked at the other women. They stared at me.

'How many did she take?'

Apron said, 'They're just aspirins.'

'They're diazepam. How many did she take?'

'I don't know.'

I turned to the short one. She was quiet, pale with fear. She shook her head.

Apron said, 'There were only a couple in there.'

'She's had something to drink,' the short one said. She turned to her friend. 'I gave her some gin. I thought she needed it.'

'There were only a couple in there,' Apron said again.

'How long have you both been here?'

'An hour.'

Cole's men had been here two, three hours earlier.

'What about before you got here?'

'Shit,' the short one said. 'Dunno.'

'Did you call an ambulance after she'd been beaten?'

They looked at each other. Neither of them had thought of it. Probably, they were used to violence, up to a point, and wouldn't call an ambulance for anything short of a decapitation.

'Just a couple,' Tina mumbled.

'What?'

'Just wanted to... put it... put it behind me.'

After that, she was quiet.

'She's talking about the pills,' the short woman said.

'We'd better call an ambulance,' Apron said.

That was the last thing I wanted.

'No. It's only diazepam, it won't kill her.'

'Are you sure?'

'Yes.'

They were quiet for a moment, but then the short one stood and made for the phone. I had to stop her. When I did that, Apron rushed over and started to shake Tina, yelling at her to wake up. The walls of these places were paper-thin and if I wasn't careful, I'd have neighbours banging on the door. I wondered when the police were going to arrive. I'd have to shoot out the back and hop over the rear wall. At the back was a concreted area and a row of garages. I'd left my car there.

'I know someone,' I said. 'A doctor. I'll call him. Okay?'

That stopped them for a moment. They looked at each other.

'He's legit,' I said. 'A GP.'

They agreed. I phoned Browne. He took a long time to answer. When he did, he muttered something unintelligible. He sounded drunk. I told him about the woman. That seemed to sober him up.

'Call an ambulance,' he said.

'Can't do that. There'd be a report. I don't want the law involved.'

'I don't give a damn what you want. Call for a bloody ambulance.'

'Tell me what to do for her, or I hang up.'

He was quiet for a while. He didn't know where I was phoning from, so he couldn't call anyone himself.

'I'll come over,' he said.

I didn't trust him not to dial emergency, so I told him to take the tube to Debden and then to call me. I'd direct him on the phone from there. In the meantime, he told me to give her black coffee, strong and sweet. I put the women on this. They were happy to be doing something.

I poked around the house some. I got looks now and then, but nobody tried to stop me. In a drawer, I found bills and letters addressed to Christina Murray. I found no mention of a man.

'Where's her husband?' I asked Apron.

'She's not married.'

I titled my head at the framed photo on the TV. Apron shrugged.

'Divorced.'

We spent a while pouring coffee down the woman's throat and then I hauled her into the bathroom and got her to vomit, then we fed her more coffee. I tried to get the swelling down around her eye. I didn't want the other women to get the idea that an ambulance was needed. She didn't seem badly hurt.

Browne called and I told him how to get to the house. When he arrived he looked bleary and hungover. I carried the woman into the bedroom. He pushed me out and shut the door. After a half hour, he came out and glared at me.

'Who is she?'

'Does it matter?'

'I suppose not. Did you do that to her? Beat her?'

'No.'

'You know what happened?'

'Cole happened. He wanted information from her. He set his men loose.'

He looked at his hands, and rubbed them, like he was washing them.

'They sexually molested her, you know.'

'Uh-huh. She'll be alright?'

'Define "alright".'

'Will she talk?'

He glared at me again, like it was my fault the world was fucked up. He fished around in his case and brought out a syringe and a bottle of something and went back into the bedroom.

After another hour or so, she was in a reasonable state. There'd been no law, and I thought I knew why, but I needed to make sure.

She was drinking the coffee by herself now, holding it in both hands. The other women were suspicious of me, but they could see that I wasn't a threat. They'd relaxed since Browne had shown up and I think they must have realized I had something to do with Paget. They probably had an idea what he was. They didn't want aggro. They were smart.

Browne had taken himself into the kitchen and was making coffee for himself. He was a moral doctor, didn't want to treat anyone when he was pissed.

When I thought the woman was up to answering me, I said, 'When did you call the police?'

She looked at her friends.

'I... I didn't.'

'Why?' Apron said.

The short one, I noticed, hadn't said anything, hadn't been surprised.

'Didn't want them involved.'

'Well, I'm going to call them right now,' said Apron.

'No,' Tina said. 'Don't. It's okay. I'm alright.'

The short one put a hand on Apron and gave her a meaningful look. Apron got the message. There wasn't much more the women could do. It was early morning and they looked tired.

'I'm sorry,' the woman said to them. 'I'm sorry.'

They went home soon after that. They were glad, in the end, to get out of there. Friendship will only stretch so far. People are usually the same; they start off showing how much they care because they know it makes them look kind and decent. After that, they get impatient and start thinking about their own problems and, finally, they don't give a shit about their beaten, drugged-up friend, they just want to get home to bed. Nobody gives a shit, when it comes down to it. Except, maybe, people like Browne. And Brenda. And look what happened to them.

Browne was asleep. I could hear him snoring. He must've had a skinful last night and now it had caught up with him. He'd popped a couple of pills from his bag and was crashed out on the woman's bed.

'She won't need her bed anyway,' he'd said. 'She has to stay awake for a while.'

I sat and drank a mug of tea and watched the woman as she gradually came back to life. She sat opposite me, curled up on the sofa, one hand holding the coffee, the other hand on her lap. She watched me calmly and didn't say anything. She didn't know who I was or what I wanted, but she took it all in her stride. She didn't seem to care.

She didn't look too bad, now that she was more alive. She looked pale and worn-out, fragile, I suppose they call it, but there was something there, some depth. Her eyes, I saw, were a pale blue. She was younger than I'd first thought, maybe late thirties.

'Do you know what's going on?' I said.

She nodded.

'I know Kenny's mixed up in something,' she said. 'I know he worked for that man who was killed, what was his name?'

'Marriot.'

'Yeah. Marriot. Frank Marriot.'

The hand in her lap started pulling at the dressing gown, turning it around, twisting it. She looked at the photos of the children. Her eyes flickered, flashing with some emotion I couldn't read. Anger, maybe.

'He won't come back,' she said quietly.

Her hand was still twisting that nightgown. I didn't think she knew what she was doing. I realized then that it was fear I saw in her. But it wasn't fear of me or Cole or the police. She feared Paget.

'What are you going to do to him?' she said.

'Does it matter?'

She looked back at me, and drank her coffee, eyeing me over the rim of the mug. When she'd finished drinking, she leaned forward and put the coffee on the floor. Her actions were slow and deliberate. She looked like a drunk who was trying to appear sober. She leaned back in the sofa. She pulled the dressing gown tightly about her, and wrapped her arms around her, as if she'd felt a cold chill. She gazed down, at the floor, and her eyelids dropped a little. I thought she was falling asleep, but then she spoke.

'They kept asking me, again and again, where is he? I kept telling them, I don't know. For a while, every time I said that, they hit me. Then they started... doing other stuff. There was this small blond one, he kept smiling every time I told them I didn't know where Kenny was. I don't think he wanted to know. I think he wanted to keep on... well, you know.'

That sounded like Carl.

'Who were they?' she said softly.

'They were dogs, belonged to a man called Bobby Cole.'

She nodded slightly. She knew the name.

'What's it all about?'

'Paget tried to fix Cole up for a fall, tried to take over his firm, him and Marriot. He's still got a load of Cole's heroin.'

She took it well. She was taking it all well. I had to give her that. She said, 'I knew when I saw him it must be bad. I haven't seen him in five, six years. I thought I was free of him. Then he turns up one night, a couple of weeks ago. Him and this bloke. Mike.'

'Mike?'

'Some old friend of Kenny's.'

I thought about the second man in the car at Lee Valley, the one who'd run from my sights.

'What's Mike's surname?'

'Glazer.'

'You know where he lives?'

She shook her head, her lips tightening in a frown.

'And I don't want to know. About either of them. I made a mistake years back, with Kenny. I was young and stupid. He was flash, throwing the cash about. I always knew he wasn't legit, but I never thought he was so... so vile, you know? I think I didn't want to know. I thought I was going to live in a mansion. Look at me.'

'You don't know where Paget is?'

'No. I don't.'

Paget was going to be hard to find, but I might have more luck if I went after this Glazer. If, that was, Glazer was the second man.

'You got a photo of Glazer?'

'No.'

'He's average height, stocky, shaved head?'

'He's fat and bald, yes.'

So, I had him. The other man. Paget's accomplice. I looked at the pictures of the kids on the wall. If Paget had family, he might be vulnerable.

'These kids, are they yours and Paget's?'

'No.' She snapped the word at me, using it like a weapon, and her eyes sparked anger. She'd come alive for a moment, then the fury seeped away. 'No, they're not his. I met someone else. He had a couple of grown-up children. He... he's gone .' She tilted her head at the photos. 'They're the closest I've got to a family, and they're not even mine. They never visit. They just send photos. Every time one of them has a new kid, they send a photo.'

'Got any ideas where I could find him? Glazer?'

'I don't know anything about his life. He only came here because he was with Kenny. Kenny only came here because he wanted somewhere to stay for a while.'

'Have you got anything of theirs? Any old address books? Photos? Letters? Anything like that.'

'I've got nothing of theirs. Nothing.'

'There was another man, with Glazer. Young, black.'

She nodded.

'Saw him once or twice. Don't know him. Eric, something. Or Derek, yeah, Derek. Friend of Mike's. They never talked about things in front of me. They were hardly ever here.'

'Where'd they go?'

'Oh, shit. I don't know.'

She sighed and her head lolled backwards and rested on the cushions behind her.

'Ah, Christ,' she said. 'What a mess.'

She stared up at the ceiling, searching it for something, trying to see where everything had gone wrong. We listened to Browne snore. I felt tired, my head was fuzzy. I wanted to find a dark room and lie down. I wanted to stop.

'Thank you,' she said to the ceiling.

'What for?'

'For what you did.'

'I didn't do anything.'

She didn't hear me. She wasn't listening.

'Must've been shock or something,' she said. 'Didn't mean to take so many pills.'

It was as good an excuse as any.

'Where do you think Paget went?'

'I don't know. And I don't care.'

'Give me something,' I said. 'Anything.'

She looked back at me, and there was new fear in her face, like she'd just woken and was seeing me for the first time, seeing this hulking danger, lurking, waiting to strike. She pulled back, curling her legs further underneath, holding her arms more tightly about her.

'You're one of his men,' she said. 'You're one of his fucking men.'

'No.'

'You're one of Mike's fucking men.'

'Mike's men? What does that mean?'

'You are. You're one of them.'

She pushed away from me, scrambling backwards on the sofa, trying to get as far from me as she could, pushing herself back with her legs and arms. She was like a cat with its heckles up, claws out.

'What does Glazer do?'

'You're Cole's, then. This is a trick. What do you want? Who are you?'

'I'm a man who wants to find your ex-boyfriend.'

'Why? Who are you? Are you going to help him? Are you one of them?'

'No.'

'You're after the drugs, then.'

'You've seen the drugs?'

'That's it, isn't it? That's what you fucking want.'

'I don't want anything from him.'

64

'What do you want, then? What do you want? What the fuck do you want?'

'I want to kill him.'

She stared at me, her mouth open, her face white, her eyes wide. She was panting, and her hand was twisting the life out of her dressing gown.

'Yes,' she said. 'Kill him. Kill him.'

TEN

Browne said, 'It's to do with this man, Paget, isn't it? All this.'

The sky had lightened some, but not enough to give any depth to the buildings. We sat there, in the car, not saying anything, whirring down the road with grey above and grey around and grey between us.

There was something wrong with the woman. I thought it must have been delayed shock, or trauma or something like that, but I'd seen enough of that before and her reaction didn't fit, she was too violent too quickly. If Browne hadn't been there, I could've squeezed her more. Browne would go so far for me, for old times and because he thought he owed me, but the moment I touched the woman, he would've been on the phone grassing me up to anyone who'd listen.

It didn't matter. What I needed to know right then was about this Glazer character, and that information I could get from someone else: Derek.

So, I'd drop Browne off back at his place then make a few calls to local hospitals. That was the plan, anyway. It wasn't much of a plan. For one thing, I didn't have a surname for this Derek. For another, if I turned up at a hospital and asked about a man with a gunshot wound, they'd call the law.

I switched on the radio and listened to the eight o'clock

news. They mentioned a stabbing in Hackney and a drugs bust in Bermondsey. There was no mention of a shooting in Ponders End, nothing about a man being shot. That could mean Derek ran out of blood and was lying face down in Epping Forest. Or it could mean that it was too early for the report. I wondered if anybody had yet discovered the car. If it was still there, I might find something about Glazer or Derek inside it.

I pulled over. Browne looked out.

'What is this godforsaken place?'

'Chingford.'

'And?'

I fished twenty from my pocket and handed it to him.

'Get a cab.'

He sat there for a moment.

'Did you see her arms?' he said.

'What about them?'

'Scars. Old puncture scars.'

'She was a user?'

'Once. What are you going to do?'

'You know what I'm going to do.'

'You're going to kill them. You're going to find Paget and anyone else who gets in your way or had anything to do with Brenda's death and you're going kill them all.'

'If you know, why're you asking?'

'I said once you'd been beaten by life. Remember?'

'Yeah.'

'I was wrong,' he said. 'I mean, that wasn't right, not exactly. You haven't been beaten by it, Joe. You've been gutted by it. There's nothing left inside of you.'

'What are you talking about?'

'That woman back there. I don't know who she is. I don't want to know, but she was… Damn it, I don't understand this world any more.'

If he'd only just discovered that the world was a stinking pit of snakes, each turning on the others, there wasn't much I could do for him.

I said, 'Are you telling me you don't want to be involved?'

'For Christ's sake. No, I'm not saying that. Cole went to Kid's funeral. Then he does something like that to that woman. All you people, I just don't understand it. I just…'

He sighed. He didn't seem to know what he was trying to say. He didn't understand that there was nothing to understand.

He ran a hand wearily over his head, over the thinning grey hair, over the years of wasted effort and forgotten ideals. He wanted something; order or hope or just a reason, and I couldn't give it to him.

'I know the bloke who did it,' I said. 'If I get the chance, I'll fix him.'

Browne looked at me, gazing right into my eyes. I had the feeling he was trying to find something there, trying to find an answer, maybe. Finally, he turned and opened the car door and got out and walked away.

I pulled out and turned into Kings Head Hill. When I hit the top of the hill, North London lay before me, like a slug beneath a sluggish sky. The reservoirs were the colour of dishwater. Beyond them was Ponders End.

The traffic was getting heavy and it was another twenty minutes before I got to the site where, only a few hours earlier, I'd put 7.62 mil rounds into Glazer's car. By now there would've been people who would have seen the car. If I was lucky they wouldn't have paid any attention. The car would've looked just like a joy-rider's wreck. There were plenty of those around. It was possible, though, that someone had seen the bullet holes and called the police.

I pulled into the car park and cruised slowly, ready to turn and leave quickly. There was no law. There was no car. I found broken glass and, further along, dried blood on the concrete. But the car was gone.

What did that mean? Had Paget been watching us? Had he driven the car away afterwards? No, that didn't make sense. For one, he would've had to drive to Ponders End and that meant he would've had his own car to drive, he wouldn't have been able to drive two cars. Besides, if he'd been there at all, he would've tried to kill me. Of that I was sure. And he wouldn't have gone there afterwards.

Had Glazer waited around and gone back for the car? It was possible, but I didn't think so. Why would he risk it?

I got back in my car and drove over to Enfield. I stopped at a cafe and ordered fish and chips and coffee. I took a seat at the orange plastic table and tried to work out what that fuck was going on.

The first thing I did was call Cole and ask him if he'd sent his men back to collect the car. He said, 'Why the fuck would I do that?'

I listened to the nine o'clock news. There was still nothing about the shooting, nothing about this Derek. Had Carl lied about dumping him in Epping Forest? If Derek had been picked up from there, or anywhere near there, he would've been taken to Whipps Cross Hospital or maybe to the Princess Alexandra in Harlow. I phoned both places and told them I was a newspaper reporter who'd been given a lead. Neither one had treated a gunshot wound overnight.

I thought about things, as much as I could with my head all over the place. Paget had gone to ground. He was going to be a bastard to find. Plus, Cole was after him and if I went after Paget directly, I'd have to deal with Cole's mob at some point. I wasn't sure I was in the state to take them all on. But I knew something they didn't, I knew that Paget had a cohort: Mike Glazer. He'd been at Paget's hide-out in Loughton, he'd gone armed to meet me earlier that morning. He'd know where Paget was. I had to concentrate on him. I had to at least find out who he was.

Something Tina had said was ringing bells in my head. She'd asked me if I was one of Glazer's men. Did that mean he was in the game in some way? I'd never heard of him.

I decided to call Nathan King. After a dozen rings, I heard a woman's voice over the line. She sounded sleepy. I asked for King. I heard the woman shout, 'Nat, one of yours.'

After a moment, I heard King's deep slow voice wanting to know what kind of idiot would call him at this hour. I told him. He said, 'Thought you'd be dead by now.'

'You ever heard of Mike Glazer.'

'No. Should I of?'

'He's something to do with Paget. Partner or something.'

'Well, I'm glad I know that, Joe. Next time I have Paget over for cocktails, I'll be sure and invite this Glazer.'

'I need to find out about him.'

'Yeah? Good luck.'

'You know people. You could ask around.'

'I could. Why would I? What I hear, you're up to your neck in shit right now. Cole on one side, Dunham on the other, Paget out there somewhere, them fucking Albanians running around shooting people. I don't want anything to do with that. If I start raising my head and asking about people involved in that, next thing I know, *I'm* involved in it.'

It was a good point. I said, 'There could be something in it for you.'

There were a few seconds of static over the phone. Then King's voice rumbled through the static.

'Such as?'

'Paget's got a million quid's worth of stuff that belongs to Cole.'

'Forget about it. We get hold of that and Cole will come after us with all guns blazing. We don't need that kind of grief. Besides, we don't deal in shit. You know that.'

'If I get it before Cole does, he'll deal with me, say 10 per cent finder's fee. You two get to split it.'

There was a little more thinking about that.

'I'll get back to you,' he said.

He rang off. He was going to call Daley and speak to him. They were careful, those two. When he called back, he said, 'What's to stop Cole taking the stuff anyway?'

'I'll plant it somewhere.'

'Why would he pay up? It's his stuff.'

'He'll be glad to get it back.'

'We give you legit info, we each get fifty grand?'

'Yeah.'

'Okay, Joe. We'll see what we can do.'

I put the phone in my pocket. My head throbbed and felt clogged with unclear thoughts. The neon lights in the cafe were starting to eat into my eyes, and the glare from the plastic table was making me feel sick. The waitress came over and put a plate in front of me. I looked at the food: oven chips and breaded fish straight out of a frozen packet. I pushed the stuff away then thought better of it. It might be a while before I ate again. I drowned the fish in ketchup and forced it down and ordered another coffee.

Bowker came into my thoughts. If Paget had sent Glazer and this Derek bloke to Ponders End, did that mean Bowker had grassed me up after all? I doubted it. It didn't much matter now anyway. It probably only meant that Paget was being extra careful. I cursed my stupidity for the hundredth time.

I considered going back to Bowker and squeezing him again, but that seemed pointless. If he had half a brain, he'd make himself scarce, at least until there was a last man standing. Then he'd come out and try to make peace with whichever one of us was left.

There was a buzzing noise and it took me a second to realize it was a mobile phone, switched to vibrate. It wasn't my phone. I looked around me. The only other people in the cafe were the waitress, who was leaning over the counter wiping up grease, and a heavy Turkish man sitting in the corner reading a paper, who, I supposed, was the owner. Neither of them seemed to have heard the phone.

Then I remembered. When Derek had tried to make a run for it with that hole in his back, I'd taken his phone away from him. I reached into my jacket pocket and pulled it out. It vibrated in my hand. I flipped it open and saw the number of the person calling. I made a note of the number. Finally, the buzzing stopped and the screen told me that someone had left a message. I tried to access the message, but the phone was protected by a PIN. All I had, then, was the phone number of someone trying to reach Derek. It was a landline, and a London code. It might have been Paget, or Glazer. It wasn't the same number as Bowker had used to contact Paget, but that meant nothing.

I was running short of ideas. I needed something from King, but had to wait for that. Frustration was building inside me. I found myself clenching and opening my fists, an old habit from my fight days. I drank the coffee and ordered another. I wanted to put some caffeine into my system, get it moving a bit.

With my own phone, I dialled the number. After one ring, a woman's voice said, 'Hello?'

'Is Derek there?'

'No.' There was a pause. 'Who's calling?' she said, trying to keep her voice level.

'I work with Derek.'

'Has something happened?'

'Why would you think that?'

'He was supposed to be home last night.'

There it was. Home.

'He had a job,' I said.

'I know he did. He told me he'd be an hour. Where is he? Why don't you people know where he is?'

You people.

'There was some confusion,' I said. 'Did he tell you what the job was?'

'What do you mean? Is this about Elena?'

The way she was talking, the answers she gave me – it was off somehow. Who was Elena? And why was this woman bringing her into it?

'I'm worried about him,' I said.

'Oh, no.'

'Can I come round and speak to you?'

'Come round?'

'It's important.'

'He's hurt, isn't he?'

'I don't know. Let me come round and talk to you.'

'I don't understand. Why?'

'Something Derek was mixed up in. Something to do with Glazer.'

'Who?'

She didn't know Glazer. Tina had told me Derek and Glazer were friends. I said, 'I'm pressed for time. I think Derek's fine, but I need to find him. You can help me. Can I come round?'

'Alright. Fine.'

'What's your address?'

There was a long pause now, and I knew I'd lost her. She said, 'Surely you know my address.'

As I was trying to think of a reply, the line went dead.

ELEVEN

They were waiting for me, spread around like chess pieces, one in the kitchen, in case I came in through the back door, two in the hallway. They watched me as I went past. There was no tension in them, no hands in pockets, so I knew they weren't here for a grab.

Browne was in the living room, sitting in his chair, staring at the floor. He looked moody. Eddie was opposite him, drinking tea from a mug, as if we were all in Eddie's house and he was tolerating us.

He put down his mug of tea and smiled.

'Vic would like a word,' he said.

'Is this an order?'

'Relax, Joe, will you. It's a request. Vic's not your enemy.'

'He's not my friend.'

'Who is?'

So, off we went, off to see King Vic.

I'd never met him, but I'd heard of him. Who hadn't? I didn't like organized crime, didn't want to be part of any pack, always waiting for some other pack to come along and try to take over. Dunham had held onto power better than most, and a lot of that was down to Eddie.

Dunham owned a club and casino in the West End. The

place wasn't quite in Soho, the women weren't quite naked. It was a huge place, and dark, all deep red and black, with mirrors and chrome. The casino was upstairs. The punters were toffs, footballers, Far-Eastern businessmen, Middle-Eastern embassy types, that sort of thing. They'd come in and watch the birds for a while and get pissed on free booze and then wander upstairs to the casino where they'd blow their dosh on long shots. The women were there to make sure the men knew how to get to the tables. They'd gasp and giggle and rub themselves against the men's bodies, and the men, pissed and lording it up, would blow even more dosh even more stupidly. It made a lot of money, that place.

There was a back street entrance, but we went in through the front, through the shining black granite foyer and into the club. I was getting five star treatment. They were after something.

It was too early for the main action. Or too late. One or two of the girls were sitting at tables, flicking through magazines and eating breakfast. As we went past one table, a slim blonde looked up and caught Eddie's eye and smiled at him. She looked at me and the smile soured. She looked back at her magazine. Eddie laughed and looked over his shoulder.

'You got a way with the birds, Joe.'

One of the men behind me laughed.

When we got to the office door, Eddie opened it without knocking. I followed him and kicked the door closed behind me.

Dunham was behind a large mahogany desk. He was a small man, considering his reputation. He had bulk, though, for his size, a kind of bulldog body, with a thick neck and thick strong torso. He was Irish by birth, but that was way back and he'd lost his accent and spoke now like an East Ender. He was trying to become English landed gentry if his office was anything to go by. Lots of oak and bronze racing horses and hunting prints, that sort of thing. Maybe in a few years he'd talk plummy and forget Ireland ever existed.

There were a few family photos around. There was one of a young woman, thin and pale and attractive in a posh English way. She wasn't smiling, though, and that made her look cold and somehow different, apart, as if she wasn't the same as the rest of us.

There was a picture of a young girl, ten or so, who must've been Dunham's daughter. There was another picture of Eddie in a large country garden, swinging the girl around, both of them laughing. It was odd that there were no pictures of Dunham with his daughter, or his wife, for that matter. It was like Dunham had given Eddie the role of father to his child. I looked at that picture. Eddie looked at me looking, and looked away.

Eddie walked over to a leather sofa that ran along one side of the room. He sat and watched me. Dunham watched me. I felt like I was being sized up, like I was a prize stallion Dunham was thinking of buying. I was getting tired of it, but they were up to something and I wanted to know what it was. After a while, Dunham smiled. It wasn't what they call a genuine smile. I didn't think he was capable of a genuine smile. He was trying, I suppose, and that tipped me off more than anything.

'You want a drink or something?' he said.

'No.'

He helped himself to a large glass of eighteen-year-old Jameson.

'I've heard a lot about you,' he said. 'You were a fighter once, right? Eddie here tells me you were good. That Marriot business was quite something. You were a one-man army. Tore up half of London. Well, Marriot was out to get you, can't blame you for treading on the cunt. Took us a bit of sorting out to do with the filth, though.'

'I didn't ask you to do that.'

'You were part of a fucking armed robbery, boy. You killed Marriot. In front of a dozen witnesses, for fuck's sake. You should be thanking me.'

I waited for him to say something worthwhile. Eddie was looking at the floor. I had the feeling I was here against his wishes.

'What do you think of all this shit?' Dunham said.

'What shit are you talking about?'

'With the Albanians. Them running round tryna take over our fucking turf. What do you think of all that?'

'I don't think of it.'

'You should. You're in this mess much as anyone. They might come for you.'

'I'll sort myself out.'

'You sure? From what I hear they almost wiped you and Cole out.'

I shrugged, but he was right. They'd been after Cole for the money he owed them and they'd caught us with our backs against the wall. We smoked a few and they scarpered. For a while, though, it had been a close thing.

Dunham took a sip of his Jameson's. He stood up, walked around his desk and sat on the edge of it, one leg planted, one dangling. It was an act. He glanced at Eddie.

'Cole seems to have decided to keep the million quid he owes the Albanians,' Eddie said.

I don't know what they expected me to do about that. I wasn't going to go out with a begging bowl.

'He's going all out for Paget and fucking us up,' Dunham said.

'How?'

'We had an agreement, me and Cole. We sort the Albanians first, together. Now Cole's getting distracted by this Paget shit. He's making it personal.'

'From what I hear on the news, the Albanians aren't a problem.'

'Don't you believe it. We've got word they're regrouping. We've got to sort them out before that happens.'

I nodded. It was all bollocks. I said, 'I don't tell Cole what to do.'

'No. But you could try and persuade him.'

'He wouldn't listen to me.'

Dunham glanced at Eddie. There was something there, in that look, that told me I wasn't playing the part I was supposed to. It was an irritated look, but hidden, as much as a man like Dunham can hide irritation.

He stood, returned to his seat, rested his arms on his desk, swirled his drink and looked up at me. He'd decided to give it one more try, like a salesman with a difficult customer. That's what this was, a sales pitch.

'Cole's stupid,' Dunham said. 'He's descended from

Germans, you know. Immigrants. Changed the spelling of their name. You know what Cole means in German? Cabbage. He's a fucking vegetable. He won't give up what he's got now in favour of a long-term advantage. He owes the Albanians that money for the junk. If he paid them off, they'd shut up for a bit, but Cole's got this bee up his arse. He's a Neanderthal.'

'What are you?'

He leaned forward.

'I'm God, as far as you're concerned.'

Eddie piped up.

'What we're saying, Joe, is that Cole won't give the Albanians their money until he's got his heroin back. We have to get the Albanians to calm down. If they got their money back, they'd shut up for a while and then we can hit them when they're not ready.'

It was a reason, just not a good one. I hadn't heard anything about Albanians running round London gunning people. At least, not since they came after Cole that time when I got in the way. But that was old news.

I said, 'You want me to help find Paget and get the heroin back to Cole.'

'We'll sort Paget out,' Dunham said.

'I want Paget for myself.'

Dunham shook his head a little.

'I heard you were a smart man,' he said. 'Lot of people think you're just a mug, brains bashed to shit, but Eddie told me you had something up there. He told me you were a pro, not some cunt who acts from his emotions. You get hold of Paget, you'll wipe him out. Tell us where he is, leave the rest to us.'

Eddie said, 'You could help us out, Joe. Any ideas where Paget is?'

'No.'

Dunham nodded slowly, and kept his eyes on me and let me know he didn't believe me. He wanted to know what I knew. I didn't want him to know that, but I also didn't want him to know that I didn't want him to know. In the end, I shrugged and said, 'I'm working on a couple of things. Give me time.'

Dunham leaned back in his seat and studied me.

'Time we don't have. Tell us what you got.'

They were trying too hard to sound casual about wanting to know if I knew where Paget was. They had contacts all over the place and I was pretty sure they had a man in Cole's firm. Dunham might have been tipped off that me and Cole had traced Paget to Loughton.

All that didn't matter so much, though. What mattered to me was why they were so anxious to get to Paget, and why they wanted me and Cole out of the way, chasing fucking Albanians.

'We thought we were onto something,' I said. 'We found that Paget was staying at his ex-girlfriend's place in Essex. But he's gone from there. I've asked around, but so far nothing.'

'This ex-girlfriend doesn't know anything?'

'No.'

Dunham took another sip of his Irish and nodded slowly. He glanced at Eddie. Eddie said, 'Well, if you get anything, tell us first, alright?'

'Yeah.'

TWELVE

King lived in a thirties semi a few blocks from Oakwood tube. It was the kind of house a bank manager might have. Maybe that was why he liked it. He wanted to be a regular bloke – decent car, nice street, plump wife, kids, the works. All nice and cosy and a long way from robbing jewellery stores and security vans.

The curtains were drawn. I knocked. One of the curtains twitched. Right then I knew something was wrong. I'd left my Makarov in the car, and I'd left the car a block up. I backed up a pace. The door swung open and King stood there in jeans and vest. He gripped a .38 revolver. When he saw me he relaxed and I saw the muscles around his neck ease. He kept a tight hold of the gun, though. He said, 'It's you.'

'What's wrong?'

'We're out.'

'What?'

He took a step forward, looked up and down the road. 'Did anyone follow you?'

'No.'

His dark face shone with sweat. His short blonde wife came out of the lounge and took a look down the hallway and saw me.

'Get rid of him.'

King nodded and waved her away. She didn't move.

'Get rid of him,' she said again.

King sighed heavily. He was surrounded; the wife behind, me in front. I don't which pissed him off more.

'We're out. Me and Tone. Out. I don't know what this shit is, Joe, but it's too fucking heavy for us.'

I'd known King and Daley for years, I'd worked with them on a couple of big jobs. They'd never lost their bottle. But I was looking at King and he was sweating and gripping his revolver tightly and his wife was hovering, not letting him out of her sight.

'What's this about?'

'You're on your own, man. That's what it's about.'

'Did you get anything on Glazer?'

'Fuck Glazer. Fuck you.'

'Tell me what happened.'

'Fuck off, Joe.'

'Tell me.'

He looked down at the revolver, put it in his jeans pocket, wiped the palm of his hand on the denim.

'I phoned a few people. Got nothing. Asked a couple people to ask around. Next thing I know, my wife is crying. Some cunt called up, threatened my kids, Joe. My fucking kids. I take that seriously.'

His wife was watching me, her arms crossed, her face grim and set, her mouth thin.

'It's Paget,' I said, 'that's all. He's frightened, making a lot of noise.'

'Bollocks. They were onto us half-hour after I made the

first call. This cunt knew my kids' names, where they go to school, when my wife's birthday is. Said he'd hit the kids first then come for my wife. That's heavy shit.'

Glazer had clout, then. Or Paget did.

'And it wasn't Paget, neither,' King said. 'He had a Manc accent.'

'You sure?'

'My brother-in-law's from Salford. I know the accent.'

'It doesn't matter. It's a bluff.'

'I don't give a shit. I don't get my family involved.'

'Who was it?'

'I don't know who. And I don't fucking care. Tone got the same message.'

'Did you get a number?'

'No. Fucker blocked it. I'm not going to say it again, we're out. Keep your fucking fifty grand.'

'Who did you call?'

'Fuck off, Joe. Seriously.'

'Who?'

'Nat,' his wife said. 'Get rid of him.'

He glanced back at her.

'Get packed,' he told her. To me, he said, 'We're taking off for a while.'

King's wife unfolded her arms, gave me a last lingering stare and marched off. She knew what the score was. You couldn't be married to a man like King without days like these. He turned back to me.

'I called three people, but the third I called only ten minutes before I got the message, so I reckon whoever grassed me up comes from the first two. Ben Green and Harry Siddons.'

I knew Ben Green, a small-timer out of Bow. He was into fraud, receiving, fencing, that kind of thing. Nothing heavy. He was someone you went to if you needed some information, new documents, bits and pieces like that. He was one of those blokes who knows lots of people. I suppose he was what they would call sociable, chummy. I didn't trust him, of course, but I'd never heard anything against him.

Harry Siddons I didn't know.

'Tell me about Siddons.'

'He used to do jobs, but then they diagnosed him with something, epilepsy I think. Now, he fixes jobs. Knows a lot of people. Me and Tone used him once when Ricky pissed off to Amsterdam and left us in the lurch.'

'Where is he?'

'Works as a salesman in a garage in Collier Row. The Ford place, off the A12. Know it?'

'I'll find it.'

'Right, now clear off.'

He slammed the door in my face.

THIRTEEN

I finally tracked Green down to the bakery in Stepney where he worked. I hadn't seen him in a few years. In that time he'd traded his hair for weight. He worked for the bakery as a delivery man, hauling boxes of bread and bagels to local restaurants, pubs, that sort of thing. When he saw me, he was red and sweating. He told the boss he was taking his tea break, and we went out back into a walled yard. He lit a smoke and wiped some sweat from his brow, leaving flour there instead. He sucked on the cigarette.

'Haven't seen you in ages,' he said. 'You alright?'

'Fine.'

'You hungry? Want anything to eat, bagel or anything?'

'No.'

'I get as many bagels as I want. Fed up of the bloody things.' He dragged some more on his fag. 'Been hearing a lot about you lately.'

'Such as?'

He shrugged.

'You know, rumours.'

'Go on.'

'I heard Cole hired you and Beckett to knock off his casino in some insurance job. Heard that Beckett was in with Paget and Marriot and that they decided to keep the money and make like you'd nicked it. Then I heard you didn't like that idea and went and got it back and somewhere in there Marriot and Beckett got themselves killed. That's what I heard, but I don't listen to rumours.'

So, he didn't know about Brenda. It wasn't common knowledge. That was good.

'Anything I can help with,' he was saying, 'let me know, alright?'

'What do you know about Mike Glazer? Friend of Paget's.'

Green nodded.

'Thought as much,' he said. 'When King called me, I remembered that you and him knew each other. I wondered if this Glazer bloke was anything to do with what's going on.'

'You ever heard of him?'

'Glazer? Can't say I have. Sorry.'

'Did you ask around?'

'Haven't had a chance yet, mate. I'm run off my feet here till eleven. Thing is, like I told King, I'm a bit out of the loop these days.'

'You straight now?'

'I wouldn't go that far. Man cannot live by bread making alone.' He grinned. 'I'll see what I can do, though, alright?'

'You haven't spoken to anyone?'

'Not till you got here. The boss don't like us making personal calls. He's a bit of an odd one, exacting, you know? Type who'd get out of the bath to have a piss. 'Sides, we get busy this time of day.'

He took another drag on his cigarette and looked around the yard, as if he was looking for a way to escape.

'Can't afford to lose this job,' he said. 'My wife's expecting another.'

He made it sound like it was all her fault.

'See what you can find out for me. There's a couple hundred in it.'

'I could use it.'

'Be careful. Someone doesn't want questions asked, and they know I'm asking.'

'Right. Don't worry. I still know some people to ask.'

I was about to leave him to it when he said, 'She wants to call him Jaydon. The kid. Believe that shit?'

I believed it.

'Joe,' he said, 'this stuff, it's not going to come back on me, is it? These are dangerous people and, well, I got a family.'

There wasn't much I could tell him. He was right, they were dangerous people.

FOURTEEN

I found the Ford garage easily. You could hardly miss it. You travelled down the A12 for a while and it was like you'd hit one of those American strips, all huge signs and used cars and burger joints. It looked like everyone had conspired to make it as ugly as possible, as a kind of joke on the people who came here to spend their money.

An old bloke was on the forecourt cleaning cars. I asked him where I could find Siddons. He pointed at the show-room and I could see a tall, thin man with a tanned, pinched face and a flat, pudding-bowl haircut. He had a gangly look, as if his limbs and trunk had been stretched. It made him look sly for some reason.

I went inside. He was showing a silver Ford Focus to a young Asian bloke. The car was the kind of thing half of Britain drove. Siddons had that mean cockiness that all successful salesmen have – a smugness that made them look like they had a mirror stuck in front of their eyes and they were always talking to themselves.

The young man kept glancing over at a red ST injection model, five grand more than the silver one. Siddons knew this and kept saying things like, 'The 1.6 is great at fuel economy, a nice car, really. Doesn't give you any trouble.

My brother-in-law's got a 1.6 five door. Takes the family out, every weekend, three kids.'

The young bloke was getting the idea that the cheaper car meant family and mortgage and a safe, steady, boring life. His eyes were spending more and more time on the sports model, which, after all, had alloy wheels.

There was a blonde secretary at a desk in the corner of the showroom and a small salesman who wandered around with a clipboard, making some notes on the cars there. The blonde woman glanced at me once, and then didn't take her eyes off the typewriter. The small salesman didn't want anything to do with me. I suppose I didn't look the type who would seriously want to buy a new car. Maybe they thought I was there for the pleasant surroundings.

After I'd stood around for a minute, the small salesman decided he'd better at least see if he could sell me something. I told him I wanted to speak to Siddons. When he heard his name mentioned, Siddons turned and looked at me. I could see his mind working. He could see straight off that I wasn't a customer, and he was trying to work out if he knew me and what I might want. Finally, he left the young bloke to look the cars over for himself and came over to me and said, 'Can I help you?'

'You spoke to a friend of mine on the phone. Man called King.'

'Ah, yes. A Ford Transit, wasn't it?' Not a second's hesitation. 'Come into my office and I'll give you the details.'

He went over to the small salesman and muttered something and pushed him towards the young Asian. Then he walked past me and I followed him out of the showroom and down a corridor.

'Fucking Pakis,' he said over his shoulder. 'Want everything half price.'

He took me into a windowless, cluttered office. He closed the door. He didn't sit, but went over and leaned against a filing cabinet along the side wall.

'You lot are jumpy. I only got a call from King couple hours ago.'

'Heard anything?'

'No. What's your name, anyway?'

'It doesn't matter.'

'Oh, right. One of them. Well, look, I'm doing this as a favour, yeah? I don't like doing this sort of business during work hours. I don't like people like you coming around here. So, why don't you fuck off and I'll make some calls and if I hear anything, I'll call King.'

He started to go back out of the office and I put a hand on his chest and stopped him.

'Who did you call?'

'The fuck you doing?'

'Who did you call?'

'Look, old son, you don't come into my place and make demands. Got it?'

He tried to push past me. I held him. I said, 'I won't ask again.'

'Fuck off.'

I snapped my arm out, the flat of my palm still on his chest. He flew backwards, smashing into his desk, knocking folders and paper onto the floor. He came to rest on the floor.

He stood up slowly, keeping his eyes on me. He brushed himself down. The cockiness had gone from his thin face now.

'I'm phoning the police,' he said.

He didn't move, though, and we both knew he wasn't going to phone anyone. I said, 'Who did you call?'

'I didn't call anyone. I didn't fucking call anyone. I told you, I don't do that shit at work.'

He was too angry to be lying.

'Does King know you're here?' he said.

'It doesn't matter what King knows.'

He shook his head.

'Who the fuck are you?'

'That doesn't matter.'

'Does anything matter to you?'

'Yes. Glazer.'

He watched me for a while then leaned over and started to pick up the fallen folders and papers. He bundled them together and tossed them onto the desk. Then he turned and looked at me again. His face cleared. He said, 'Wait, I know you. You're one of Dave Kendall's boys.'

'Was.'

'Huh? Oh, shit. Yeah. Someone killed him. You used to be a fighter, yeah? Joe—'

'I haven't got all day.'

'Right, Glazer. Why the fuck didn't you tell me who you were? You come in here, I don't know you from Adam. You might have been Filth or something. I mean, I can see you're not, but you might've been.'

'Glazer.'

'Yeah, right.'

He walked over to the filing cabinet and tilted it back and pulled a folder from beneath. He took it to the desk and sat down.

'Why did you want to know if I'd called anyone?'

'Someone called King and threatened his kids.'

'Shit. That's bad. Wasn't me, though.'

He didn't fidget or look away or do any of the other things people do when they try to hide something. I kept looking at him, though. I didn't want to make it easy on him if he was lying.

He said, 'Look, I've got a reputation, and I don't like it fucked with. You say someone put someone onto you, well, it wasn't me. And I don't need grief from King, yeah?'

He took some reading glasses from his desk drawer and opened the folder and ran his finger down a sheet of paper. I went nearer so that I could see. On the paper was a handwritten list. He turned the page to a second sheet and scanned this one, then a third. When he reached the bottom of that, he looked up.

'No Glazer.'

I turned the folder around so that I could see for myself. The list was coded; a surname and first name in a column on the left side, a series of letters and numbers in the middle column, phone numbers on the right. There was no order to the names that I could see, but the earlier entries were more faded and had more amendments and crossings out, so I supposed that the whole thing was an ongoing record.

I saw Daley's name at the bottom of the first page. Next

to it was a note that read, 'See King, Nathan', followed by a group of letters 'R, B, AR, AV, JS, NT, 3, 5'.

I pointed to Daley's name.

'What does it mean?'

He smiled.

'My own invention, old son. Fucking epilepsy. Used to know all this stuff, but now I can't remember my own birthday so I write it down. But I gotta be safe, so I use this code. See, anyone who wants to be fixed up with a job, or who wants contact with someone else who does, I put on the list.'

He waited for me to congratulate him. I nodded. I suppose it was a good system, a kind of criminal's yellow pages. It would take the law about two minutes to crack the code, but they probably wouldn't be able to prove anything in court. Siddons could claim the letters and numbers meant anything at all.

'You'd be on the list if you hadn't worked for Kendall. Daley has a note about King coz they always work together. Then I give them codes according to what they do, like AR is armed robbery, B is bank, JS is jewellery store, AV is armoured van. The NT means no time served. The first number is my mark out of five for the size of the jobs. Daley gets three out of five, meaning about fifty to a hundred grand. The last number is my mark for how high I rate them; reliability, professionalism, that sort of thing. Daley and King are fucking good.'

He regarded his work for a moment. It pleased him to think he had brains.

'You want to go on the list?' he said.

'No.'

I finished scanning the pages. There was no Glazer. There was no Derek. But there was a name, close to the end, that meant something to me.

'What's this?'

'Kohl?'

'Yeah.'

'Know him?'

'What's the C stand for?'

'Carl.'

Carl. Carl Kohl.

'Anything to do with Bobby Cole?'

'He's Cole's nephew. They're descended from Germans, or something. One brother changed his name, made it British. The other didn't.'

That explained a lot. No wonder Cole looked annoyed when that Carl was mouthing off.

There was another name alongside Carl's; Doug Whelan.

'Tell me about Kohl.'

'Fancies himself, but if it wasn't for his uncle he'd be nothing. Did some small time stuff with an old mate of his – that one there, Doug Whelan. Now I hear he's working for Uncle Bobby.'

Back outside, I sat in my car and fished out my phone. I didn't think it was Green who'd threatened King, and I didn't think it was Siddons. Both had said they hadn't yet called anyone. That meant one thing; it was the third person King had called, the one he'd dismissed because of the timing. He'd said that he'd called this third person only ten minutes before receiving the threat on his kids. Someone, then, had clout.

I tried King first at home. There was no answer. That didn't surprise me. I tried his mobile.

'Yeah?'

'It's Joe.'

I could hear background traffic and thought that King was probably on the road.

'Come on, man. Can't you leave me alone? I'm in enough shit because of you.'

'Who was the third person?'

'Huh?'

'After you called Green and Siddons. Who did you call then?'

'Bloke called Bowker. Jim Bowker.'

FIFTEEN

I trawled around the snooker clubs and pubs and bookies and couldn't find Bowker. I went to his flat and banged on the door. There was no answer. I hadn't expected there to be. He was smart enough to make himself scarce. After crossing me and grassing King up to whoever, he was probably halfway to China by now.

I'd told Bowker that I knew what he'd done to Brenda. That was stupid. He must've feared I'd want revenge for that. I'd forced him to pick Paget's side. When King called him, he would've known it was me who wanted the information. He would've called Paget and told him about King's interest, and then Paget would've called King and Daley and warned them off.

That was how I reckoned it must have been. But there were two things odd about it all. The first was that Paget knew Cole was after him, so why would he be bothered if King wanted him too? The second was that whoever had called King knew details about his kids, and knew it almost straight away. That didn't sound like Paget.

There were only two ways into Bowker's flat that I could see: kick the door in or smash the window. Either was going to cause noise and get attention, but I took the chance that people around here, in this block, wouldn't call the law. If they did, I'd hear the sirens and get out quick.

The door looked easier. It started to give after the fourth try, the frame splitting and warping. I heard the next door neighbour's door open. An old lady in curlers peered out at me.

'What are you doing?' she said.

'You know the man here?'

She made a sour face.

'I know him.'

'He owes money,' I said. 'I'm collecting.'

She nodded and her thin lips got thinner. She seemed to think it fair that I should smash his door in.

'He owes me twenty quid,' she said.

She faded away and I kicked the lock and sent the door inward in a shower of splinters.

The flat smelled of stale cigarettes. The walls were yellowed with tar, the carpet worn.

I pulled the place apart, starting in the small square living room. I emptied drawers, riffled through papers, tore apart the few books. I tried the kitchen and the bathroom and found nothing. I moved into the bedroom and went through clothes in the wardrobe, a chest of drawers, a box of oddments. Finally, I saw a cordless telephone on the floor, by the side of the bed. I snatched it up. It was a landline, not a mobile, and I supposed that was why he'd left it behind. Being a gambler, he'd made sure of having a phone on him all times and probably didn't use the landline much. I looked around some more and found nothing and left.

Outside, the old lady from next door was waiting. She

had removed her curlers and put on a thick woollen coat. When I came out, she said, 'Has he gone?'

I shrugged.

'Did you find it?'

'What?'

'My twenty quid.'

I left the door open for her and walked off.

Back in the car, I looked through Bowker's cordless phone. There were dozens of stored numbers, all with what looked like coded contact details, abbreviations that meant nothing to me. I turned the thing off and drove out.

I found a small pub and ordered some food. I got a pen and some paper from the girl behind the counter, found myself a quiet corner table and began scrolling through the numbers, noting down all the details I could get from the memory. After a while, I had two sheets of paper with numbers listed. There was no Paget in the list, no Glazer, no Mike or Michael, no Derek. Instead, the details were all combinations of letters; JG, ATC, and abbreviated words like Tag and Mac. It looked like a simple code, but it was probably just Bowker's way of being discreet. They were only abbreviations of names. Tag was something like Taggart. Mac could be anything Scottish. There was no KP, though, and no MG.

I already had one number for Paget stored in the memory of my mobile. I checked the numbers I'd taken from Bowker's phone against the one I had. None of them matched.

The food came over. My head was throbbing now and

I felt a clammy sickness getting a hold of me. I must have looked ill because when the girl brought my food, she lingered and looked at me.

Something was wrong. Something inside me was squirming and clenching my guts and wringing them, and an ice-cold hand gripped and squeezed my head. It wasn't anything I'd known before, but I recognized it for what it was: fear, of a kind. Not a fear of Paget, though, or of Cole or Dunham or any of those cunts – that kind of shit I was used to dealing with. They were just men, and I could face them and take my chances. And it wasn't like the fear I'd felt as a fighter, covering up because my face was mush and I knew that my brain was being thrown around more than it could cope with. And it wasn't the fear of a boy ducking to avoid Argentinean machine guns and knowing that we were going to have to advance towards them. I'd known that kind of fear, but knowing what was coming, the fear isn't so bad. This, though, was something else, a sickening hollowness. I didn't know what was causing it, but my mind kept creeping back to Brenda and how she'd been in those last weeks I'd known her.

I picked at the food for a while then pushed it aside.

I started to call the numbers I had. I went alphabetically. The first one was listed as AL. After a few rings, a man's voice said, 'Hello.'

'I'm trying to reach Kenny Paget or Mike Glazer.'

'You've got the wrong number, mate.'

'Jim Bowker gave me this number.'

'Bowker? What the fuck did he do that for?'

'He told me—'

'I don't give a shit what he told you. You've got the wrong number.'

He hung up.

It went on that way. Most of the numbers belonged to bookies, pubs, that sort of thing. Some were individuals and most of those didn't seem to know what I was talking about. They'd never heard of Paget or Glazer. Some were more guarded in their answers, some were hostile, some didn't bother talking to me at all. I made a note of those ones, for what it was worth. I hadn't planned very well how I would try to get information from anyone, and I had to change my approach as I went along, pretending that Bowker had been taken ill and that I had an urgent message from him for Paget or Glazer. I don't know if anyone believed that; I wouldn't have believed it. Most of the numbers were mobiles, and they were untraceable save for fancy tracking gear which I didn't know how to get hold of. So, I plodded on with my story.

I'd gone through the numbers from A to F and I was tired of the whole fucking lot. It was lunchtime now, and the pub was starting to fill up. People sat at the tables and ate lunches and laughed and talked loudly. I tried another number. The hum of the place started to seep into my head, the pain piling up around it. I closed my eyes for a moment and when I opened them I saw Brenda. She sat opposite me, gin and tonic on the table in front of her. She looked at me with wide empty eyes.

I blinked. She was gone. The pain wasn't.

I was into the H's by now. I dialled another number.

Something happened. The phone in my pocket vibrated.

I pulled it out and looked at it. It took me a moment to realize the phone belonged to this Derek character, and I'd just dialled his number. I had him. Or, at least, I had an abbreviation of what I thought was his name: HAY. That was something, but not enough. Too many names started HAY. If it was his name. I remembered the phone call I'd answered from Derek's wife or girlfriend. I still had her number. I went to the public phone in the corner of the pub, fed in some coins and dialled the number. I recognized her voice when she answered. Some of the concern had gone from it now, but it was still wary. I said, 'I'm trying to reach Derek Hay...'

I paused, like I was fumbling with an address book or something.

She said, 'Hayward.'

'Yeah, Derek Hayward. Is he there?'

'No. May I ask who's calling?'

'Is this his wife?'

'Yes.'

'Do you know where I can find him?'

There were some seconds of silence. Then the line went dead.

I had his name, though. Now I was looking for Derek Hayward, who must've been admitted to a hospital within the last few hours. Unless he was dead.

I started calling the hospitals. There was nothing. No Derek Haywards. I tried the pub's phone book and directory enquiries. I had a home number, so if any of the D. Haywards they'd given me had been the right one, I'd have known. I tried different spellings of Hayward, and different initials, in case Derek was a middle name or something. After a couple of hours I still had nothing. By now, the pub had cleared and my head was thick with pain. I couldn't think straight. I quitted the pub and drove back to Browne's.

When Browne saw me, he said, 'You're still alive, then.'

He didn't bother to ask if my head hurt. He just handed me a couple of his knockout pills.

The last time he'd seen me, Eddie and his men were taking me to see Dunham.

'Trouble?' he said.

'Huh?'

'From Eddie. Is it trouble?'

'It's something.'

I downed the pills.

'I thought he was a friend of yours. Well, as much as you can have a friend.'

'He works for Dunham.'

'What does that mean?'

'It means he doesn't have friends when Dunham wants something.'

'And what does Dunham want?'

'I don't know. Something's going on. They want Paget.'

'They want you to get Paget?'

'No. They don't. They want him, but they want me out of the way.'

'Why?'

It was a good question. Why?

I hit the sack and let the pills work on me.

She came to me again, in the dreams.

SIXTEEN

One day, she said to me, 'Do you think there's a god, Joe?'

It was late summer and still hot. I'd taken her up the West End to see a film, and then we had a meal in Chinatown. She was wearing the dress I'd bought for her at the market. I could see now that it was too small for her, too short on her tall body, and too tight. It clung to her and she'd have to pull it down every now and then when it gathered. It would fit her to a T, the geezer in the market had said. Bastard. He must've seen me coming.

Brenda didn't complain.

Her skin was like black velvet against the dress which clung to her tall slim body so that she seemed unreal to me, a flowing thing, like she and the cotton were part of the same thing and a breeze would float her away. She held my hand. I was almost scared of touching her, scared that I'd crush her.

After we ate, we wandered along Regent Street and Bond Street, Brenda stopping every five feet to gasp at a dress or piece of jewellery in some posh shop window, dragging me by the arm and saying things like 'Look, Joe, isn't it beautiful' and 'Look how expensive it is' and stuff like that.

When she saw Liberty's, she pulled me towards it.

'I came here once, years ago. They have such lovely cloth. You should see it.'

I saw it. It was cloth, alright. The place was still open so we went inside. It smelled sweet with all the soaps and scents. It made my nose itch. Brenda was wide-eyed with it all, stroking silks, sniffing candles, hefting cotton, and showing it all to me.

'Isn't it beautiful?' she kept saying.

She saw some handbags and went off to look at them. My back was bad by this time, so I found one of their small chairs and took a seat. After a while I couldn't see Brenda and I knew I was in for the long haul. It didn't matter. I sat and watched the people, tourists gaping at the colourful cloth and looking awkwardly about, city blokes buying silk ties, dusty old women trying on scarves, thin women dabbing perfume on their wrists, all of them like they were in some kind of wonderland. I suppose it was an escape for them, for Brenda too.

Every now and then, one of the security guards would walk slowly past, looking at me directly. I got the message. After a while, I had an idea. I remembered all the cheap creams that Brenda had bought at the market that time.

I got up and wandered over to the cosmetics section. The woman at the counter was polite, but I could see she wanted to be rid of me as quickly as possible. I couldn't blame her for that. I must have been a bad advertisement for them. I asked her for a gift box of some kind, something a beautician might like. She brought out a few. I paid eighty quid for some purple thing with an Italian name. I got the woman to wrap it up for me.

I went back to my seat and waited. A half hour later, the lift doors opened and Brenda came out. She stopped short when she saw me. She looked at the bag at my feet. She said, 'What on earth have you got there?'

'Beauty stuff.'

She looked from the bag to my face and burst out laughing.

'You're gonna to need a bigger bag,' she said.

Then she burst out laughing again.

I stood and gave her the bag and she said she'd open it when we got back. She reached up and kissed my cheek. I think she was happy then, at that exact moment. We went home.

She was quiet on the tube back, gazing at nothing, thinking, I thought, about those dresses and necklaces and handbags, dreaming, like people do, about how one day she'd buy one of them for herself. Every now and then she'd look down at the bag or lift it up and weigh it.

It was when we were walking down the Caledonian Road, back towards her flat, she tottering by my side in her high heels, one arm in mine, the other swinging the Liberty bag, that she asked me if I believed in a god. I said, 'No.'

She said, 'I mean, don't you think it's even slightly possible?'

She'd asked me all this before. I'd told her I thought it was all bollocks and she'd told me the same thing. Now she was asking me again and I wondered why. What did she want me to say?

'You didn't go to church when you were young?' she said.

'I went sometimes, while I was too small to do anything about it.'

'Why did you go?'

'My parents took me.'

'But they didn't give you religion.'

'They gave it to me till I was black and blue.'

'They beat you?'

'My old man did. My mum didn't do anything to stop him.'

'Why'd he hit you?'

'Drunk,' I said, 'or full of hatred for everything. Himself, mostly.'

'But he was a Christian.'

'He said he was. Lots of people do.'

'And your brothers and sisters?'

'They got it too, not so bad.'

She was quiet for a while. She'd stopped swinging the bag. It was stupid of me, I knew, to talk of these things. I wanted her to stay happy. I should have lied, I suppose.

'That doesn't make any sense,' she said, 'Beating a child.'

'You think it should make sense?'

'Christianity's about mercy and tolerance.'

'Yeah, well, my old man tried to beat mercy and tolerance into me.'

We were silent after that, walking along in the cool of the dusk, the low sun spreading light over everything and giving it all a glow. When we neared a pub called the Winston Churchill, Brenda pulled me in.

'I need a drink,' she said.

We'd been in there before. Brenda seemed to like it. It

was a sixties building, too new to have any character, too old to look new. The red carpet had worn away in places, the tables and chairs looked like they'd been bought second hand.

It was mostly empty. A few people sat in groups of two or three. It was a long way from Bond Street jewellers and the rich mob we'd seen in Liberty's. Nobody here had anything to prove, or maybe they'd given up trying. They had their own problems. I think that's why Brenda wanted to go there. She wanted to try and push the rest of it out of her mind. She wanted to get back to the real world. She wanted to stab the dream to death before she could start believing it. Anyway, she hadn't dragged me in there for the booze; she had plenty of that at her flat.

I bought a couple of drinks and we took a seat at a corner table. Music was crackling out from battered speakers. The light was dim. There was laughter and chatter. There was a smell of crisps and beer and mildew and furniture polish.

Brenda was quiet. We sat there, her stirring her gin and tonic with her finger, me looking at her, waiting, looking around at others. I wondered if she was going to tell me we were over. I suppose I always half expected that, anyway. I tried to tell myself it didn't matter, but I felt a coldness grip my stomach when I thought of it.

Finally, she pulled her finger from the gin and sucked on it a moment. Then she looked at me and saw that I was looking at her. She smiled, but she couldn't make it look real. It was just too hard for her to do.

'I've got to work tomorrow,' she said.

She tried to make it sound casual. I said, 'Uh-huh.'

It was something in the way she said it, the way she looked away from me, the way she went back to stirring her gin with her finger. There was something else about the job, something wrong. Or, rather, something worse than normal, something beyond lonely old men who only wanted a fumble because they couldn't get it up, or drunk businessmen who wanted to display a bit of their power by buying a tart for an hour, or married men who wanted someone else, anyone else.

'What is it?' I said.

She'd stopped stirring the gin, now, and just watched it, like she was looking at something she'd lost and could never have again. After a minute, she looked up and around at the other people in the pub. Finally she looked at me and forced a shrug.

'A film.'

She'd made films before for Marriot.

'What about it?' I said.

'It's a special.'

That was how she said it. 'A special.'

Something inside me went cold.

I didn't push it. I suppose I should have. I didn't have the words. I didn't have whatever I should have had. I was just a lump.

I don't know what I would have done anyway. I don't know if I could've changed anything. I might have done nothing, I might have done everything. I would have tried to help her, maybe, for what that was worth. I'd tried to get her to leave the business before but she'd fought me. I hadn't understood it at the time.

I suppose I might have saved her. I might have killed her, like I later killed Kid. I touch something, it dies.

I think, then, sitting there in the Winston Churchill, Brenda was caught between telling me the whole of it, spilling everything, wondering, probably, if I could help her. Maybe she knew better than me what my reaction would've been. Maybe that's why she didn't say anything. Or maybe she wanted me to ask her, take the responsibility out of her hands.

Anyway, we sat there and listened to the crackling music and the tar-filled laughter and throaty chatter of the people around, and at the silence of our thoughts. We smelled the crisps and the beer and the mildew and the furniture polish and the dankness that came with it all. We looked at faded prints on faded walls and at the people, the old, young, empty, faded people, clinging to this moment of escape, more real for them than all that bollocks up the West End. We looked at all that and, sometimes, we would look at each other.

We walked back to her block of flats. The lift was working for once, so we took it up. She pushed herself close to me. It was warm in that metal box. She shivered and I put my arm around her.

'I feel safe with you,' she said.

'Good.'

When we got into her flat, she didn't bother turning on the light. She kicked her shoes off and turned the fan on and fell onto the sofa. She hugged the Liberty's bag and closed her eyes. I went and made us a coffee. When I brought it back, she hadn't moved, and her eyes were shut. I put her mug down by her foot and took mine over to the window and looked out over North London. It was dark now and from Brenda's place you could see the reservoirs up by Chingford and Edmonton, lights reflected in them. You could see Ally Pally up high and White Hart Lane and all the roads with bright insects crawling along them. It wasn't something for the tourists, it wasn't for those dusty old birds in Liberty's or the young thin ones who'd be dusty in thirty years or the fat white men with fat white bank accounts who these women wanted to please. It wasn't anything you could care about, but in the dark you could forget all the concrete and crowds and endless exhaust fumes and for a moment, if you were with your bird in a flat up high, you could think it wasn't so bad.

I felt Brenda's arm curl around my waist.

'Thank you,' she said.

'For what?'

'For everything.'

She held me. We looked at the view.

Later, we were sitting in front of the TV. She was curled up next to me, holding me. The smoke from her cigarette was floating like a cloud in the middle of the room, just hanging there, as if time had stopped.

She said, 'Tell me something, Joe.'

'About what?'

'I don't know. Anything. Tell me something about you. Tell me something nobody else knows.'

'Why?'

She let her cigarette burn. The sound of the TV muttered into the silence.

'I don't know why,' she said finally. 'I just want you to tell me something.'

I started to tell her about my time in the Paras, about the slog of the Falklands, tabbing in that ankle-breaking terrain, the weight of the packs. I was going to tell her about the Argentine conscript, about how he still came to me, all these years later, in dreams or in dark moments, but she stopped me.

'Not that,' she said. 'Tell me something else. Tell me a story.'

I thought about that a while. I said, 'There was this fight once—'

She put a hand on my stomach.

'No.'

She looked up and put her hand onto my cheek and turned my face to her so that she could look at me in the eyes. She said, 'Not that.'

I understood then. I nodded. I tried to think what to tell her. I couldn't think of anything. I felt clumsy, my mind breaking down, words not coming to me. I looked around her flat. I saw the print she had of Turner's Fighting Temeraire. I said, 'When I was fifteen I made a boat. Out of wood. I stole some bits of pine from the woodwork class and I whittled a hull and sanded it. I made the masts out of a wooden coat hanger I found in a skip. This old bloke lived in a flat near us and he used to say hello to me when he saw me. I gave it to him.'

When I finished, she nodded.

'That's good,' she said. 'That's a good story. Now I'm gonna open my present.'

She sat up and grabbed the package and ripped the wrapping off.

'Blimey. This musta cost a bloody fortune.'

She took the lid off and picked out the bottles and tubes. She looked at them and read the labels. Then she leaned over and kissed me on the cheek.

'Thank you.'

She got up and went to a corner of the room, near the drinks cabinet. There she knelt and lifted a corner of the carpet away from the skirting board. She turned to me.

'My secret hideaway.'

She fiddled about a bit and prised up a large white tile. There was a hole underneath, chiselled out of the concrete. She put the box I'd given her in there, then she peeled off the dress and folded that up and put it in. Her skin was like the night, endlessly dark, the darkness lighting the white strap of her bra. Her ribs rippled, her spine pushed at her skin. She looked so thin, so breakable.

She put the tile back and laid the carpet back on top. She made a drink then came back and curled herself up on the sofa, folding into me.

'Only you know about that place,' she said into my chest.

'What do you keep in there?'

'Oh, this and that. Stuff. You know. Nothing worth much to anyone else but worth a lot to me.'

'So why hide it?'

She thought about that for a while.

'That story you told me, about making that ship and giving it to that old man, you never told anyone else?'

'No.'

'But it's not something you should be ashamed of, is it? I mean, there's no reason why you shouldn't tell anyone.'

'No. No reason.'

'I think it's like that, Joe. I think I need to keep something secret from everyone, something away from everything else. In a way, I think it's something I need to keep away from me. If you see what I mean. But I want you to know where I keep it.'

She turned her eyes up to me so that when I looked down at her, she looked like she was pleading with me.

'You understand,' she said, 'don't you?'

'Yes,' I said. 'I understand.'

But I didn't. Not really. Not then.

SEVENTEEN

By the time I woke up, it was almost 4 p.m. and getting dark. I crawled out of bed. My head was better, but I felt dopey. I forced myself to do a few sets of press-ups and sit-ups and followed those with a long shower, switching the water from hot to cold.

Browne had some food ready for me in the kitchen. He sat at the table and watched me eat. My head was clearer now, but the fear was there, lingering, twisting my guts slowly.

'Are you alright?' he said.

'Yeah.'

'Your brain still there, is it? Still working?'

'Yeah. I need to find someone. He was injured, probably taken to a hospital.'

'Where?'

'Somewhere near Epping Forest.'

He thought about that for a moment, wiping a hand over his head.

'What kind of injury?'

'Gunshot.'

He muttered something, probably cursing me. Then he sighed and said, 'It'll be Whipps Cross or the Alex in Harlow. Too far for Middlesex.'

'What about private hospitals, clinics, that sort of thing?'

'If he had a gunshot wound, they'd take him to an A and E. Private hospitals won't deal with something like that.'

'Some doctor, then.'

Browne shrugged.

'An honest one would call an ambulance. And then call the police.'

I knew he was right. I wondered if Glazer or Paget had picked Hayward up and taken him to some bent quack. But they wouldn't have known where to find him; Cole's men had dumped him in the middle of nowhere and I had Hayward's phone. It was possible he'd managed to get to the road and flag a car. But Carl said he was bleeding badly. He surely would've phoned for an ambulance.

All that meant I was a long way from finding him. And I was nowhere near finding Paget or Glazer.

'Have you tried the ambulance stations?' Browne said. 'They have logs of all calls.'

I got the number for the Essex Ambulance Service and made a call to the main station. I told the woman who answered that I was calling from Whipps Cross Hospital, and that we'd been told that a man with a gunshot wound was being brought to us by ambulance. She asked who I was and why I wanted to know. Browne had told me what kind of thing to say. I gave the woman a load of bollocks and she checked with her log and told me that I'd got it all wrong, a man had been picked up from the side of the Epping New Road, near the Wake Arms roundabout at 3.18 a.m. with a probable gunshot wound to the right shoulder, broken collarbone, hypovolemic shock. He'd been taken to Princess Alexandra.

I had the bastard.

'Oh, hold on,' she said. 'No, not Princess Alexandra. Addenbrooke's.'

'What?'

'He was taken to Addenbrooke's. There's a note here.'

I told Browne what the woman had told me.

'Addenbrooke's? What the bloody hell is he doing there?'

'Where is it?'

'Cambridge. Bloody NHS.'

I grabbed my coat.

'You're welcome,' Browne said as I left.

It took me an hour to get to the hospital, which sprawled on the south edge of Cambridge. It was like an industrial complex mixed with a council estate, all concrete blocks and chimneys. I took my time and drove slowly around the hospital, through the car parks and along the roadways, looking for police cars. If he'd been admitted with a gunshot wound the hospital would have made a report. He would've had emergency treatment and then, when he was able to talk, the law would've been waiting. Cole's men dumped him about 3 a.m. By now, the law might've left, or they might still be waiting to speak to him. After a couple of circuits, I saw no sign of them.

I stowed the car in the car park, near to the exit. I got out, pulled on my woollen hat and my large coat and headed towards the main lobby. I stopped at the help desk. A bald man sat there and stared at his computer screen and clicked his mouse. His name-tag read 'Bryan'. A mug of coffee rested on the desk. He kept his eyes on the computer screen and held up a finger up.

'With you in a minute,' he said.

He threw the mouse around a bit, then picked up his mug of coffee and sipped from it. When he was happy he'd kept me waiting long enough, he looked up at me.

'What can I do for you today?' he said, trying hard to look like he cared.

'I'm looking for a friend of mine. Derek Hayward.'

'Hayward. When was he admitted?'

'This morning.'

He clicked and typed and slid the mouse around. While he was doing that, he sipped more coffee. Then he reached a hand into a desk drawer and pulled a biscuit from a packet. It was when he put the biscuit back that I knew something was wrong.

'Um. Now, Hayward, you said. No. Nobody here called that. Sorry.'

He wouldn't look at me, but started to glance through some of the papers to his side, like they were suddenly important. I turned and walked away, back out to the car. I tried not to run. It had been a mistake, coming here. I'd let myself become careless. My fucking head again, all fuzzy and clogged with the desire for blood. Like I'd said to Eddie, it was a mug's game. Stupid.

I hadn't seen a closed-circuit system in the lobby, but I'd seen enough of them outside to know they'd have a rough idea of my face. In the car park, I scanned for cameras and saw one a dozen yards from me, aimed at the entrance. I'd have to ditch the car. I opened it up, wiped down the steering wheel, handbrake, gearstick and the few other parts I would've touched. I grabbed my Makarov from the glove compartment, gave the car a last once over, locked it and threw the keys into a hedge.

Over in the distance, a woman was getting into her car. It would take her a few minutes to get out of the parking space and then out of the car park. I scanned the road she'd have to take. I walked out of the car park and along the road. I stopped by the corner of a large building, which looked like the generator station. I waited. There were no cameras here, no witnesses.

I heard her car get near and then, as she rounded the corner, I moved into the middle of the road. She braked slowly, a puzzled look on her face. I held out my hand like I was an official of some kind. She stopped, put on her handbrake and opened the window. I walked towards the open window and leaned down.

'I paid,' she said. 'At the machine.'

She was in her late middle-age, maybe mid-fifties, and neat, but dully dressed, as if she'd left the house in a rush to run a quick errand. When I held the Makarov up, she looked at it, not quite understanding. When she got it, she said, 'Oh.'

'I'm going to get in the passenger side,' I told her. 'You're going to drive me out of here.'

'Yes,' she said. As an afterthought, she said, 'Don't hurt me.'

They came in as we left: two patrol cars with sirens screeching, both Cambridgeshire police. So Hayward was there, then, and they'd been waiting to see if someone would try to see him. Probably, the man on the desk had hit his name into the computer and some flag had come up. The woman shrank from the sound of the cars, and I could see her hand shake as she made the gear change. As we came to the roundabout, she said, 'Which way?'

I had an idea. Risky, though.

'Which way?' she said again, looking left and right, as if the direction she should take was all she had to worry about.

'Go all the way round.'

'We'll go back into the hospital.'

'Yeah.'

She hesitated, looking to see if any traffic had right of way. Now she was all nerves, and the shock of having a thug with a gun in her car was getting through to her.

A van came up behind us and started hooting. That made her more nervous, and she stalled the car. I waited while she got it started. The van overtook and the driver gave us the finger.

'I'm sorry,' the woman said. 'I'm not very good at driving. My husband...'

She burst into tears and I had to wait a few seconds before she could get a grip.

'I'm sorry. He's ill and I have to drive, there's no buses where I am.'

She babbled a bit – a reaction to the shock – but she managed to get the car started and drove us back to the hospital. I directed her, and we passed a patrol car parked outside the main reception. Through the glass doors, I saw uniforms talking to the bald man at the desk. I looked for the other patrol car and saw it for a moment ahead of us, turning slowly, cruising around the hospital grounds, looking for me. I told the woman to park up the road from the first patrol car. I moved the rear-view mirror so that I could watch them.

If Hayward had talked, they'd know he was in with serious people, and they'd want to grab those people. If he hadn't talked, they'd wonder if he was still a target. Either way, they'd have to go and check on him.

The uniforms came out, and spoke to each other. Then one of them keyed his radio and spoke into that. They got into their car and pulled out and came past us slowly. I kept my face down, like I was texting someone on a mobile. When the patrol car was fifty yards ahead, I told the woman to follow it slowly. She did and in a minute I saw the car stop at a smaller two-storey building. The uniforms got out of their car and walked in. We passed the building. It was called the Gardenia Wing.

I got the woman to drive us out of the hospital then. We stopped in a quiet residential street, a quarter mile away. The street was wide, with grass verges and thick-trunked trees. A few cars passed us, followed by a couple of people trundling by on bikes. I told the woman to give me her purse. She did and I fished through it for some ID. I looked at her name and address and handed the stuff back to her. I forgot it all the second I gave it back.

'Now I know where you live,' I told her. 'Don't tell anyone about this.'

After she'd driven off, I walked into town. I'd have to give it a while before I went back. Visiting time was until 8 p.m., which gave me a couple of hours.

I found a small dark pub, and a small dark corner to hide myself in.

What Browne had said was plaguing me. He was right to wonder why Hayward had been taken to Cambridge when there were hospitals closer to Epping Forest. Maybe they'd decided he wasn't that badly hurt. Maybe all the other Accident and Emergency places were busy or closed or on holiday. It seemed wrong, and I didn't like it.

I bought some flowers and, at half past seven, I waved down a cab. It was dark and drizzly, the rain floating in the air. The night helped me, and the rain gave me a reason to turn up my collar and bury my face. I told the driver to take me to the hospital. As we neared, he asked where I needed to go. I told him the Gardenia Wing. He dropped me off. I had twenty minutes till visiting hours were over. I told the driver to wait for me. He wanted money up front, so I bunged him a tenner. He turned off the engine and sat back to read his paper.

The building was long and narrow with small windows evenly placed on both floors. It looked more like a prison block than a ward. I walked in through the double glass doors and into a white reception hall. On my left was a nurses' station. A woman in blue uniform was at the desk, filling out some form. I walked past her. I was just a man visiting someone.

On my right was a stairway and, next to that, a lift. Ahead of me was another double door, with glass panels, leading to a long corridor with doors on either side. Those, I guessed, were the rooms. So, it wasn't an open ward, which was good. There were fifteen or so on each side.

I turned right and took the stairs. Upstairs was a repeat of the ground floor without the nurses' station. Halfway along, a small female cleaner was on her knees, her upper half out of sight through a doorway. I walked slowly down along the corridor, looking at the nameplates on each door. Some doors were open. I passed a man in his room sitting next to his bed, reading a book. I passed a room with the radio playing. I passed the cleaning woman, an Asian, maybe Filipino. She glanced up at me and saw the flowers and smiled. I carried on walking, looking left and right at the nameplates. Lawrence, Enid; Jones, Paul A.; Bromley, R. D. A door opened and a woman and child came out. The child waved to whoever was in the room. She closed the door as I passed; Sanger, John. I came to the last three names; Zimmer, Wilcox, Thomm. There was no Hayward anywhere. At the end of the corridor was another staircase and another lift. I had to go back down and along the ground floor corridor, back towards the nurses' station.

I trudged down the stairs, trying to look casual.

More open doors, more closed ones, more names. Floyd, Khan, Ambrose. The closer I got to the nurse, the more obvious I'd look, the more like the freak I was. I was a walking wall with a bunch of pansies and I had to act like a concerned friend. The corridor was funnelling me into a trap. I had to hope the nurse wouldn't look up and see me and know, as she surely must, that I was out of place. Jenkins, Kerr, Peters.

She'd seen me, a quick glance up and then back to the forms. Watson, Matheson, Patel. If I took her out, I'd risk discovery. There were the other visitors, for one thing. She might have calls to make, for another. Maybe someone else would be along soon. It might be an hour before someone realized she was missing. It might be a minute.

She was watching me now, not bothering with the paperwork in front of her. A few doors left. A few doors. My brain was screaming at me to think of something. I was too far inside hospital grounds to get out without a fuss. If the law was alert, they could swarm the area before I managed to get a few streets away. Lewis, Turner, Burton. I'd tripped the alarm earlier by asking for Hayward's room, so that was out, and if I left, she'd start wondering and she might remember the police bursting in a few hours earlier.

I was at the end of the corridor now.

'Lost?' she said.

'I thought my friend was here,' I said.

'What's his name?'

My mind went blank. I'd seen a dozen names and I couldn't remember a single fucking one. She stared at me.

'Zimmer,' I said finally.

'Oh, Mrs Zimmer. I... uh... who are you again?'

'Never mind.'

I turned and went back to the stairs and climbed them slowly, trying to think what I should do now. I knew the nurse was watching me, wondering, probably, why someone like me would want to see some Jewish lady who, for all I knew, was a hundred-and-eight-year-old Hungarian. I didn't think it would take the nurse long before she made a call or two.

Back up the top, I started walking along the corridor,

the flowers crushed in my hand. I passed the cleaner again and she looked at me and smiled uncertainly. I stopped and went back to her. She was scrubbing the floor of a small toilet. She stopped scrubbing, but stayed on her knees.

'I can't find my friend,' I said.

'You go to the nurse,' she said, pointing back to the stairs.

'She's not there.'

This surprised the woman.

'No?'

'No. My friend is black, tall and slim.'

She thought about this for a moment. Then her face cleared.

'Black man? Young?'

'Yes.'

She stood up. She wasn't much taller standing than she'd been kneeling. She looked along the corridor, towards the far end. She walked that way and stopped outside a door and pointed to the nameplate: Zimmer.

'A man,' I said. 'Not woman. Black man.'

She was confused now. She pointed at the nameplate again.

'Black man. Young.'

And I knew I'd found him. And I knew I was in trouble. The cleaning woman was going to go back to her work and she was going to stop and wonder how it was that I didn't know my friend's name. And then she was going to wonder why the nurse wouldn't be at her station. And, meanwhile, the nurse was calling the law or security and telling them that someone had come to find 'Mrs Zimmer' who was, in fact, a man under police protection. Yes, I was fucked. But I'd found him. The cleaner looked at me curiously as I opened the door. Then I saw I was really fucked.

There were two of them, one each side of the bed. They were looking at Hayward, who was sitting up, bandaged from his shoulder to his torso.

They were white, one tall, about six-two, in his late thirties, early forties, the other shorter, older, maybe late fifties. Their suits were of a type; one in grey, the other blue, both plain. The ties around their necks were loose, their top buttons undone. The taller one was in the blue suit. He had thin hair and puffy eyes. The one in grey had short grey hair and a greying moustache. He was grey all over. Both were unshaven. I could smell stale cigarette smoke in the room. I could smell cheap aftershave and booze. I could smell the sameness and endless disappointment of life. It was a uniform, of sorts.

They looked like middle-managers who'd become stuck in middle-management hell, too old to move up, too young to retire, too fat to do anything else. They looked like a million men, washed-up and wasted and worn out, but I knew them for what they were, I smelled it on them. They were the law. They stank of it. They were the fucking law and I'd walked right in on them.

Hayward saw me first and his eyes widened. The others turned. Their dead eyes flickered. Nobody said a thing, nobody moved. We all just looked at each other. There was something unreal about the whole thing, something not right, and I thought, This is a trap.

The room, the building was closing in on me. The stench of the place, the putrid air, sweet with the smell of urine and antiseptic, seeped into my nostrils. It was suffocating me. The cloying heat made me want to tear off my jacket and shirt just so that I could breathe properly. But I stood there, like the fool I was, rooted to the spot, staring at two plainclothes coppers.

Then Hayward said, 'That's him.'

They moved as one. I dumped the flowers and reached for my gun. The cleaner screamed. The one in blue charged me and slammed his shoulder into my stomach. It threw me off balance and I crashed back against the doorjamb and lost grip of the Makarov, which clattered to the floor. I drove my elbow down into his back and he yelled in pain and collapsed at my feet. Grey Suit was at me now, smacking his fist into my face, his mouth twisted in fury and effort. I took his pounding and batted him off as best I could while I tried to move. Blue Suit realized what I was trying to do.

'His gun,' he said.

He scrambled along the floor, reached for the gun. I kicked him in the stomach. I was off balance and hadn't connected, but I caught him enough to double him up. He sucked deeply and clambered to his feet and came at me again. The cleaner was at my feet, balled up and covering her head. The nurse downstairs must have called for the police by now. If I didn't get out quick I was done. I put my right foot flat against the wall and pushed with every-thing I had, flinging both men backwards. We crashed onto the bed and Hayward cried out as we landed on him. Grey Suit was up again, staggering but balling his fists, ready to strike. I took hold of his jacket and smashed him in the jaw. He went down cold. Blue Suit was struggling to right himself and Hayward was crying out in pain. I jumped up and grabbed the cleaner and threw her at the three men. She shrieked and she landed on them heavily and I had the gun in my hand.

Grey Suit was coming to. The cleaner scrambled off the bed and balled herself up in the corner of the room. Hayward's bandages were soaked through with blood and there was a glazed, sick look on his face. Blue Suit was staring at me. I levelled the gun at them, spitting blood.

'We know who you are,' Blue Suit said. 'You won't get far.'

I backed out and took the nearest stairs down. I barged through a fire exit and onto the street. The cab was still there, the driver leaning back smoking. I walked up to the car, opened the driver's door and pulled him out. He yelped when he hit the ground. As I got in, I could hear sirens screaming towards me.

The first police car rounded the corner as I shot away from the kerb. They slewed their car across the road, blocking my path. There wasn't enough pavement to go around them. On one side was the brick side of the building I'd just come from. On the other was a grass verge with trees. I skidded to a stop and threw the car into reverse. When I saw flashing lights in my rear-view mirror, I knew I was fucked. I swung my car round to block the road and took the keys out of the ignition. The second patrol car pulled up behind me, trapping me. Something in my mind was telling me something was wrong, somewhere. Everything was pushing in on me, squeezing me. If these boys were tooled up, I didn't have a chance. They looked like regulars to me, but I couldn't be sure. I thought, Fuck it.

I opened the door and got out and walked up to the first cop car. Both coppers got out and started to walk towards me; their batons were out, but they weren't armed. That was a mistake. I pulled my Makarov and added ten years to any stretch I'd ever do. The gun opened their eyes. They scrambled for cover. I got in their motor and gunned it away. Behind me, I could see the other patrol car trying to nudge past the cab.

EIGHTEEN

I was in south Cambridge. I hit the side roads, going through residential streets, avoiding traffic cameras. After a half mile or so I eased the speed down and looked for a place to ditch the cop car. I left it beneath a large cedar tree. I could hear sirens in the distance. It wouldn't be long before they got the chopper over here. The car would be hard to spot from the air and it would take a while before the patrols found it. That meant I had a bit of time, but not much. The station was about a mile north of me with the city centre another mile further. The police would be all over there by now. If I went south, it was a short way to the edge of town, but then I was exposed, a lone figure in fields. It was dark, but I'd show up on infrared. They'd get me easy. I pulled the collar of my coat up and started walking towards the station.

I spent an hour ducking down side roads, turning back on myself the moment I heard a siren up ahead, twisting this way and that like a worm on a hook. When I finally got to the road leading to the station, I saw police all over the place, coppers on foot standing at the station entrance, patrol cars parked. I kept walking.

I was on a main road now and it was busy. Buses and

cars and trucks whirred past me, people on bikes and foot all around. I could see the steeples and taller buildings of the town centre ahead. That was where I had to get to. A patrol car turned into the road a hundred yards up and headed my way. I ducked into a pub and waited for it to pass by. After that, I was okay. Once I was in the centre, I got my bearings and made for the old part of town.

It took me another hour to find what I was after. I thought it was too late in the day, that I must have missed them. Then I saw them coming out of one of the colleges, a dozen people, mostly old, following a tour leader. I tagged on at the back, getting slowly closer as the group stopped before one place and another. I got a few odd looks, but nobody said anything. After a half hour, they stopped for a bite to eat and I pulled the tour guide aside. He was a stuffed shirt type, more interested in showing off his knowledge than keeping the people interested. He hadn't even known I wasn't supposed to be there. I told him I was on another tour group but had got separated. I asked if I could tag along. He thought that was against policy or something. I pulled some money out of my pocket and handed him a score and policy went out of the window. After that, he told everyone I was joining the group. I had to put up with them for another couple of hours, traipsing round museums and that sort of shit. I saw a few patrol cars cruising, but they were looking for a lone figure. Finally, with the dark fully upon us, we went to a park and climbed aboard a coach. I took a seat at the back and pushed myself into the corner. I'd found out the group was from Birmingham, so that's where I was going.

By the time we got onto the M6, I was tired. I listened to the hum of the wheels, the soft twitter of music coming through the small speaker above. I watched the shadows blur by, the lights of cars and lorries.

But I couldn't sleep because something nagged at me. It was that bunch at the hospital. Something was wrong and I couldn't put my finger on it. The two suits were law, but they weren't behaving like they should've been. They had a man in custody and that man had been involved in a shooting incident, but they'd shipped him out to a hospital in Cambridge, when he should have gone to Whipps Cross or somewhere near the incident. They were protecting him for some reason. It could have been that Hayward was an informer. But the coppers' manner bothered me.

I thought of these things and of the conversation I'd had with Hayward's wife or whatever she was. The first time I spoke to her she was agitated. She hadn't heard from Hayward, she thought he might be hurt. The second time I'd spoken to her, she'd seemed calm, as if, by then, she'd got news of him. But if her old man was nicked and in hospital, would she be calm? Then there was Glazer; when I mentioned his name, she gave no sign of recognition. No, I was missing something.

For a moment, I thought the whole thing had to have been a set-up, that they'd used Hayward as bait to lure me after him. But that didn't make sense either. Why hide him in Cambridge if they wanted me to find him? Why were the detectives unarmed if they expected me to hit Hayward? But that, of course, that was the last thing they wanted. When I'd walked into that room they'd been as surprised as me.

Those detectives hadn't been quizzing Hayward, either. There'd been no notebooks, no recorder. It was all wrong.

I leaned back in my seat. It was darker now and the coach was hot and stuffy. The people in front of me were quiet, some resting, some talking softly, travelling back to their dull lives in their dull homes. Christ, I wished I could be them. To be able to go home, go to work, live quietly, boringly. That was what I wanted.

I watched one middle-aged couple a few seats in front of me. The woman was rabbiting away about her friend Wilma who'd done something to someone for some reason. It was the bloke that got me, though. He was bored, but there was something else. He was trying not to look bored, trying to look like he didn't mind being there even though he was itching to escape. It was like he was doing his duty, putting up with it all. Something about that snagged in my mind and I realized that he reminded me of the detectives in Hayward's room when I'd first seen them. There had been that half second when I'd first barged in and everything had stopped and I saw the men in front of me like a scene frozen from a film. Those detectives had the same expression then as this bloke did on the coach.

Then I realized. They weren't there to question Hayward. They hadn't nicked him. They were visiting him. Hayward was one of them. Hayward was a fucking copper. Now I understood that conversation I'd had with his wife. And I understood too why he was in Cambridge, why the gunshot wound had been hushed up. They were protecting him, protecting their own.

NINETEEN

It was late when we hit Birmingham. I found a chain hotel near the station and paid for a single room, high up so I could get away from the traffic. Things were building up and I needed to sort them out. I took a shower in the room and popped some pills to sort my head out. After all that I lay on the bed and stared at the ceiling. I could hear the drone of the traffic from the street, six floors below. My head throbbed. I had to think.

Paget was at the root of it. We all wanted him – me, Cole, Dunham. All for different reasons. Cole wanted to get his heroin back and restore his reputation. Dunham wanted something else, but I didn't know what. I wanted something simple. I wanted revenge. And the law? What about them? What the fuck did they want with Paget? Was Hayward a plant of some sort? And if he was, what was he after? One thing I knew, the law wasn't interested in arresting Paget. If Hayward had been attached to him for a while, which he must have been, why hadn't he nicked him? And Glazer? What of him?

My mind was going round in circles. I stared at the ceiling until it seemed to come down and meet me. The throbbing was duller now, but so were my thoughts. I needed to work this shit out. I needed to reach through the dullness, the fog.

I kept thinking about the hospital. Things didn't make sense.

When the ambulance had picked Hayward up, it should've taken him to Whipps Cross, the nearer hospital. Instead it had been diverted to Cambridge. If he was a copper, someone he worked for could have arranged the diversion. Once in Cambridge, he was hidden under a different name. That meant that his people thought he was still a target. If he was undercover, it made sense. Then Hayward's superiors would have alerted the local force, let them know what was going on. When I'd gone to reception and asked for Hayward, there'd been a flag on the name and the bloke behind the desk had hit a button and the law had turned up.

All that was fine, as far as it went. What didn't make sense was what happened later, when I'd gone back. They hadn't expected me to do that – that much was clear from the reaction of the men in Hayward's room. But what didn't fit was the response from the Cambridgeshire police. They'd sent a couple of patrol cars, but at the first sign of my gun they'd hit the dirt. Which meant they didn't know what they were dealing with. By rights, I should've walked out into an armed response unit. It was like two things were going on; the first was Hayward's mob, protecting him. The second was the Cambridge law, reacting to something they didn't understand.

The law didn't operate that way.

Something else. When I'd called Hayward's bird the

first time, she'd asked me if this was about Elena. What was that about? Who was Elena?

My head was starting to bang away again. All this thinking was making me ill. I took a couple more of Browne's little white pills. That was a mistake. I needed a clear mind. Instead, I got wiped out.

But I slept badly, my mind turning things over and around so that it all became lumped together and murky. I slept for a few minutes, then woke and slept again and woke again. In the end, I gave up, picked up the bedside phone and called Ben Green.

'Know what time it is?'

'I need you to find someone for me.'

'Go on.'

'Derek Hayward. He's a copper, Met.'

'Where does he work out of?'

'I don't know.'

'Anything you can tell me about him?'

'Mid-thirties, six-two, black, slim. He's mixed up with Paget and some bloke called Mike Glazer.'

'Glazer? That's the one you wanted me to find out about before.'

'Yeah.'

'What's this all about, Joe?'

'I don't know.'

'Is there anything you do know?'

'No.'

'You're a great fucking help.'

I dropped the receiver back onto the cradle and went down to the hotel's lounge.

136

There were booths and tables scattered about. The odd small group of business people sat around and pretended to have something worth saying, a straggler or two sat by themselves staring at the carpet or at their drink. The light was dim, the music was low, the talk was hushed, the furnishings were faded. It was all designed to relax you into a coma. That was fine with me. I could have done with a coma just then. I dropped myself onto a stool at the bar and ordered a couple of beers. The bartender had some rule about serving drinks one at a time so I downed the first while he was still ringing it up. He got me my second and when he put it down I ordered a third.

There was a television behind the bar. They were onto the sport before I realized there'd been some kind of shoot-up in East London. They'd said something about a gang-related crime. They'd shown a large house, bullet-ridden, and a wall, half blackened by fire. The world was cracking up. I heard more words, but by then my head was coming apart, like the rest of the world, and I had trouble staying upright in my seat. The barman came over and asked if I was okay. I told him I was fine. He didn't believe me and lingered a while. Then he was gone and so were most of the others. I didn't know what time it was, or what day. A bit later a bloke in a suit came up to me and asked me to leave. I don't know why. I showed him my room key and he suggested I go and lie down. I suggested he go and fuck himself, but he was right. I weaved between tables as best I could and took the lift back up and staggered out and found my room and aimed myself at the moving bed.

I dreamed of Brenda, her smile bright, her eyes young.

She stood in front of me and held out her hand and I took it, but what I held was a dead dried-up stump and when I looked up the smile was set by rigor and the eyes were white and dead and it wasn't Brenda any more but that Argentinean kid, frozen in death a dozen yards from my foxhole. I wanted to go out to get him, even though I knew he was dead. I couldn't stand to see his face there, staring back at me, hour after hour.

I didn't know where I was. My head was fuzzy and I was on my back staring at darkness. I could feel dampness beneath my head. I thought it must have finally cracked open. I heard a ringing and my mind was telling me to get up before I was counted out for good. Then I realized the ringing was wrong and everything else was wrong. The ringing stopped. The dampness was still there.

It took me a moment to work out where I was. Light came through the orange curtains. I traced a crack on the ceiling and counted how many heads I had and managed to work out that those large things in the distance were my feet. I climbed off the bed and threw up in the waste-paper bin. When I'd done that I had a shower. I felt better. I was fresher and my head had cleared. I wasn't feeling pain so much, the alcohol was thinning out, the pills had lost their muddled effect. I began to think again.

I took a few bags of peanuts out of the mini-bar and ate them and made a cup of coffee. Then I reached over and picked up the phone and called Ben Green.

'Did I phone you last night?' I said.

'You don't know?'

'Yes. I think so. I asked you to find Hayward.'

'You okay, Joe?'

'Fine. Did you just call here?'

'Yes, I did. About Hayward; I can't find him, couldn't find anything out on him. But I might have something.'

'Go on.'

'Copper I know knew someone who worked with him.'

'When?'

'Way back, seven years maybe.'

'Did he give you an address for this bloke?'

'A bird, Joe. Not a bloke.'

'Go on.'

'Well, this copper I know works out of Harlesden, and his old governor was a woman who had a thing with Hayward for a couple of years. Bit of a talking point, apparently. She was married and left her husband, that sort of thing. That's all he knew. Bird's name is Sarah Collier.'

'What do I owe you?'

'You're after Paget, right?'

'Yes.'

'And this might help?'

'Yes.'

'In that case, it's on the house, old son. I told you about my kid? I don't want him in the same fucking world as Paget. Got me?'

'Yes.'

'Look, Joe, I know this is none of my business, but from what I hear, Paget's got a shitload of Cole's smack. That right?'

'Go on.'

'Have you thought that he might need to unload it, get

some readies? If I was looking for someone on the run, I'd ask around, see if anyone's bought a load of dope.'

I should've thought of that myself.

'Want me to check around?' Green said.

'Yeah.'

TWENTY

She wasn't a copper any more. She hated it. The whole fucking force was prejudiced against women, especially successful women, especially successful women who had affairs with other officers, especially black officers. They didn't like that sort of thing, even if it was none of their fucking business. And when they didn't like something about you, that was it. You were finished, dead in the water.

She told me this. Repeatedly. She didn't really want to talk about it, she said. She didn't know who I was or why I'd be interested. She told me this too, over and over. I'd told her I worked for a solicitor and that Hayward had been named in a case. It was a shit story; what did I know about solicitors? She didn't believe me from the word go, but she didn't question it, didn't even ask for an ID. She didn't care who I was. She took my money, though. She was fine with that. And she was happy to talk. I let her get on with it.

We were in a semi-detached in Acton. I could see from the photos that she'd married. I had a feeling she'd divorced too. There wasn't any sign of a bloke living there. Her husband had probably got sick to death of her yammering.

There was a kid wandering around. It was about three

or four. I could see it wasn't Hayward's, so there was nothing there for me to use.

She made another couple of mugs of coffee and put them down on the kitchen table and sat opposite me.

'What was your rank?' I said.

'I was a DI. I was only thirty-two. There weren't many DIs at that age. Hardly any women. I joined straight from school. Eighteen. Three A-levels. And that was when A-levels were hard to get.'

The kid had been settled in the corner of the kitchen, dribbling on an empty egg box it was pushing around. It got up now and shuffled over to its mother and held the box out to her like some kind of offering. She took the box and patted the kid on the head and put the box on the table. All that while, she didn't stop talking, going on about her brilliant career. I drank my coffee.

She'd been attractive once. I knew that because she had plenty of photos of herself looking attractive. And young. She wasn't so young now.

'This was in Barnet,' she was saying. 'Del was only a Detective Constable then.'

'Only?'

'Huh?'

'What is he now?'

'I heard he got promoted. Did alright for himself.'

'You heard he did?'

'Yeah. This was after we split up. After he split us up, I should say. Got promoted to a DS couple of years after that. I hear he's an Inspector now. Positive discrimination. That's fine. If you're black.'

'When was the last time you saw him?'

'Must be eight years ago, something like that. Yeah, it was. Eight years last January.'

'You left?'

'He left. Asked for a transfer. Too awkward for him, see. About then he decided he had a fucking career to get on with.'

'Where'd he go?'

'Some specialist unit.'

'Which one?'

The kid was back and wanted its mother to pay it some attention. She stroked its hair.

'Huh? Oh, I dunno.'

I took a roll of notes from my jacket pocket and peeled off another hundred quid.

'Which one?'

'What does it matter?'

'Which one?'

'You're persistent. Who are you anyway?'

'Nobody.'

'Well, nobody, you think money's going to help me remember?'

'You remember. The money's so you'll tell me.'

Her hand froze on the kid's head.

'God, you've got a fucking nerve. What makes you think I know about something that happened eight years ago?'

'You know when he got promoted. You know the month you last saw him.'

Her mouth became thinner. She stared at me, trying to get even for all the shit that men had done to her. After a few seconds, she gave up trying to scare me and shrugged. She wouldn't have lasted as a copper. She looked at the money instead, like it was to blame for her failures. She snatched it up.

'Something to do with Vice.'

'Where?'

'I don't know. I really don't. It was a vice unit in Peckham or Brixton or somewhere. He's black. Lot of crime down there is black crime, so they're always looking for good black coppers.'

Vice. I felt a tightening in my gut. There was a connection, then, between Hayward and Paget. South of the river, though. That didn't fit so well.

'You ever heard of Kenny Paget?'

'Who's he? Another copper you lost?'

'Mike Glazer?'

'No.'

'Did you ever hear anything about Hayward after he went to Vice?'

'Like I said, he got promoted. I left the force soon after that so I couldn't tell you. It took me years to get from Sergeant to Inspector and he did it in a leap and a bound.'

And off she went again. Even the kid was sick of it by now. It shuffled out of the room and disappeared. I would've gone with it, but I still needed some information. I didn't want to get heavy, so I put up with it.

Finally, she said, 'If I never see him again it'll be too soon.'

It took me a second to realize what she was talking about.

'So you wouldn't know where I could find him?'

'Find him? You want to find him?'

'Yes.'

'Why didn't you say? Course I know.'

As I walked back to the bus stop, I thought about what she'd told me. There was so much of it, it was hard to put it in order. But something stuck out, rang a bell.

By the time the bus came, I knew what was ringing the bell.

It was Elena. But Elena wasn't a person. Elena was a thing.

And I knew, too, that Hayward had to be bent.

I knew everything. I was a fucking genius.

TWENTY-ONE

The car was parked outside Browne's. The nearside window was open a crack and cigarette smoke wafted out. They weren't worried about being seen, which meant they weren't expecting any grief from me, which meant Dunham must've thought I'd go quietly. On the other hand, they were here, waiting for me, which meant Dunham must have been getting jittery or something.

The car doors opened and they climbed out wearily. The driver was a short man. I didn't know him. The one my side had red hair and freckles on his face. I'd met him before. He looked at me like I'd fucked his wife, threw his fag on the ground and opened the back door.

Browne must've been keeping a look out for me too because his front door opened and he stepped out and looked over at us.

I was going to tell these blokes to fuck off, but I changed my mind. I didn't need grief from Dunham.

There was another reason why I decided to go along. I wanted to know why Dunham was paying me so much attention, why he was so bothered about finding Paget. A meeting with him and Eddie might not be a bad idea.

I waved Browne back. Red Hair held his hand out for

my Makarov. I wasn't giving that up and Red Hair let it go, which meant he was under orders to be polite.

We didn't go up the West End this time. Instead, we went for a ride in the country. The drive took forty minutes and all that time the two up front didn't say a word. Every now and then one of them would look at the other and they'd grit their jaws or sigh. They must've been waiting outside Browne's a long time and they weren't going to blame Eddie or Dunham for sending them there, so it was all my fault and now they were giving me the silent treatment like a pair of old women. I wondered where the fuck Dunham got these clowns.

We slowed when we came to a village. I thought we were in Hertfordshire, or Buckinghamshire. The village was one of those stockbroker-belt type places, full of mock-Tudor houses and fat men with fat faces and their thin tight-arsed wives who stared at strangers.

We slowed in front of a wrought iron gate, brick pillars on either side, a security camera on one pointing down at us. A ten-foot-high brick went in both directions from the gate. I guessed it must encircle Dunham's entire property. On top of the wall were black iron spikes.

Red Hair got out of the car, went up to the gate and pressed some numbers into a panel on the lock. The gate opened slowly and we drove in. I surveyed the grounds as best I could from the car. On both sides, there was open land, grass running from the front of the house to the high wall.

The house was a cube the size of a factory. It was a lot like Dunham: a squat block that shouted power, flattening everything else around it. I suppose they'd call it a mansion, Dunham's country seat.

The car stopped and we all got out. From there I could see a wooded area that ran from the wall and stopped fifty yards from the rear of the house. All around the rest of the house was the grass.

The front door opened and Eddie came out and met us at the top of the steps. I glanced up and saw another security camera. Red Hair trotted up the stairs and whispered something in Eddie's ear. He was telling him I hadn't handed over my gun.

Eddie dismissed the troops with a nod and they faded away. Eddie wasn't worried that I was tooled up. He still thought I was playing along. Above us, in the wet grey sky, crows tossed and fell and screeched, like they were crying out something to me, a warning maybe.

'Welcome to the country,' Eddie said. 'Like it?'

He smiled at me, but there was something forced about it.

'Should I?'

'People do, you know. They come out here for holidays.' He nodded over his shoulder at the building. 'Vic paid three mill for this pad. What do you think of it?'

'Ugly. Dunham should feel at home.'

He laughed. I wondered why.

He led me into a hall that was bigger than my old flat. The ceiling was twenty feet up and the staircase contained enough marble to build another house. The place was full of antique furniture and old oil paintings and stuff like that. All very expensive and tasteful. Dunham was trying hard to forget who he was and how he'd managed to pay for everything.

We wandered through the hall and then through a door and into a living room. The room was too large. Only a corner of it was used. There, a TV was on. A kid's cartoon was playing. A woman sat in a large chair, half facing us. Her legs were crossed, a glass of something colourless in her hand, a magazine on her lap. On a small side-table a cigarette burned in an ashtray.

Her light hair was pulled tightly away from her face. Her cheekbones were strong, her eyes were large, her nose was straight. She was good looking, and she looked like she'd never smiled in her life. Eddie glanced over at her. She sipped her drink and turned the page of her magazine. Her actions were too well timed, and I knew she knew Eddie was looking at her, and he knew she knew it. Everyone knew everything. We were all so fucking smart, all so cool.

Facing the TV was a huge white sofa. A small blonde girl was perched on the edge of it, lost in its size. She kicked her legs as the cartoon characters ran around. I remembered the photo in Dunham's office. There'd been a picture of Eddie and a girl, taken in a country garden, which, I supposed had been here. The woman ignored us as we passed, but the girl looked up for a moment. Eddie waved. She smiled and waved back. Then she saw me. She stopped kicking the sofa. Her hand fell.

At the far end of the room was another door, solid oak, half a foot thick. We went through this and into a library. The walls were lined with leather-bound books. There was a heavy desk at the far end and beyond that a window

overlooking the garden. Two leather seats were this side
of the desk. Eddie pointed to one of the leather seats. I
sat. He sat. We waited. We looked like we were waiting
for the headmaster. Eddie crossed his legs, then uncrossed
them, then stood and walked over to the window. I saw
his eyes glaze over for a moment as he looked out of the
window at the garden. Then we heard a door close and
Eddie blinked.

Another door opened and Dunham came in, walked
slowly over and sat behind his desk.

'Got anything?' he said to me.

'No.'

He looked at Eddie, but it took Eddie a while before he
turned away from the garden, as if he had to do something
he didn't want to do, and was delaying it.

But he ignored whatever it was and said, 'You've been
gone awhile, Joe. Where've you been?'

'Around.'

'Around where?'

'Here and there.'

'And you didn't find Paget?'

'No.'

Eddie nodded.

'What did you find?'

'Nothing.'

Dunham smiled.

'You just had a short break?'

'Yeah.'

'I don't believe you.'

'I don't care.'

'Can he read, Eddie? Coz we don't seem to be on the same fucking page.'

That crack smelled like a routine, like I was being treated to an act. I'd felt that since the first time I'd met Dunham.

'We just want to find Paget, Joe,' Eddie said.

'I'll find him.'

'And hand him over to us?'

'You can have what's left of him. There won't be much.'

'I thought we had a deal,' Dunham said. 'You let us know what you get, we fix Paget, get the junk back to Cole, he pays the Albanians their money. Everything's settled.'

'And what do you get out of all this?'

'We get peace,' Eddie said.

'Since when are you interested in peace?'

'It's just strategic. We let the Albanians calm down for a while, then we get rid of them, Cole and us.'

'Why would you care about the Albanians? They don't stray on your turf. Unless you've moved into prostitution and people trafficking.'

Dunham leaned forward. I could see a vein throbbing in his forehead.

'It would be a mistake to fuck with me. I'm not some cunt like Cole.'

'What kind of cunt are you?'

He wasn't smiling now, but he hadn't exploded either. That was interesting. I was still getting the treatment, then.

Eddie said, 'Take it easy, Joe. We're on the same side.'

'I'm on my side.'

'Not if the Albanians come for you. Then you'll want to be on the strongest side. Which is us.'

'They won't come for me. They've got problems of their own.'

I caught something then, a flicker of a look between Dunham and Eddie.

'You didn't hear about Cole, then?' Eddie said.

'What?'

Even as I said it, I felt a tug in my guts that said, Yes, I know.

'He got hit last night.'

'While you were on your short break,' Dunham said.

It came back to me like the taste of bile. I was in the bar in that hotel in Birmingham. I was watching the news on TV. They mentioned a shooting in East London. They showed a house riddled with bullet holes. It was Cole's house. My head had been so fucked up with pills and booze I'd watched the pictures and listened to the voice and seen right through all of it.

Dunham was smiling grimly. He was enjoying himself. I was wrong and he was right and he loved it, the power of it.

'Is Cole dead?' I asked Eddie.

'No. Nobody was home.'

'They're not quite the finished mob you seem to think, are they?' Dunham said. 'Maybe now you'll start trusting us.'

There was nothing I could say to that. They'd scored a point off me and I was on the back foot. Now they wanted me to block up and go to the ropes. Instead, I thought I'd try and land a punch of my own. I said, 'What do you know about Glazer?'

Eddie's eyes narrowed and glistened with that amused expression he sometimes had. He smiled thinly. Dunham didn't look so happy now. I thought I'd hit him on a sore point, but now he looked like he didn't give a shit. Or tried to, anyway. That was interesting.

'What do *you* know about him?' he said.

'Fuck your games.'

'You're in over your head, Joe,' Eddie said. 'If you've got a lead on Paget, tell me what it is.'

'Why?'

'What does Cole know?' Dunham said.

That was a mistake. I could see it in Eddie's eyes. He was still smiling, but the glint had gone. Dunham had split with the script. We were supposed to be making plans for Paget and the Albanians and all that shit, and suddenly Dunham's forgotten all about them and wants to know about Cole. That was strange. That mention of Glazer had hit home.

I was sure I was right – they were playing some kind of game – but the more I saw Dunham, the more I knew of him, the less I thought he was the type to play games. He was a knot of power, a man with a mission, serious and vicious. People like that didn't fuck about. No, the more I watched them both, the more I knew they were playing Eddie's game. Dunham had gone along with it for a while, but I'd hit him with the fact that I knew about Glazer and he'd dropped his guard a moment and let me see that I'd hurt him, if only a bit.

Whoever Glazer was, then, they didn't want me to know about him.

Dunham was tired of games now. His face seemed to cloud over, his eyes became hooded and dangerous. He was becoming himself, creeping out of the daylight and back into the slimy dark pool.

'How would I know what Cole knows?' I said.

'Now you listen to me,' he said, his voice thick as mud, 'you're gonna forget about Paget.'

'We need you and Cole to concentrate on the Albanian threat,' Eddie said, still trying to make like the Albanians were dangerous. I kept my eyes on Dunham.

'Paget's mine,' I said. 'I want to watch him bleed for what he did.'

Dunham said, 'I don't give a fuck what he did.'

Eddie turned to him.

'He killed a woman, Vic. Cut her up.'

'My heart bleeds.'

'The woman was Joe's bird.'

'I know it. She was grassing Marriot to the filth, wasn't she?'

I'd hit him with Glazer and he'd staggered. Now he was hitting me back. He sank into his seat and watched me from behind his large desk and smiled at me.

I turned and walked out of the room and past the woman with coldness in her eyes and past the kid who stared at me. I walked through the hall with its antiques and paintings that made the place taste more sour, more rank. I walked out into the dark day and looked at the gloomy sky and felt the cold air blast me in the face. I watched the crows above whirl and fall and screech their murderous cries.

Eddie had followed me out. He put a hand on my shoulder. I didn't try to break it off. I had a grip on myself.

'Don't take it personally. He gets carried away sometimes, likes to stick the knife in a bit too much. He didn't mean what he said in there, about your bird. He has a wife. Has a daughter too. You saw them, in there. He loves the girl, always talks about her. That must tell you something.'

'Sure.'

He was trying too hard to make like Dunham was a saint, which, I thought, might mean that whatever Dunham had going on, Eddie didn't like it.

Whatever it was, it was bad.

TWENTY-TWO

By the time they dropped me off outside Browne's, I felt like I'd done ten rounds. My body weighed a hundred tons. My arm throbbed but it was a dull and distant pain. My head was fuggy.

On top of all that, I felt an emptiness that was more than hunger, it seemed to start in my gut and work its way through to my fingers.

I told myself I just needed a change of clothes and a shower and a shave. I told myself to shut up and get on with it. I told myself to find Paget and kill him.

The car stopped and Eddie's boys waited, keeping their eyes ahead. It took all I had to open the door and climb out.

I stumbled into Browne's house. He heard me and came out of the lounge and grabbed me by the arm. I almost pulled the both of us down, but he held on. He pushed me into the lounge and steered me to the couch. I fell onto it. He disappeared. When he came back, he was carrying a tray of food and a cup of tea. He put the tray on my lap. My hands shook with the effort of picking up the knife and fork. Browne took them from me and cut the food up and fed it to me. I didn't know what he was shovelling in my mouth. I couldn't taste it. I could feel the blood pulsing around my head, though, and the emptiness swelling and sucking me in.

'You can't go on like this,' Browne was saying. 'You know that, don't you? It'll kill you.'

'No choice.'

He was right. I was right. It didn't matter.

He disappeared for a while. When he came back, he had a syringe in his hand. He stuck me with it, pressing the plunger quickly. I don't know what it was he shot in me. He told me, but I didn't take it in.

'Need a clear head,' I said, stupidly.

'Well you're out of luck there, aren't you? You haven't had a clear head since I've known you. We in the profession call it being bloody stupid. It's a form of brain damage. There.'

He pulled the syringe out and unscrewed the needle.

'Now, no exertions, understand? Don't even sneeze for the next twelve hours.'

I sat there and felt my head fall and dip and whirl, like those black crows. Browne went and sat in his chair and watched me.

'Bad, huh? Well, you were almost killed a couple of weeks back. I'm not surprised your body's reacting like this. You need to be hospitalized. But then you know that. You should at least go and rest.'

'Can't.'

'No. Of course. Places to go, people to kill. Right?' He smiled darkly. 'That's what it's all about. Aye, that's it. I patch you up so you can go out and slaughter. Is it revenge,

Joe? Is that what you're after? Don't you understand that doesn't work? That's like trying to cut out a cancer with a meat cleaver. You destroy yourself as much as the thing you want to destroy. Revenge isn't about getting justice or closure or anything. It's about satisfying your lusts, your base desires. It's ego, man. Bloody ego.'

I saw his lips move. I heard the words a minute later. I just kept staring at him.

'It doesn't matter,' I heard myself say.

'Och, what's the bloody use.'

He got up and left the room. I thought he was gone for good, but he came back straight away with a glass of Scotch. He grabbed the TV remote and took it and the drink over to his chair. He sat down and flicked the TV on. He made an effort to watch whatever they were churning out. To me, it was all noise and blur. He took some gulps of his drink and switched channels. He was angry with me. I didn't know why.

I opened my eyes. The light from the sky had gone. I must have passed out. There must've been something in that brew Browne gave me. There were no lights on, but I could see Browne by the glow of the TV. He was in the chair still, but he wasn't solid like he'd been. Now he was a lump of clothes. A bony hand at the end of a sticklike arm gripped a drink. The few grey hairs he had left were a mess. He was staring at some programme about sea birds. They dived into the sea and swam around under the water. I thought again of those crows, their screeching, mocking cries. A murder of crows. Wasn't that what they called them?

Murder. Damn right.

I moved. Browne looked over at me. He looked a dozen years older than he had a few hours ago. I saw the bottle of Scotch by his foot.

'Decided to carry on living, did you? Well, let us rejoice.'

He turned his head back in the direction of the TV.

'Not that you care,' he said, 'but I've decided on something. I'm going home.'

My head was still fuggy. Wasn't this his home?

'Home?'

'To Scotland, I mean. North of London a bit. You know where that is, don't you?'

Did I? I wasn't sure.

'Why?' I managed to say.

'Why? I can't take it any more, that's bloody why. I can't live here, be amongst these people. You have a system for coping; you just bull your way through, go after what you want and if someone gets in your way you smash them. Maybe that's the way the world is these days; take what you want and damn everyone else. It's Darwinian, I suppose. Fundamentally. Anyway, it's not my world. Probably never was.'

I didn't have it in me to tell him to shut up so I just sat and waited for him to prattle on some more. He didn't. Instead, he took some of his drink and watched the birds. We both watched the birds. Seagulls were gathering in gangs and swooping down on fish. They were murdering them. Maybe Browne was right; everything murdered everything else.

Time crawled. My head floated to the ceiling and came

back slowly. Browne got drunker. The day got older. The sky got darker.

'I miss her,' Browne said. 'Stupid, I know. After all, she was only here a few days, wasn't she? And she hardly spoke. But I miss her. I suppose because she was so...'

He sighed and ran a hand over his hair. I didn't understand what he was talking about.

I said, 'Brenda.'

He didn't hear me. I don't know if I even spoke. I saw a shadow out of the corner of my eye. I tried to turn my head, but I couldn't make it. I thought it was Brenda, and then I remembered the girl, Kid, and I thought it might have been her.

I realized that was who Browne had been talking about. A small girl, thin, alone.

'There was that time,' he said. And then nothing more.

There was that time.

Yes, there was that time we'd gone to the market. Or was that Brenda? Yes, it was Brenda. I'd bought her a dress. The dress was too small. She took it off and put it somewhere.

Where? Did it matter? For some reason it did.

And I thought about the market, too. There were lots of people there, and she was nervous, looking around her. When I asked if she was okay, she told me that she didn't like crowds. But she'd been the one who'd wanted to go there, to the market.

It played in my head, that stuff. Lots of things did. My life was on some kind of loop, bringing the past back around every now and then. But sometimes the past had changed or was unclear and I couldn't work out what was real and what was in my head, what was memory, what was dream.

Anyway, Brenda, Kid – they'd both gone. They were both dead, both victims of the world that bore them and mutilated them and tried to destroy their hearts. Now they've got a lot more in common. Now they're just memories. Browne remembers them, most of the time. But he's old, and when he's gone, there'll be three of them, living as only the dead can live, in memories, And who'll remember them? I will, while my mind holds out. And what then? Then nothing. Not a fucking thing.

But even in my head, they would become confused and I'd see Brenda as Kid and Kid as Brenda so that the girl was trying on the shoes in the market and the woman was staring in wonder at the shiny trinket.

They were born decades apart on different sides of the world, but they shared things, as if they'd lived one life, split into parts, broken, like that mirror, like my memory. But, in death, in my head, they became one again.

I opened my eyes. Had I been dreaming? I didn't know.

'There was that time,' Browne was saying, 'do you remember? When we couldn't find her and she'd hid in the cupboard. Christ, I was terrified we'd lost her. Do you remember?'

He was talking about Kid, about the time she'd had a flashback, been traumatized and had hidden in the wardrobe upstairs, taking shelter there in the same way she'd hidden at the house where I'd found her.

I remembered. Of course I did.

She'd shot me with a gun she'd found. When she realized

I hadn't been there to hurt her, she helped me out. I wouldn't have made it out of there without her.

After that she got it in her head that I'd gone there to save her. I hadn't. I'd gone there looking for Cole's money. But she wouldn't leave me. She was like some small animal that was afraid to come closer to the dangerous thing, but afraid to be alone.

I knew what Browne was doing. It was what I did with Brenda; it was torture, self-inflicted.

'Do you miss anyone, Joe? No, I don't suppose you do. Well, I'm not like you. I can't shrug off all this insanity, all this... this hopelessness. So, I'm going back to where I came from. More or less, anyway. My sister's up there. Elgin. Nice place. I thought I might go and stay with her for a while. I haven't got much, but I've still got this house. That must be worth something.'

They were both shadows now, Brenda and Kid. I could only see them from the corner of my eye.

I was about to say something to Browne, but when I looked at him, his chin was down and his eyes were closed and I thought he was asleep. Then I saw that his chest was heaving and I realized he was sobbing. He got a hold of himself and wiped his nose on the sleeve of his shirt.

He carried on drinking, staring at some cookery programme that was now on the box, sinking lower into his seat. After a while, his head bolted up.

'I know you,' he said, throwing his arm towards me, spilling his drink. 'You think I don't, but I bloody well do.'

He was slurring his words now and his accent was stronger. That happened when he got drunk. The more

162

Scotch he poured into himself, the more Scottish he became. He wiped some dribble from his chin.

'You think nobody knows you,' he was saying. 'But I saw what you did for her. Almost bloody killed yourself going up against Merriot, Marriot, whatever his bloody name was. Oh, I know you claimed it was for your reputation and all that maloney, baloney. But I know you. I know there's something there, Joe. I know it.'

He put the glass to his lips and tilted it up. There was only a drop left, but he didn't seem to notice.

'He keeps telling himself it doesn't matter,' he said to the cooks on the TV, 'because that's how he survives, by not caring. But I've heard him scream at night. I know what haunts him. I know what he did. He can fight the whole bloody world, but he can't fight what's inside him.'

He shook his head from side to side.

'No, he can't fight that.'

'Yes,' I said. 'I miss her.'

'Ah,' he said. 'I see.'

He didn't say anything else.

I stayed there a while longer, letting my head clear some more. Browne drank and we watched whatever it was on the TV. At some point I looked over and saw that he was asleep, the empty glass in his lap.

I hauled myself up. I put his glass on the coffee table and left him to his hangover. I had things to do. Places to go, people to kill.

TWENTY-THREE

It took me a while to find Cole. I tried his mobile and got no answer. I got through to his club and someone there passed me on to someone else and they wanted to know who I was and what I wanted. All this time, I was in Browne's car, driving towards Cole's house. I wanted to get a look at the damage.

I called some other places and some other people and got nowhere. I turned into his road in Chigwell. The place was quiet enough. There didn't seem to be any patrol cars around. I cruised along slowly. Lights were on in Cole's house. I saw a few cars in his driveway. I parked at the kerb and walked towards the front of the house. Before I'd gone a few yards, I could see the front door open. A man came out and looked towards me. He spoke to someone behind him then disappeared back inside. I must've had a dozen eyes on me.

After my trip to Dunham's country place, Cole's house looked like a doll's house. Maybe that was why Dunham had dragged me out there.

There wasn't as much damage as I thought there might have been. There were a few dozen bullet holes in the brickwork, and the holes weren't big. Not large calibre, anyway. I guessed the holes had been made from a couple of bursts from assault rifles. The holes were scattered over the whole front of the house and one of the large bay windows was boarded over. The double garage, separate from the rest of the house, had an area of charred brick-work, more so at the bottom.

I went up to the front door. It opened without me knocking and the same small bald gammy-legged man who'd let me in before stood and peered up at me.

'Cole?'

'Upstairs.'

He moved aside to let me in. Men were scattered around the place. They glanced at me. The last time I'd seen those men, they'd been sitting with drinks in their hands, watching Cole do his chief boss act. Then they'd seemed uneasy. Now they held guns, not martinis, and they didn't have to pretend they were enjoying themselves. Now they looked like they belonged.

I went upstairs. The landing was as plush as his lounge, and as fake. The white carpet was two inches thick, and on the walls hung more of those splurges of colour that he thought were art. From there, a half-dozen doors led to the bedrooms. From the furthest, at the back of the house, I could hear Cole snapping instructions to someone. I moved that way.

Cole was throwing things into a suitcase with one hand and holding a mobile to his ear with the other.

'I don't give a flying fuck how much they get,' he was saying to the phone. 'Just sell them.'

He looked tired. There was thick stubble around his chin and dark circles beneath his eyes. He was feeling the strain.

When he'd finished with the phone, he tossed it onto the bed. It was only then I noticed that Cole's wife was in the room. She sat with her back against the headboard of the bed and her feet out in front of her, and I thought she had the look of someone who had taken Valium. She didn't seem to know where she was or why.

'Where the fuck have you been?' Cole said to me.

He was striding around the room, collecting underwear from the chest of drawers, shirts from the wardrobe, chucking everything into the suitcases.

'Trying to find Paget.'

'You still bothered about that cunt. Fuck him. We got other problems.'

At this, his wife let out a short laugh. Cole glanced at her.

'Whyn't you help?' he said to her. She shrugged her reply.

'Who did it?' I said.

'Who d'ya think? Fucking Albanian cunts.'

'Why aren't the law here?'

'Them wankers? They questioned me for hours. I told them I didn't know nothing.'

'They believe you?'

'Course they fucking didn't. What can they do? I told them nobody was home. That bit was true, as it happens. The wife and I were up in the West End. So, no witnesses. I swore blind I didn't have an enemy in the world. So they took some statements and made some measurements. Then they fucked off. In the end, if I want to live here, they can't stop me.'

'What was the damage?'

'Are you blind?'

'They shot the place up and threw a petrol bomb at the garage.'

'You sound disappointed it wasn't more.'

'They didn't storm the place? Didn't throw anything through the windows?'

'You can fucking see, can't you.'

He turned to his wife.

'Where's my address book?'

She blinked.

'Downstairs,' she said. 'By the phone.'

'They didn't concentrate their fire,' I said. 'That petrol bomb wouldn't have done any damage, so why throw it? Why just shoot the place up bit?'

Cole stopped packing his cases and looked at me.

'What's your game?' he said.

'I thought you said the Albanians were finished.'

'I was wrong, wasn't I?'

'Were you?'

'What's that supposed to mean?'

'There's something wrong with all this. Haven't you noticed?'

'I tell you what I noticed, I noticed my fucking house getting shot to shit. That's what I fucking noticed.'

'You can't find Paget. I can't find him. No sign of him. Nothing.'

'So?'

'And these Albanians; why would they hit you now? They've got the law all over them. Why would they risk it?'

'Because they're fucking nuts, that's why.'

'All because they want you to pay up a million quid. How is this going to make you pay up?'

'What the fuck you on about? It was a warning. That's why there was no real damage.'

It was possible. I didn't like it, though.

'Who said this was the Albanians?'

'Who else would it be?'

'Who said it was Albanians?'

'I got the word. You think I just sat on my arse and wondered why my house was developing holes? I got my boys out and they put the screws on a few people.'

'It's not that easy,' I said. 'There's something wrong. They wouldn't risk coming out of the woodwork just to set fire to your garage. There's something else going on. Something to do with the law.'

Cole looked at me steadily for a while. Then he turned to his wife.

'Fuck off a moment, will you?'

She tutted and made a big gesture out of swinging her legs round and climbing off the bed. She gave us both a dirty look as she walked unsteadily from the room. Cole walked over to the window and looked down at the back garden, oaks and shrubs and half an acre of perfect lawn.

'You've been busy,' he said. 'And you've been holding out on me. I should be angry with you.'

'You didn't think I'd let you get Paget before me.'

'No,' he said. 'I suppose I didn't. Now, perhaps you'd better tell me what's been going on in your life recently.'

I hadn't wanted to give him too much information. I

wanted to keep one step ahead so that I could get to Paget first.

But now things had changed. Now I thought I might need an ally, and Cole was as good as I was going to get. But he was about to go to war, and if I wasn't careful he'd get wiped out and I'd be left alone. I had to clue him in to a point.

'The law's involved somehow,' I said.

'What?'

'The one you took that night I'd gone to kill Paget – Derek Hayward.'

'The one you shot?'

'Yeah. He's a copper. I found him in a hospital in Cambridge.'

He thought about that.

'We dumped him in Essex. What the fuck was he doing in Cambridge?'

'His friends on the force fixed it. They put him there with a false name, cleaned up the mess at Ponders End. They didn't want the local law knowing about it.'

Cole pulled a hand across his chin. The whiskers rustled.

'What do you make of it?' he said. 'Are they bent? Putting the screws on Paget?'

'Something like that. There's more. That night there was another man in the car. You missed him. He scarpered before you hit us. His name's Glazer. He's connected to Paget somehow, but I don't know how.'

'And you didn't think to tell me about this Glazer?'

'No.'

He sighed.

'Well, what does he matter?'

'I don't know who he is.'

'Who cares. If he gets in my way, I'll wipe him out too.'

'And I don't trust Dunham. He's up to something. He's pulled me in a couple of times for little chats, trying to send me and you round in circles.'

'He was right about the Albanians, wasn't he? I should've finished them off when I had the chance.'

'It's wrong,' I said. 'There's something mad about it all, something twisted.'

He turned and looked through the bedroom window at his garden below. He didn't say anything for a long time. I could see his shoulders rise an inch, fall an inch as he breathed heavily. Then he put a hand on the glass as if to steady himself.

'When I was a kid, sixteen, seventeen, I used to do manual labour. I used to work for a firm that put in swimming pools. I used to go to houses like this one and get filthy from the mud. I had a job out here once, one of these houses. I thought, that's what I want. I want to be the bloke who hires someone to dig for him. Now I'm that bloke, I got the house. My wife wants a swimming pool. I tell her to dig it herself.'

I think he believed what he was saying, that this was his dream, away from the hardships of his youth. Like Dunham, he was trying to justify his life. Or hide from it, make like he'd succeeded through graft and brains, not from the blood he'd spilled or the lives he'd ruined. In the end, they all pretend they're clean.

'Why was this other bloke there?' he said, still looking

out over his dream. 'This Glazer character. I know what you arranged with Bowker; he was supposed to tell Paget you were going to be at Ponders End and he was supposed to go and kill you, right?'

'That was the idea,' I said.

'So why would Glazer show up instead? He must work for Paget.'

'So why haven't we heard of him? There are things going on that I don't understand and I think I'm being played, we're being played, and I want to know why.'

Now he turned to me, and the strain wasn't showing so much. Now he was feeding off his anger, or his fear.

'Look, Joe. I'm hitting these cunts.'

'Give me time.'

'It's funny. I got people telling me you've got brain damage, that you're paranoid or fucked up somehow. I look at you and I think they're right. You look like you've been stitched together from broken bits. What do you care about me anyway?'

'I don't.'

'Then why not let me carry on?'

'Because for the moment we're tied together and I might need you, and I'll need you in a state to help me. Right now, you're acting stupidly and you could get yourself in trouble.'

'Could I?'

'You want revenge. At any cost.'

'A few days ago, I was thinking the same thing about you. You were going mad for blood, like some wild dog.'

'You're right. I was. Now I'm thinking.'

He looked at his garden some more.

'Whatever people think of you,' he said, 'I know there's something there. You ain't dumb.'

He turned and went over to his suitcase and snapped it shut.

'I've got people out looking for the Albanians. It might take a while. I'll give you twelve hours.'

TWENTY-FOUR

The street was one of those seventies suburban jobs; the kind they used to show in TV sitcoms and magazine adverts, with rows of neat bungalows and neat kids playing on the neat grass verges, and family cars, neatly parked in the driveways, and the odd small thin tree swaying neatly in the wind.

It was pissing down now and the trees had gone and cars were parked solid along both sides and what grass verges were left were sodden and torn up with tire tracks and the pavement looked slick and dark like an oil spill and all the neat people were shuttered in their homes. It was still a popular kind of place, just not good enough to feature in adverts and sitcoms.

There was no movement, as far as I could see, no flickering lights, no odd shapes. No cars went past, no people. There was no sound except the distant blur of traffic and the endless pattering of rain.

I was starting to put things together, but I was still groping. I didn't have anything on Glazer. I didn't know where Paget was or what he was up to, or what Dunham wanted with him. I didn't know Hayward's role, but I was pretty sure he was bent. Things made sense that way. Still, something was wrong. So now I was trying the only thing I could think of.

I found the house I was after: a detached bungalow, halfway along the road. There was a light in the front room, but the curtains were drawn. I walked past and carried on around the block to recce the area. It was all the same, all fucking neat, nothing out of place.

When I reached the house again, I edged past the car in the driveway and stepped over the wrought iron gate. I stopped and waited. Nothing happened. No alarms, no shouts from neighbours, no barking dogs. Rainwater had pooled on the asphalt and I stepped over the puddles, keeping my footfalls as quiet as possible. The back garden was a large dark mass, shrubs and bushes around the edges, a large lawn, trimmed. Neat. There were no kids' toys, no mess.

There was a door at the back, which opened into the kitchen. The door was glass panelled and I could see through to the hallway. All the lights were off except the one in the front room. When I was sure there was nobody in the darkened kitchen, I tried the door knob. The door opened and I pushed it slowly. Warm air pushed past me. It was heavy with the smell of cooking and laundry. I eased in and let the door back slowly, and closed it quietly. I took the gun from my pocket.

I stood a moment and waited, listening. The only sound was the murmur of the television coming from the front room along the hallway. I moved slowly towards it, letting my feet roll on the carpet. The lounge door was ajar, the light was on inside. I peered through the crack in the door and saw the television in one corner facing towards the wall on my right. That meant the sofa was there, along the wall out of my sight. I pushed the door open and stepped in quickly, raising the Makarov.

The blow hammered into the back of my head and sent a shaft of pain through my neck and into my skull. A woman yelped. A man grunted. My legs buckled and I staggered and fell to one knee. When I tried to swing the Makarov round, it fell from my hand and skittered across the carpet. I tried to stand, but the floor moved and spun about me. I tried again and my head exploded for an instant and I lurched forward and saw the floor rushing to slam into my face.

TWENTY-FIVE

I was on my back. I saw a white ceiling. It took me a moment to remember where I was. I thought my hands and feet would be tied, but they weren't. I guessed I'd been out for only a few seconds. Pain moved around my head, as if it was full of molten lead. Shapes went in and out of focus.

I shifted my sight and Hayward came into view, looking down at me. He had my Makarov in his left hand. His right arm was in a sling. At his feet was a blackjack. He must've put all his strength into it.

Behind Hayward was a woman who stared at me. She was small and thin. Her eyes were large and brown, and her dark skin looked pale. She was scared, but she was staying close to Hayward, trusting that he was in control.

'I've called for support,' Hayward said.

Hayward was on the other side of the room, a good distance. But, because he'd hit me when I came in the door, the only way he could cover me and feel safe was by boxing himself into the corner of the room. Behind him was a cabinet with fancy plates, and a heavy armchair.

He was calm enough, but wary.

'Don't try anything,' he said. 'The only reason you're

not tied up is because my arm's not too good and my wife won't go near you.'

I tried to say something, but it came out in a slur and I had to shake my head to try and clear it. I'd been there a hundred times before. When the world is swirling around, you keep still and wait and hope that it'll stop moving some time.

I rolled over and pushed myself up. The woman took a step back, but Hayward didn't move. He was confident with my gun in his hand.

'I want to talk,' I said.

He held the gun up.

'With this? You come into my home with this and you want to talk?'

'Precaution.'

'Do you know him?' the woman said.

'He's the man who shot me.'

Her hands went up to her mouth, but she didn't scream, didn't get hysterical. I had to give her that.

'We had a feeling you'd come here.'

The woman shot a glance at Hayward. There was some small surprise in her look. I thought it odd that Hayward would expose her like this. I thought I might have something I could use. I said, 'We?'

'Never mind. Did you come alone?'

'Yes.'

'Well, if anyone comes through that door, I'll shoot you and nobody in the world would condemn me for it.'

'Like I said, I came to talk.'

'About?'

'Paget.'

'That's funny. That's exactly what I want to talk about.'

The woman was looking from one of us to the other as we spoke, like she was trying to follow a new language.

'Who do you work for?' Hayward said.

'Nobody.'

'I know you don't work for Cole. It was Cole's men who hit us in Ponders End. That probably means you work for Dunham.'

'I don't work for anybody.'

'What does Dunham know?'

'You're not listening, I don't work for him.'

'Masterminded my kidnapping by yourself, did you? That's a longer sentence, you know.'

He was biting his lip. He wasn't sure. I thought he was out of his depth and knew it. But he'd said he'd called for support, which meant his confidence was based on that.

'I'm going to stand up,' I said.

'Stay there.'

I didn't think he'd do anything, but I had to test him. He was calm, but not cold-blooded. I got up slowly. Hayward took a step back from me. He tightened his grip on my gun.

The room tilted and my head went wonky, but I managed to stay upright. I couldn't feel any pain now. That should have told me something. Hayward was still three yards from me. I had to be careful. He was a wounded man protecting his wife from a dangerous beast. He'd be jittery. I didn't need a hole in me.

He said, 'You move again, I'll use this.'

'Does your wife know about you?'

'Leave her out of it.'

'Does she know you're bent?'

'What?'

It got him, but not in the way I thought it would. He looked more wary now. His wife looked confused. She said, 'Derek? What's he talking about?'

I moved a half step forward.

'Nothing.'

'Derek?' She was looking at him now, pawing his gun arm. It was enough to distract him a bit.

'He doesn't know what he's on about,' he said.

Still he wouldn't take his eyes off me.

'Where's Paget?' I said.

'How would I know?'

'You were with him a few days ago.'

'So?'

We were circling each other. I was getting nowhere. Something was banging away inside my head. Something wasn't right. He was bent, and his wife thought he was a knight. He thought I might come here. His men were on the way. He had my fucking gun.

I said, 'I know about Elena.'

His face betrayed him. There was surprise there, and uncertainty. I took another inch towards him. He didn't move.

'How?'

I looked from him to the woman.

'She told me.'

It took her a while, but then she got it.

'Oh my God,' she said, shooting her hand to her mouth again. 'You were the one who called.'

'What?' Hayward said.

He glanced at his wife, then back at me. His eyes weren't off me long, but he was wavering, beginning to get distracted, forgetting that I was a threat.

'What has this to do with my wife?' he said to me.

'She called your phone.'

I put my hand in my jacket pocket and took out his mobile and tossed it to him. He followed it for a second with his eyes, but let it fall to the floor. She stooped and picked it up.

'Yes,' she said. 'I did. When you didn't come back that night, I called and he answered.'

'And you mentioned Elena to him?'

'Yes. I think so.'

'Alright, so you heard her say it, you still don't know what it means.'

'I know what it means,' I said. 'I remember it.'

'What do you know?'

'I know Elena was an investigation run by the Met six years ago. Some anti-prostitution thing. Paget was one of the men you would've been investigating; instead, you're working for him.'

'What's he talking about?' the woman said. 'Who's Paget?'

She was confused, but there was also anger in her voice, her expression.

'It's complicated. I'm working a case.'

'A case?' I said. 'You get shot, snatched out of a car and

the next day the whole place is cleaned up, the car gone, nothing on the news, no crime scene. What kind of case is that?'

'You don't know what you're talking about.'

'You take a round in the shoulder and you lose a gallon of blood and your friends pull strings and get you to a hospital in Cambridge? Bollocks. You couldn't go anywhere local, you couldn't go where people would know who you were. That's why you had an alias.'

'Derek?'

'Wait in the kitchen,' he told her. She looked at me. She didn't know what to do. 'I said—'

'I'm not leaving you,' she said.

Something occurred to me. I said, 'I don't see a panic button.'

'What?'

'You said you thought I might come here, but you don't have a panic button.'

'For God's sake, Derek. What's he talking about?'

'If there was a threat,' I said to her, 'your husband would have a panic button connected to the local law. They'd send an armed response unit.'

She looked at her husband. His face was grim.

'Did you know he'd come here?' she said. 'With a gun?'

'No,' he said, flustered now. 'It was an idea, that's all.'

'What's Elena? Who's Paget?'

'Nothing. Nobody.'

I took another half inch.

'Paget's a murderer,' I told the woman.

'Leave her out of this.'

'He was a pimp, a pornographer, a drug dealer.'

'Del, what's he talking about?'

'He doesn't want you to know,' I said to her.

'Shut up.'

'Derek?'

'It's nothing. It's complicated,' he said. Beads of sweat were on his upper lip. 'He's wrong.'

'Paget uses kids in porn movies. He—'

Hayward was snarling.

'Shut up.'

The woman grabbed his arm and he turned sharply to her. I moved. He saw me too late. The woman screamed. I slammed into him. We smashed into the cabinet, destroying it, shattering the plates. The Makarov went flying. I didn't want to hurt him too bad. I wanted him to talk. I wanted my gun. I wanted to be in control. I pulled myself up. My head went sideways. The room spun. Hayward was a wreck, holding his shoulder and crying out in pain. I turned and saw the woman hunched in the corner of the room whimpering. I scanned the place for my gun. I saw two of them. I felt a pressure in my head, like my skull was being squeezed. I moved forward and held my hand out for one of the guns. The guns wobbled and my hand weighed so much it pulled me forward and there was nothing I could do about it. No exertions, Browne had said. Shit. I saw the fucking ground coming towards me again.

TWENTY-SIX

When I came to this time, they'd taped my ankles and wrists together. I was on my side on the sofa, my feet overhanging the arm rest. I watched the room from an angle. Hayward stood in the corner of the room, by the shattered cabinet. He was gripping his shoulder and grimacing, his face sheened in sweat. Two other men were with him. I could see them side on. All three talked to each other. Their voices were low and I couldn't make out what was said, but I could see enough to know there was a disagreement of some kind. The woman was gone.

I closed my eyes and tried to work out if my head was still on top of my neck. I wasn't sure. I pulled at my tied wrists. There was no give. When I opened my eyes again, the men had stopped chatting and were looking at me and I had the feeling that I'd said something. I swung my legs over the edge of the sofa and pushed myself upright.

It took me a moment to place the two that Hayward was talking to. It was the suits they wore that brought it back. They were the ones from the hospital; one with greying hair and moustache, the other with the thin hair and puffy eyes. They looked better now, less tired and bedraggled, but there was still an urgency about them, something desperate.

Moustache said something finally to the others and crossed the room to sit in a wooden chair opposite me. They must have brought the chair in from the kitchen. Moustache watched me for a moment. The others waited for him to speak.

Now that I was looking at him clearly, I could see he was younger than I'd thought, early fifties maybe. I saw also that the moustache almost covered a hair lip.

'You've been out quite a while,' he said. 'Delayed concussion, I'd say.'

Hayward lurked in the corner of the room and glared at me. My gun was in his waistband. The one with puffy eyes tried to look bored, but he was too jittery to pull it off.

'What are you going to do with me?' I said to Moustache.

'Dunno.'

'You going to kill me?'

He smiled.

'Could we? Is that even possible?'

'We bloody should,' the one with puffy eyes said.

Hayward didn't say anything. He seemed to be the lowest of the three, and since he was an Inspector, the one I was talking to was a CI or higher.

'The woman,' I said. 'She's a witness.'

Moustache laughed at that.

'My wife,' Hayward said. 'Not a bloody woman.'

Moustache stretched his legs out in front of him and crossed his ankles. He leaned an elbow on the arm of the chair. He was nice and cosy and relaxed as hell, or so he was telling me. That was fine while I was tied up.

'You're a problem alright,' he said to me. 'But you've

got us all wrong. We're not in the business of killing people. You're name's Joe, isn't it?'

He waited for me to say something. When I didn't he said, 'You're a big bugger, aren't you? Took all three of us to get you on the couch. You were a fighter, I think. You look like you were. You ever done time?'

'You're the law. You tell me.'

'No, I don't think you have. And yes, you're right, we are the police.'

'Bent.'

'Like I said, you've got us all wrong. We're on the same side.'

'No one's on my side.'

'Let me rephrase; we want the same thing. More or less.'

'Do we?'

'I think so, yes.'

'What's that?'

He wiped a hand over his moustache. I tugged at the tape around my wrists.

'Let's approach this from another direction,' he said. 'Why don't you tell me what you're after?'

'Fuck you.'

Puffy Eyes said, 'I told you, John. Let's dump him and get on.'

'Hear that?' Moustache said. 'My colleague wants me to throw you in the nick and let you rot. We could put you away for decades, you know.'

'You won't.'

'Oh? Why?'

'You can't risk me going down. I know too much.'

'Well, there is that. But not for the reasons you think.'

'You telling me you're not bent?'

Hayward said, 'For Christ's sake. Why are we bothering with him?'

Moustache held a hand up to Hayward, but he didn't take his eyes off me.

'I wonder.'

'He's a thug,' Hayward said. 'Comes into my home with a fucking gun. Frightens Jan. He's a damned thug. Hasn't got the brains to grasp what this is about. Bob's right. Let's get rid of him.'

Moustache waited him to finish, then he said to me, 'What if I told you we were straight?'

'You're not.'

'What makes you so certain?'

This one – Moustache – was in charge. He wanted to talk.

'If you were legit, you would've had the Cambridgeshire law protecting you with an armed response unit. But they didn't have a clue, did they? Which means you lot are some rogue outfit. If you were legit and you thought I'd come here after Hayward, he'd have a button to the local nick, but you can't let them know what you're doing. You're way off the radar. Are you putting the screws on Paget? Taking his money? Maybe you want to grab the smack he nicked off Cole.'

Moustache smiled. He shouldn't have been so calm. He should've been worried sick. He turned to Hayward.

'Del, how about a drink for our friend here?'

'Yeah,' Puffy Eyes said. 'Hey, I know, let's all go down the pub and have a pint. We could get a game of darts in.'

Moustache ignored him and waited for Hayward to speak.

'What do you want?' Hayward said finally.

I looked at Moustache. I didn't get his game.

'I can't drink with my hands tied.'

Moustache turned to Puffy Eyes.

'Bob?'

Puffy Eyes pulled himself off the wall he was leaning against and walked over to me. He pulled me forward and drew a lock-knife from his jacket pocket. I felt my hands go free.

'And my feet?'

Moustache smiled and shook his head.

'What do you want to drink?' he said.

'Beer.'

'You got a beer in the house, Del?'

Hayward gave me a sour look and headed into the kitchen. We waited for the drinks. I pulled at the tape around my ankles, but there was no give and I'd need a knife to get free.

Moustache was wearing his jacket open. He wasn't wearing a holster, didn't have a gun in his belt and with his legs out in front of him, I could see he didn't have an ankle holster. I wondered if he was deliberately showing me he wasn't tooled up. Maybe he expected me to hug him. I looked over at Puffy Eyes. His jacket was buttoned up.

I thought things through, as much as my mind would let me. If these men were bent, as I'd thought they were, they might decide any time to get rid of me, or give me to Paget.

If they were legit, they had enough on me to bang me up for years. So why weren't they doing that? And what then did they want? Did they expect me to roll over on Cole? Did they think I knew where Paget was?

Either way, for the moment, I had to play along with them.

Hayward came back in with four cans of bitter and handed them around. He disappeared again. When he came back, he had two more of the wooden chairs and a saucer. He put the chairs down and he and Puffy Eyes sat. He put the saucer on the ground and Puffy Eyes pulled a pack of cigarettes from his jacket pocket. He lit one and handed the pack to Hayward who pulled a cigarette out and borrowed Puffy Eyes' lighter. I had three of them playing games now.

'Right,' Moustache said, 'let's try and have a friendly chat. That okay with you?'

I didn't know what he expected me to say to that.

'You might want to remember he shot me,' Hayward said.

Moustache ignored that.

'Why don't we start with you? We know you're working for Cole. That car you abandoned in Addenbrooke's Hospital was registered to one of his firms.'

'I'm not working for Cole. He thinks I am.'

'Okay, you say you don't work for Cole. Well, we know he wants Paget dead and to that end it was his men who took Derek – DI Hayward – and questioned him. So what's your role?'

'Independent.'

'Meaning what?' Puffy Eyes said.

'Meaning fuck you.'

Hayward exchanged looks with Puffy Eyes. Moustache pulled his lips back over his teeth and puffed his cheeks out. Here they were, trying to be nice, and the dumb bastard didn't want to play. What could you do?

'You know your problem, Joe,' Moustache said, 'I'll call you Joe, if you don't mind – your problem is you don't trust anyone. You see a person and straight away you think they've got an angle, they're blagging someone, they're double-crossing, they're stealing. You're so busy seeing the worst in everyone, you never see anything else.'

'Get to it.'

'We're not bent. We're not working with Paget or Glazer. We're not putting the screws on anyone, as you say. You're right about Operation Elena, but for the wrong reasons. We do have an interest in it, but not the one you think we have.'

He'd mentioned Glazer. Why? I hadn't mentioned him. Or had I? I couldn't remember. Still...

'You haven't told me anything,' I said.

'No. I haven't. I want to be able to trust you. I think we can help each other, and I think you want what we do, more or less, but I'm not going to spill confidential information without being sure. You understand that?'

They sat there and watched me. I took a long pull on the beer can. I hadn't realized how thirsty I was. The beer was cold. I felt it going down my gullet. By the time I was through with that, I'd made a decision. I looked at Moustache.

'It's personal,' I said.

'What is? Your gripe with Paget?'

'Yes.'

'Go on. We're all ears.'

He slurped his beer. I wanted to ram it down his throat. He knew that and smiled.

'I've got a score to settle.'

'It's like pulling teeth,' Puffy Eyes said.

'We're getting there,' Moustache said. 'We're doing okay. Right, big man? What score?'

'I'll go on when I get something from you lot.'

Moustache thought about that for a while. He took another gulp of beer and wiped his moustache. He nodded.

'That's fair,' he said. 'Within reason. I'll give you my name. Okay?'

'Fine.'

'I'm Detective Superintendent Compton. I believe you're already old friends with Detective Inspector Hayward—'

'Funny,' Hayward said.

'—and the miserable bugger over there is DI Bradley.'

'Bollocks,' Bradley said.

'Prove it,' I said to Compton.

He fished in his inside jacket pocket and pulled out a wallet, flipped it open to show me his warrant card. I held out my hand. He tossed it to me. It was his name all right. It was real.

'It's fake,' I said.

He just smiled.

So, two DIs and a Detective Super. For Paget? That didn't work. I threw the wallet back to him.

'I'm putting a lot of faith in you by showing you that,' he said. 'Now I want something from you. Why are you after Paget?'

I had to give him something, but I didn't want to tell him about Brenda. I didn't want him that close to me.

'I knew a girl once,' I said. 'A small girl. She was African. Paget used her.'

'He used a lot of people,' Bradley said.

'And Marriot?' Compton said. The bastard was ahead of me.

'Who?'

He smiled. The others smiled.

'Bollocks,' Bradley said.

'Frank Marriot,' Compton said. 'I think you've heard of him.'

I had the feeling they knew everything about me.

'Yeah.'

'Marriot,' Hayward said. 'He's dead.'

'Yeah.'

'Know how he died?' Compton said.

'No.'

'Slowly, I hear,' Bradley said. 'Gut-shot.'

'Uh-huh.'

'You have anything to do with that?'

'Why would I tell you?'

'We got intel that it was some dispute with an Albanian gang. That they'd got word that Marriot had fucked them over some smack deal.'

'Uh-huh.'

Bradley snorted. Compton glanced at him.

'That never sat right with us,' Compton said, looking back at me. 'Not their style.'

'No.'

He leaned forward, elbows on knees.

'You knew Marriot, didn't you?'

He waited for me to confess everything. When I didn't, he smiled and sat back.

'Not that I care,' he said. 'They can wipe themselves out as much as they want, as far as I'm concerned.'

While they'd been tag-teaming me with their questions, I'd remembered something Tina had told me. When I'd questioned her, she'd told me that she didn't know anything about Hayward, except she'd said that he was a friend of Glazer's. Not Paget's.

The desire, the need to destroy Paget was in my blood. It had infected me, clogged my mind, choked me, blinded me to everything else. And now, looking at these three, listening to their vague answers, watching them skirt around, I knew I'd been wrong.

Compton talked for a bit, but I wasn't listening. I kept thinking, why did he mention Glazer? And then I knew, and realized what a fucking fool I'd been. Yes, I had been blind to everything except getting Paget. Once I took him out of the mix, things made more sense.

'It's not Paget,' I said. 'It's Glazer. That's who you're after.'

Compton flicked his eyes over at the others and I knew I was right.

'What do you know about Glazer?' Bradley said.

'Where is he?' Hayward said.

They'd picked up where they'd left off, but now they weren't fucking about. Well, I'd taken their combinations all I was going to.

Now it was my turn.

'Undo my feet and I'll tell you,' I said.

Compton nodded to Bradley. Bradley mashed his cigarette in the saucer, stood, took his knife out and ambled over. He leaned down, sliced through the tape. I grabbed the back of his head and slammed it down as I brought my knee up. He was quick enough to move his face away. I felt cheekbone as I connected. He cried out, raising his hands in a reflex action. His blood spurted over my leg.

Hayward said, 'Fuck.'

He was struggling to get my Makarov out of his waistband.

I ripped Bradley's jacket open, reached in under his left shoulder and tore out his gun. I jumped up, shoved my hands in Bradley's armpits, lifted him up and threw him at Hayward. Bradley flew, sprawling, onto Hayward, who gurgled a cry. The two of them crashed onto the wooden seats.

All this time, Compton had stayed where he was. His face had gone white, his eyes wide. He stared at Hayward and Bradley. I walked over to where Hayward was curled up, crying in pain, blood seeping through the bandage around his shoulder. I pulled my Makarov from his waistband. He looked up at me and recoiled, raising his good arm to defend his face. Bradley was almost out cold. He stirred a bit and murmured.

Bradley had been carrying a short-barrelled .357 Smith and Wesson revolver. I opened the chamber and let the cartridges fall to the ground. Then I checked my Makarov.

'Why did you do that?' Compton said, still staring at the other two. 'Why the hell did you do that?'

'I wanted my gun back.'

'You're mad.'

'Yeah. Now tell me what the fuck is going on.'

He looked at me, his eyes fierce.

'What are you going to do if I don't? Kill us all?'

'Maybe.'

He shifted in his seat.

'You're not that stupid.'

'I might be that mad.'

The anger in his eyes lifted. He shook his head slowly.

'No you're not.'

I put the Makarov in my jacket pocket. Bradley moved groggily and hefted himself up onto his hands and knees. Hayward wasn't making such a noise now. He was curled up still, holding his shoulder.

'I'm going to get these two seen to,' Compton said.

It was as much a question as anything. He wanted to see what I'd do. I shrugged. He got up and went over to his men. Bradley waved him away and sat back on his ankles. He shook his head to clear it. There was a gash under his right eye. He wiped some blood off with his sleeve.

'I'm alright,' he said.

Compton knelt by Hayward. The bandage was soaked through now.

'He needs stitches,' Compton said. 'They both do.'

'I know someone,' I said.

TWENTY-SEVEN

It took me a half hour to get Browne out of his drunkenness. He was still bleary, but he could work okay. He complained for an hour, but I think he was glad to be doing something instead of brooding.

'I suppose this is your doing,' he said to me when he saw the men laid out in his lounge.

He went to work quickly on Hayward, stitching him back together again. Then he took a look at Bradley and put a few stitches in his face.

I wanted to clear my head a bit. There was a lump at the base of my skull where Hayward had bashed me. I didn't tell Browne about it. I didn't want him fussing. I told him I was going to lie down.

'They're law,' I said to him. 'Don't tell them anything.'

'I know, I know.'

I stared up into the darkness and let my mind clear, trying to work things out.

Everything went back to Brenda. Everything circled her, like those crows, flying around screaming, looking for carrion to feed on.

And these coppers; why were they interested in Glazer and not Paget? Surely Paget was the greater catch. He was involved in shit up to his neck. He was well known. Glazer? Nobody had heard of him. And Operation Elena was about people smuggling, using children. Paget had his hands dirty there. But Glazer...

When I went back into Browne's lounge, everyone was watching TV. On the coffee table were empty plates and mugs, a pack of cigarettes, a couple of half-full ashtrays and a lighter. The room was foggy with cigarette smoke. I thought I'd been gone thirty minutes. From the look of things, it was more like three, four hours.

Nobody was talking. Bradley and Hayward were on the sofa. They glared at me, but I got no lip from them so I guessed Compton had told them to shut it. Browne was in his armchair, Compton in the other one. Browne was asleep. I nudged him and he blinked his eyes open. He looked around at the others.

'Oh,' he said. 'Now I remember.'

He stood with an effort and told us all he was going to bed. He shuffled off.

Compton hadn't taken his eyes off the TV. There was some film on. Some clean-faced kid was running around with a gun too big for him. I sat down where Browne had been.

'How are you feeling?' Compton said.

'Fine.'

Now he looked at me.

'What say we start again?'

'Fine.'

Compton flicked a look at Hayward and Bradley.

'Can I have my gun back?' Bradley said.

I'd left my jacket in the bedroom. I went and grabbed

it and took it back to the lounge. Bradley held out his hand. I took his Smith and Wesson and my Makarov and put them on the coffee table. Compton looked at the weapons and nodded.

'Good,' he said. 'Now maybe we'll get somewhere. We've all made mistakes. You've made a few. You really shouldn't have gone to Del's house like that, not armed, not with his wife there. And we, well, we underestimated you.'

If Compton thought I was going to clap him on the back and shake hands all round, he was wrong. He shifted in his seat.

'He's a good man,' he said. 'Your doctor friend. He is a doctor, isn't he?'

'Sort of.'

'Well, he's a good man.'

Bradley leaned forward. I thought he might go for his gun, but he took a cigarette from the packet and the lighter. He lit up and leaned back and blew smoke rings.

I still had the feeling that I was being played, used. Bradley blowing smoke rings, Compton making small talk; it was too casual, too false. I knew the law, knew how their minds worked. I didn't trust them.

Besides, things still didn't make sense. Something gnawed at the back of my head, something about this lot, about Paget and Glazer, about their interest. They were too senior to be bothered with vice, surely. And I still didn't get the secrecy thing, why they'd had to keep their activities quiet from the London law.

'He told us about the girl,' Compton said. 'Kid? That was her name?'

'Kindness.'

'Right. Anyway he told us about her. Why did he do that, do you think?'

'He was drunk.'

'Maybe, but he told us anyway, and I believed what he said. He said you rescued her from Marriot, that you shot the place up just to get her.'

'Bollocks,' Bradley said. 'We know about the robbery on Cole's casino. We know that Beckett was behind it and that Marriot and Paget were behind a double-cross and scalped the money off him. Cole hired you to get the money, didn't he? Eh?'

Compton put an innocent expression on his face.

'That true, Joe?'

'You went after Beckett first.' This from Hayward. 'We know Beckett liked little girls. You knew it too so you used the girl to get you in and then you killed him and Walsh and Jensen. But they didn't have the money. Marriot had it, so you went after him. That's why you wrecked his club. That's why you killed him.'

'I don't know what you're talking about.'

Bradley said, 'Did you use her, Joe? That little girl. Was she your way in?'

Compton shook his head at his two men. He looked at me.

'I don't think he used the girl,' he said. 'I think she was just caught up in the middle of it.'

I said, 'Was she?'

They'd figured it wrong, but they were close. They didn't have me for the original robbery and they didn't know that

Marriot had used Kid's junky sister to force her to get to
Beckett and open the door to let Paget in. They didn't know
Paget wiped out Beckett and his crew and took the money
back to Marriot. Or maybe they knew everything and were
just fucking with me.

We were fencing with each other again, and I was tired
of it all. They'd shown they knew a lot of stuff about
Marriot and Paget, and me, and it was more than I wanted
them to know. Now I was going to have to do a bit of
figuring myself. I said, 'Anything you got on Cole or Beckett
or Marriot, Hayward must've learned from Paget. You
know shit, which means Hayward wasn't with Paget that
long or wasn't close enough to him.'

I looked at Hayward.

'Right?'

Hayward looked at Compton who frowned.

'Some of what you say is true. Del here picked up some
of it from Glazer, yes. The rest we've pieced together. But
it's true, Hayward was with Glazer and only recently hooked
up with Paget, probably when Paget was in trouble. So,
Hayward was connected to Glazer, and he's—'

And then I had it, and I felt a fool not to have seen it
before. It all fell into place, it clicked.

'He's a fucking copper,' I said.

It was like I'd pulled my gun. They went still, not
breathing, not looking at each other. Bradley's cigarette was
halfway to his mouth. Hayward had gone rigid. Nobody
said anything.

I was right.

'Glazer's one of you.'

Compton had recovered enough to say, in a bored voice, 'What makes you say that?'

'If you're not bent, it's the only thing that makes sense.'

'We're not fucking bent,' Hayward said. 'Can't you get that in your thick head?'

'Then Glazer's a copper.'

'I say again,' said Compton, 'what makes you say that?'

'A Detective Super and two DIs after one man? Bollocks. Unless that man's bad for your lot. He must have clout too. That's why you can't trust the local law. That's why Hayward had no panic button, which he would've done if you thought I might come for him. It's why you put Hayward in a hospital in Cambridge. You must have called on some favour from someone you knew there, but you couldn't tell them the truth, which is why their coppers there weren't armed.'

Compton chewed his lower lip.

'You're guessing.'

'You want facts?' I pointed to Hayward. 'He was a copper at Barnet. A DC. He had an affair that went sour, got a transfer to a vice squad south of the river, made Detective Sergeant a couple of years after that, then Inspector.'

I looked at Hayward. He stared at me, his lips tight. When he glanced at Compton he looked like he was seeking help.

'Okay,' Bradley said, blowing smoke out, 'so you know a bit about Del's background. So what?'

'I know more than that. Elena was a special operation, a vice unit targeting immigration crime. I remember it. Was Glazer involved in that? He must have been.'

I was guessing now, but from the stony looks on their

faces I knew I was right. Now things were fitting into place. I thought about it, about how it might've worked. I said, 'Glazer was bent. He got in with Paget and Marriot, probably taking pay-offs. The Elena thing was years ago. You lot can't be part of that still, so you must be investigating it.'

There was no reaction there, and I thought maybe I had it wrong after all. Unless...

'Unless you weren't investigating the running of operation Elena specifically. Unless you were investigating Glazer right from the start.'

And then I saw how it fit. I had to be right. I said, 'You pulled Hayward from his vice unit and placed him with Glazer's squad to try and get something on him for the Elena investigation. That makes sense. If Glazer was bent, he'd be savvy about men joining his team. You used Hayward because he was already a vice cop. It was natural for him to go to another vice unit. How am I doing?'

Bradley stared at me through cigarette smoke. Hayward looked at the floor miserably. Compton, though, seemed to be enjoying himself. He was leaning back in his seat with his left ankle on his right knee. He brushed his moustache with his fingers.

'Or maybe you recruited Hayward after he'd already been posted to Glazer,' I said. 'It doesn't matter.'

Compton smiled, but this time it was a grim smile, his eyes were hooded, a muscle twitched in his jaw.

'We really did underestimate you. How did you reach these conclusions?'

'It doesn't matter.'

'It matters a hell of a lot if other people know.'

'They don't.'

'So you worked it out? All by yourself.'

'Like you said, when I see a person, I think they've got an angle, they're double-crossing. You lot are no different.'

'You think we're double-crossing you?'

'I might as well.'

'Your lack of faith in the police force of this country is disappointing.'

'Uh-huh.'

'Well, we could go on like this all night. What you know, what we know, if this, if that. What I'd like to talk about is you, Joe, and us. Or, more specifically, what you can do to help us.'

'What do you need me for?'

'Well, now that DI Hayward is otherwise incapacitated – thanks, I might mention, to you – we've lost contact with Glazer and Paget. Maybe you can help us there?'

'If I knew where they were, I wouldn't have gone to Hayward's.'

'That makes sense. Still, you might know something, or you might learn something.'

'You want me to work for you?'

'We want you to cooperate.'

'How?'

'Tell us what you know.'

'I don't know anything.'

Bradley said, 'We've made guesses about your involvement with Marriot and Paget and Cole and all that, but I happen to think we're not far off the mark and some of the people we know would be very interested to hear what we've come up with.'

'You'd have the serious squad coming out of your arse,' Hayward said.

'I don't care about Glazer. You can have him. I want Paget.'

'You know that we're police officers,' Compton said, 'and that legally we cannot be a party to the commission of a crime, or to the conspiracy to commit thereof, et cetera. You know all that, right?'

'Sure.'

Bradley sucked some smoke down and blew it at the ceiling.

'He only wants to talk to Paget, don't you Joe?'

'Sure.'

'Well, that's alright, then,' Compton said. 'As long as we understand each other.'

'Sure.'

'Good.'

'Tell me about Glazer.'

'We can't tell you too much, you must accept that.'

'Go on.'

'He's smart. And dangerous. What else do you want to know?'

'What's his rank?'

'Detective Super.'

'Vice?'

'Yes.'

'You know he's bent, but he's still there. That means you got no evidence.'

'Right.'

'But even without evidence, suspicion would be enough to get rid of him. So he must have friends high up. Who are they?'

'You don't expect me to answer that?'

'Fine. He's got connections, though. He must have if you don't trust the local law.'

'All we know is he may have connections. He has a lot of friends in Manchester, we don't know about here.'

'Manchester?'

'That's where he's from. Why?'

I thought about what King had told me. I said, 'I asked someone to do some digging about. He doesn't scare easily, this man, but he got frightened off by someone who knew about his kids, his wife. The bloke who warned him off had a Manc accent.'

'This someone you asked to do the digging – he has form?'

'No.'

'But he's known to the police? Been suspected of something?'

'Yes.'

'What? Heavy stuff?'

'Armed robbery.'

'That's Glazer, then. He's got access to all sorts of intel at the touch of a button or at the end of a phone.'

It made sense. I got King to ask around about Glazer. He'd called Bowker who must've called Glazer, not Paget. Glazer got scared, suddenly finding that some hard case criminal is asking about him. He hits some buttons, gets details on King and King's family and makes the call. What

I didn't understand at the time was why he would bother to do that. Paget knew that Cole and I were after him, and if Glazer was working with Paget, he'd know too. Why, then, would he have been bothered about King asking questions? He would want to keep his connection with Paget quiet. But, in that case, why would he have turned up at Ponders End that night? Why would he involve Hayward? Unless...

'Maybe they're not working together,' I said.

'Who?'

'Paget and Glazer.'

'Sure they are. We've been over this. We know they are.'

'No. You told me they were tied together. It's not the same thing. Paget would've known that my friend's inquiries weren't important, not with Cole already on their tails. Paget would've known that I was probably behind the enquiry. If Glazer was working with him, he would know it too. But maybe Glazer didn't know.'

I thought back to Ponders End when I'd been waiting with my rifle, waiting for Paget to show. Paget must've suspected a set-up, or Bowker grassed it up to him. That was why he didn't turn up. But why send Glazer, then? Unless he just had nobody else. That didn't sit right. Paget wouldn't have worried about using someone else to get rid of one of his problems, though. I looked at Compton.

'I don't think Glazer knew what Paget got him into.'

Compton looked at Hayward.

'Del, is that possible?' he said.

Hayward looked at me, considering what I'd said.

Compton watched him, and waited. Bradley held his burning cigarette.

'Yes,' Hayward said. 'Yes. It's possible.'

'Tell me about your role in this,' I said.

He looked at Compton.

'Tell him,' Compton said.

'I was with Glazer,' Hayward said to me. 'You're right, I was working vice with him, his second in command—'

'Never mind that.'

'Right. Well, a couple of weeks ago, Glazer gets spooked. I mean, one minute he's fine, then he goes out and when he comes back he's not the same, he's panicky, sweating. I knew then this could be what we were after, hard evidence, a link. We spent months on my cover and I spent months more worming my way in till he thought I was as bent as him. So, anyway, he tells me he has to do something, help an old friend, off the books, and he needs help, someone to watch his back. I didn't see much of him then for a while, but one night he calls me up and asks me to drive him to see someone. That was when I met Paget. I knew of him, of course, and knew he'd worked for Marriot, and I knew this was to do with Elena, had to be.'

'You met him in Loughton? At this Tina's place?'

'Yeah. Paget was hiding out there.'

'Go on.'

'So, Paget tells Glazer that he's in trouble, tells him that Marriot got some money from a job on Cole's casino and that Cole's now after him.'

'The rest, we put together,' said Bradley.

'So that's why Glazer panicked when he found out your

friend was making enquiries about him,' Compton said to me. 'A known blagger starts asking questions, and Glazer thinks Cole's going to think he was involved in the robbery.'

'Could be,' I said.

They weren't even pretending now that they knew about my involvement. They could smell blood – Glazer's, Paget's – but not mine.

'Did Paget say anything about drugs to Glazer?' I asked Hayward.

'What drugs?'

'Never mind. Go on.'

'The next time I saw Glazer was when you shot me.'

'Did Glazer say anything about that? About going there?'

'No. He just tells me he needs a driver, tells me to take him to Ponders End. To the car park. We get there and he's looking around—'

'Was he armed?'

'Was he? Fuck, yes. He had a fucking magnum in a shoulder holster and a pocketful of shells and an ankle piece. And he was sweating.'

My mouth had gone dry. They looked at each other.

'Are you alright?' Compton said.

Bradley was leaning forward now. Hayward stared at me.

I felt it in my gut, a sickening, empty hole.

Brenda, I thought. It all went back, back.

Compton was half standing. Bradley looked at me like I'd gone mad.

'Joe,' Compton said. 'Joe, what is it? What's wrong?'

'What does it mean?' Bradley said. 'What the fuck's wrong?'

I felt it in my head, the blood draining away.

'Tell me about Elena,' I said, my mouth dry, my voice cracking.

'Elena,' Bradley said to Compton. 'Fucking Elena.'

I felt it in my balls, tightening in fear.

'Has to be,' Compton said. 'You know something, Joe. What? What is it?'

I felt it in the cold sweat seeping from my body and in the hair on the back of my neck.

'Tell me about Elena,' I said.

'You said they were tied together,' Compton said. 'Is that it? Do you know why?'

I felt it in my lousy fucking heart, what was left of it, hammering away, pumping that black blood. I spoke, and when I did the words crept out of some dark place.

'Tell me.'

They stared at me. Hayward edged away.

'Take it easy, alright?' I heard him say

Compton's eyes were wide. He wet his lips. He breathed heavily.

'What do you want to know?'

'Just talk.'

He nodded to himself.

'Alright. Well, you were right about us investigating it.'

'Start from the beginning.'

'Fine. Yes. Operation Elena. A good name, to be sure. About the only good thing about the whole mess. Elena was the name of a girl the Met picked up once, a long time ago, seven, eight years. She was a Latvian, worked in King's Cross for some Russians. She was fourteen. She wandered into a station in Stoke Newington. She'd been beaten, and she was thin, but she had guts. Yes, she did. They got her to testify and some pretty hard cases went down. They rehomed her, sent her up to Northampton, gave her a new name. A year later they found her body in a skip.'

His face was grim. Hayward and Bradley were waiting for him to spill it. I had the feeling that it was personal for Compton, but not so much for the others. I think he knew what revenge meant. I think he could taste it like I could, the bitter sweetness always with him. He glanced over to Bradley.

'Give us one of those, will you.'

Bradley gathered his cigarettes and lighter. He half stood and reached over to give them to Compton, who snatched a fag and lit it. His hands were shaking.

'It was in the papers,' he said, the words coming out with the smoke. 'There was some fuss over it. Someone high up decided to target immigration-related prostitution and sex crimes – trafficking, porn, that sort of thing. Specifically, East European related crime. Glazer was senior in the vice unit and he got the job. Needless to say, the operation was dodgy from the word go. They made some arrests, sure, but when the papers forgot about it, nothing much had changed. I was in an anti-corruption squad at the time. I didn't like what I heard about Elena. A year or so ago, I was given charge of a small squad to investigate it. What you see before you is most of the squad. We needed someone on Glazer's team. You were right, he was wary about who he was stuck with, so we got young Del here from another vice unit and stuck him with Glazer. For most of the last year, we've not had a sniff of anything. And then the whole thing went stratospheric. Marriot was killed. Paget went missing.'

He paused and took a drag of his cigarette.

'They've got something, Paget and Glazer. We don't know what, but we've an idea. They've got pull, in high places. Glazer's dangerous, and if Paget's working with him, or has him under his thumb, that makes Paget dangerous. But then, you already know that.'

After he'd finished, we were all silent. The TV mumbled in the corner, the clean-faced kid having his final showdown with the clean-faced villain. Bradley, another cigarette burning in his fingers, looked into space, a pained expression on his face. Hayward looked at Compton with the kind of eyes a dog makes at its master, a sort of longing, a sort of fear.

And me... well, now I understood.

'He was after me,' I said, my voice hoarse. 'Glazer, that night, at Ponders End. He was after me. That's why he was there.'

It seemed like another life. I glanced at Hayward. He was looking at me, waiting. I don't think it even occurred to him that I was talking about the night I'd shot him.

'I don't understand,' Compton said. 'Why would Glazer be after you?'

'Paget told him who I was. Paget knew it was an ambush. But he also knew I wouldn't stop till I'd killed him. He needed to take me out, and this was a good opportunity. But he was alone, no men, nobody to call on and he couldn't raise his head, not with Cole hunting him. But he knew

Glazer would fear my existence. He told Glazer that I was supposed to meet this grass called Bowker and Glazer took it from there. He went there to kill me.'

Bradley said, 'Why would Glazer want to kill you?'

If I told them, they'd have something on me. I knew that. But I didn't care any more. I was past that. I didn't care what they got on me, what they would do with it. If they sent me down for a hundred years, it didn't matter. All I cared about was my vengeance, boiling now, bubbling and writhing. Compton felt it, like me, I was sure. His eyes glistened, unblinking. He knew what I'd done, and why. Maybe Bradley and Hayward did too. At any rate, they respected Compton, I could see that much. I said, 'I knew a woman. Her name was Brenda. She was a pro, worked for Marriot. She was grassing him up to the law. I think Glazer was the copper she was grassing to and I think Glazer told Marriot what she was doing. Paget sliced her face off for it.'

Compton nodded.

Bradley said, 'That why you killed Marriot? And why you want to kill Paget?'

Hayward put a hand on him.

'We don't want to know.'

Bradley nodded. We wanted Paget. We wanted Glazer. We all had our own reasons. What they knew about me didn't matter. Nothing mattered, except that sweet bitterness inside us, that cancer, that lust that crept up from our balls and through our guts and into our chests. Vengeance. We wanted it. We could taste its sourness in the backs of our throats.

I got rid of them around midnight. Compton wanted me to stay in touch, to let them know what I was up to. I told him I would. He didn't believe me. It didn't matter.

After they'd gone, I switched the TV off, then the light, and I sat in darkness and tried not to think about it, about Brenda and what they'd done to her and why. There was a sickness inside me when I thought of it all, that rotten black blood pumping through my veins. I don't know how long I sat like that. I looked up when I heard a noise at the door. Browne's figure stood there, shadowy and stooped.

'Bad?' he said.

'Yeah.'

He went into the kitchen. When he came back he had two mugs of tea. He gave one to me and took a seat. We sat facing the blank TV screen.

TWENTY-EIGHT

One time, we went to a pub near the Angel tube station. It was a Saturday night and crowded. She was 'off duty', as she called it, and wore jeans and a jumper. The short skirts and high heels were part of her job, the uniform. Out of hours, she didn't go near that sort of thing. I suppose she could cope better if she split the two parts of her life.

I was working in the casino, back then, as security. She worked around there too, sometimes in the casino itself, picking up the odd out-of-town businessman who'd had too much to drink or was on a winning streak or wanted company for a bit. She said she wanted to go somewhere away from all that. The Angel wasn't far enough.

There were booths in the pub, and you could have some kind of privacy. It mattered to her, that sort of thing. She liked to sit and be separate from people, as if she needed life around her, but couldn't face being a part of it.

There was a jukebox in the pub, and she'd been listening to some song, tapping her fingers on the oak table. She was chain smoking, and downing one gin after the other, trying, I suppose, to dull the knowledge she carried. After a few minutes of silence, she held out her hand and said, 'Give us a quid, will you.'

I gave her the money and she got up and squeezed out of the booth and wandered over to the jukebox. She couldn't walk straight, and she bumped into a table, but she made it to the jukebox and placed her hands on the glass dome and started scrolling through the CDs. From where I sat, she looked like a million other women on a night out, nearing middle-age, tall, thin, trying to look young, trying to forget life for a while, trying to be just like everyone else. She looked tired, though, and her eyes were dull.

And then her face lit up for an instant and she looked at me, and there was that smile on her face, the one that made her look young. She beckoned me over. She was looking at the CD covers.

'There,' she said, pointing at one of the covers.

It was an old Motown compilation, full of the usual stuff. I looked at it and she looked at me looking, waiting for my reaction.

'It's a CD,' I said.

She sighed theatrically, and nudged me in the ribs.

'I know it's a bleedin' CD, fool. I mean, look at the name there. That song. See?'

I looked, but all I could see was the usual list of singers and groups.

'Brenda Holloway,' she said. 'See it?'

'Yeah.'

'That's who me mum named me after. Brenda Holloway. That song there, "Every Little Bit Hurts". It was a hit when me mum was pregnant with me.'

She pushed the pound coin into the slot and selected

that song. She had a couple of other choices for the money so she selected the song a couple more times.

'"Every Little Bit Hurts",' she said again. 'That's bloody right.'

And then her smile was gone, and the spark of her eyes, and the dullness was back and she looked hollow and wasted. She turned away from me and lurched back to the booth to wait for her song.

The heat in the pub was getting to me, and the smoke was stinging my eyes. I'd never liked herds of people. Even when I was fighting, I hardly ever sat in the crowd and watched. Here, the people heaved and laughed and shouted to each other from a few feet away and I felt like they were closing in on me, trapping me with their straight and normal lives. My neck was starting to stiffen and I could feel another headache beginning to get a grip. I pushed my way through the throng and into the Men's room. I spilled a few tablets down my throat and splashed water on my face. I waited a while and wondered why, but then I realized I was waiting for her songs to come and go.

By the time I came out, Brenda was back in the booth, facing me, but not seeing me. Her shoulders were hunched and she'd pushed herself into the wall. Sitting next to her was a man. From where I was, on the other side of the pub, I could see the man's dark blond hair and thin, long mask-like face. I could see his small mouth and his expensive suit. I could see the thick gold bracelet on the hand he was using to hold Brenda's wrist. Mostly, what I could see were his eyes, narrow and dark, slashes in the white face. He was telling her something, his hand squeezing her wrist, and he was leaning close and she was leaning as far away as she could. I could see she was in pain, gritting her teeth to keep from crying out.

I knew the man, of course. His name was Kenny Paget.

At the time, Brenda was pimped by Marriot, and Paget was his hatchet man. That was the way it was, and Brenda had stopped me several times from changing it. I hadn't understood why she wanted to stay. I didn't push her on it. But I didn't work for Marriot or Paget, and I didn't have to take their shit.

The pub was thick with people now and even with my weight, it took me a few minutes to push my way through to Brenda. By then, Paget had gone. Brenda hadn't moved, though. She was still pushed up against the wall, her shoulders still hunched, her eyes shut.

'What did he want?'

'Nothing.'

'What?'

She opened her eyes and looked at me. Her face was empty. It was like she was somewhere else, seeing someone else. Then something clicked and she looked at me as if she'd only just realized I was there. Whatever was in her thoughts, it wasn't me. I turned and searched Paget out. He was at the bar. I started to move towards him, but Brenda grabbed my arm.

'Don't, Joe. Leave it. Please.'

I nodded. But I wanted a drink, now, and Paget was at the bar and if I happened to stand next to him, well, that's just the way things happen.

He was sitting with some fancy drink in front of him.

He wasn't a big man. He was quite tall and thin, wiry. I could've snapped him in two right then and there. I should've done.

I wondered if it was coincidence, him being here. I thought back, too, to the time we went to the market and Brenda was uptight, nervous, looking around her.

Paget was a vicious bastard, and he was also cunning. He and Marriot were dangerous enemies. Not that I cared for myself. I would've been happy to wipe them both out and take my chances. I don't think anyone would've blamed me. They were hated, even amongst the underworld. But they were powerful.

I'd already had run-ins with them a couple of times, both to do with Brenda. Once, they'd warned me off her. Once, I'd gone to Marriot's office and told him to leave Brenda alone.

He'd been a dull-looking bloke, Marriot. Until I smashed his face in, that is. That was after Brenda had been killed. That had been blamed on a john – just another assault on a prostitute. Still, I'd smashed Marriot to pieces, just for someone to blame. If I'd known the truth, I wouldn't have left him alive.

Up till then, though, he'd looked like a boring small businessman; grey suit, grey face, like that. He had thick-rimmed glasses and a habit of wiping the lenses with his tie.

'Young couple like you,' he'd once said to me, 'in love, whole world ahead of you, full of promise.'

Back then I thought he was just taking the piss, saying it for effect. Paget was there that time, and he'd found it funny. I knew how people thought of us. I didn't care. Later, though, I learned what he was planning to do to Brenda, what he tried to do to me. And those words were singed into my head. Full of promise. Yeah.

So, there we were, me and Brenda, out for a nice drink. And there was Paget, smoking a cigarette, elbows resting on the bar counter. And the music played and people chatted and drank. And I was going mad with the urge to hurt him.

He didn't look at me, but he knew I was there. The young barman saw me and came over. He didn't look old enough to be drinking in his own pub. There was a woman serving too, but she was way up the other end.

'What can I get you?' the boy said.

'Pint of bitter. Gin and tonic.'

'Ice and lemon?'

'No.'

Paget glanced up at the barman.

'On me,' he said.

The barman moved over a few feet to pull the pint. Still without looking at me, Paget said, 'Hello, Joe. They serve your kind here, do they?'

The barman's look was wary, like he wasn't sure if this was a joke. Paget had spoken quietly, but there wasn't much humour in it.

The pub was loud, but near the bar it wasn't so loud that the people near us couldn't hear. There were two men standing next to us. They were big, working men, builders maybe. There were plenty of sites around there at the time. They'd been talking about football, about how Arsenal were losing out to Chelsea and United. They were Gunners fans, and they were narked that their club wasn't making the buys they needed for the season.

'I thought this was a decent kind of pub,' Paget was saying. 'Now, I dunno. If I'd known they served nigger whores, I woulda found a better place.'

Conversation between the men next to us had stopped, and the barman was looking around him, trying to find someone, the bouncer, I guessed.

'What do you want with her?' I said.

'Who? Your bird?' He shrugged. 'We work for the same man. Why shouldn't I say hello?'

It seemed like the whole pub had gone quiet apart from the music, which played in a kind of mocking way.

The two men next to us were moving away now. The barman, still unsure if this was all a bad joke, brought my drinks over. Paget fished for some money in his pocket and held out a tenner. I held out a tenner of my own. The barman looked from one bill to the other. His face showed fear, and he kept glancing around. Finally, seeing the look on my face, and maybe deciding I was too big to fuck with, he took my money, gave me change and went off to find help.

I took a few gulps of the beer.

'You look like a nice couple, Joe. Like beauty and the beast.'

I knew that whatever I did to Paget, Marriot could revisit on Brenda. Paget knew that too. He knew people's weaknesses. Brenda, I suppose, was mine. Maybe my only one. But something was going on, and I wanted to know what it was. I felt stupid, unable to outmanoeuvre him. I didn't play games, and he was very good at them.

I said, 'I want to know what you want with her.'

He laughed.

'You're starting to repeat yourself. Brain mushy? That it? All them blows on the head making you stupid?'

I downed the rest of the pint. I didn't care if he thought I was punchy. Lots of people did. It didn't matter. What bothered me was that he could say it to my face, and get away with it. The more he spoke, the more dumb I felt. I was hamstrung by Brenda, and he knew it, and he was enjoying himself.

'She tell you what she's been up to?' he said. 'Huh? She's a star. Did you know that? Didn't she tell you what—'

I saw it out of the corner of my eye; a flash of light, a crack, shattering, crunching. His head jerked forward, his glass flew across the bar and smashed into the bottles on the other side. He staggered and tried to stand and fell back on his seat. Blood poured from the back of his head, seeped into his hair and spilled down his neck.

I spun round. Brenda stood there, broken glass in her hand. Her face was vicious. People stared, horror in their eyes. I turned and saw the young barman speaking into the phone. I looked at Brenda, and she was looking at Paget, staring at him as he tried to stand. She staggered back a step. She gripped the broken glass, blood poured from her hand. I grabbed her wrist and pulled her. The crowd parted and we barged through, Brenda like a rag doll now, limp and loose.

We hit the street and I hailed a cab and we fell in. I told

the driver to take us to Tottenham. It was the first time I'd taken Brenda to my flat. She was shaking.

'What was it about?' I said.

'It doesn't matter.'

'What was it about?'

'Please, Joe. Please.'

'You knew, didn't you?'

'Knew what?'

'You knew he'd be there.'

'Did I?'

'Don't fuck about, Brenda. He won't forget this.'

'You scared of him then? You? Scared of what he'll do to you?'

'He won't do anything to me. He'll do it to you.'

'It doesn't matter about me,' she said.

She put a hand on my cheek. The tears fell.

'And anyway,' she said, 'you'd do something, Joe, wouldn't you? To protect me?'

'Do what? For you? What's going on?'

But then she wiped the tears away and half smiled and I knew she wouldn't tell me anything. It was another of her secrets.

'Don't worry,' she said.

I left it. I told myself it didn't matter.

Then we were in the market, and I felt something pulling at my mind; a weight, dragging it down somewhere.

TWENTY-NINE

I held Brenda's face. It came apart in my hands.

I woke sweating, shaking, my heart pounding. I didn't know where I was and the fear of not knowing pushed into my stomach. I couldn't breathe. I gasped for air. Brenda was going to die, I thought. Brenda was in danger. I looked around me, trying to work it out; where I was, when I was, why I was.

The dead face of the TV glared at me, glowing grey in the dark room, and I remembered and with that memory came the knowledge that it was all too late. Brenda was dead. I fell back in the chair, breathing deeply, feeling the lightness in my head fade. Gradually I came back.

And I remembered the dream. Only it wasn't a dream at all, but real, a memory. It was fucked up in my head and confused, sure, but it was a memory anyway.

Then I knew what the weight had been. I knew what my mind had been trying to tell me. It was about Brenda, and her secrets.

I saw Browne, asleep in his chair, his head forward, his chin on his chest. He was snoring slowly. I heard a car go by outside, its tyres zipping in the wet. I tasted the stale cigarette smoke and remembered Compton and Hayward and Bradley. There was a fug in the room and the lingering smell of sweat and cheap aftershave and Scotch. It was like the inside of a Saturday night.

I got up and went into the kitchen. I splashed cold water on my face and ran it through my hair. I found a bottle of Browne's throat-burning Scotch and swigged from it.

I went back to the lounge, took my Makarov from the coffee table and left.

THIRTY

The block of flats was still there. The lift was still broken. I climbed the stairs, stopping now and then to catch my breath. I passed a group of teenagers on one of the levels. They watched me go by in silence. One of them said something and the others laughed. This was their world and they were watching it crawl past, spitting at it as it went. I felt a million years old. I felt like I was always slowly climbing towards my own death; tabbing towards dug-in Argentinean troops, stepping into the ring with pain already pounding in my head, doing another blag for another vicious bastard, always heading towards another destruction.

'Poor old Joe,' she used to say to me. 'Poor old Joe, heading for the breaker's yard.'

But this time it wasn't my own doom I was trudging towards. It was hers. Maybe that's what had made me stop on the stairs.

The door to the flat had been painted since I'd last been here. It was blood red now, the paint thick and uneven. I banged on it and waited. I didn't know what time it was. Somewhere in the middle of the night. I banged again. A light came on. I banged again. An old man's voice said, 'Yes? Who is it?'

I reached into my pocket and pulled out a bunch of twenties. I pushed them through the letter box and waited. The door opened a crack, pulling the chain tight. Old eyes looked up at me.

'What do you want?'

'I want to come in.'

'You can't.'

He pushed a thin hand through the gap and dropped my money onto the floor. The door slammed shut.

I took some more money from my pocket and pushed it through the letterbox. This time I heard a younger man talking to the old man. Their voices were low, but urgent. I heard the old man say they didn't know who I was. I heard the younger man say he didn't care, it was free money. I banged again. The talking stopped. The door opened a crack and a man in his forties looked out at me.

'Why do you want to come in?' he said. 'Who are you?'

'I used to know someone who lived here,' I said.

I pulled more money from my pocket and held it up. He looked at the money. I could see his eyes counting it.

'So why do you want to come in?'

'I won't nick anything. I won't hurt you.'

'I want to know.'

'No, you don't.'

I held out some more money. He thought about it for about a second.

'What about that?' he said, nodding to the cash on the floor.

'Keep it.'

He closed the door and I heard the chain slide. I heard

the old man say something, his voice scared. The young man told him to shut up. The door opened and I walked in.

The smell had gone. That was what I noticed first. Her smell. Without it, the place was cold, just another flat in another tower block. They'd done something with it, painted it, put up pictures, but it didn't matter. There was nothing there for me. I suppose I'd been expecting some reminder of her. I felt empty. Emptier.

The old man had backed away from me and was standing close to the curtained window, watching me. He was in his pyjamas. He looked small and weak. The younger man had disappeared somewhere. Maybe he'd gone to count the money.

The floor was covered in some fake wood cover and they'd put their TV in a different corner so that threw me off for a second. I thought back and placed everything in my head as it had been. I went into the kitchen and opened a couple of drawers looking for something to use as a tool. I came up with a screwdriver. When I went back, the old man looked at it.

'What are you going to do?'

I went over to the corner of the room and started hacking away at the laminated floor. It was hard and I couldn't get anywhere with it. The young man came out then. He said, 'What the fuck?'

I hacked away, chipping the flooring, trying to get some leverage. The old man was in a seat, watching me, his eyes fearful. The younger one stood in the doorway. There was a gleam of hunger in his look. I pushed past him and went back into the kitchen. I came back with a larger screwdriver and started chopping away at the glue beneath the flooring. It was a bastard of a job and I was sweating by the time I managed to get some kind of clearing. Now I could see the old black and white tiles. Another twenty minutes of scraping and I'd hacked enough of the new floor away. I pushed the screwdriver into a crack between two tiles and prised up a white one and saw the hole.

I didn't know what I thought I'd find. I didn't know if I'd find anything at all. When I saw the box, I didn't recognize it. It was just a purple box with some foreign name written on the side. And then I remembered. I reached in. The old bloke was close to me, peering over my shoulder. I heard the younger one move forward.

I opened the box. Inside were all the creams and lotions, all untouched as far as I could see. She hadn't used any of them. Paget had even taken that from her.

There was something else in the box. Between the bottles and tubes was a small brown padded envelope. I took it out and opened it up. Inside was a DVD in a plastic sleeve. On the DVD were two words: 'For Joe'.

I drove back to Browne's with dread in my gut.

I suppose I should've thought before of her secret place. She'd shown me it, and she must've thought I'd go there and open it up if anything happened to her. But she would never explain it all properly because she knew I'd do something to stop her. Probably I would've.

I would've gone there, I guess, if I'd known Marriot and Paget had been behind her death. I would've figured things out.

THIRTY-ONE

Back. Always back.

Those crows were circling again. Time was circling. I was circling, going around, going back to Brenda.

When I got back to Browne's, he was out. I wondered where he was, if he was alright. But, I knew, sometimes, this late, he'd go to an offy or the twenty-four-hour super-market. Usually, he went for booze, and then he'd stop off at a late-opening pub or three on the way back. Anyway, I was relieved he wasn't there, though I didn't know why.

I put the DVD in the player and sat on the sofa. I grabbed the remote control, tuned the TV to the DVD channel and pressed play.

The room looked familiar, but I couldn't place it. It was small and like a hundred other lounges. The camera was still, placed at one end of the room so that the sofa was centre, face-on. The lens was wide-angled and took in most of the room, but some blurred dark shadows fogged part of the image. The picture was in colour, but poor quality. There was no sound. My guts were clenching again and cold sweat seeped from my body. The fear was back. A lanky black woman came in and walked towards the sofa. Her back was to the camera. She wore a short skirt, high heels, white blouse. She turned then and sat awkwardly on the sofa. She held a cigarette in one hand and a tall glass of clear liquid in the other. I knew what was in that glass. It was gin.

A man entered then, walking heavily towards the sofa. With him, was a small girl with long blonde hair. She must have been ten at most. She walked slowly, with small steps, so that the man had to coax her. She kept her head bowed, not wanting to look at anything, just in case it was all real and not some fucking awful nightmare.

From behind me, Browne's voice said, 'So, you're back.' He was quiet for a second, and I knew he was looking at the TV. 'Hey, isn't that... what's—'

I paused the DVD. My hands were trembling. I couldn't look at Browne. I stared at the screen, at Brenda's face, looking frail and scared and trying to look strong, like I knew she was, like she must've been.

Browne said, 'Jesus Christ.'

'You don't want to see this,' I said.

For a long time – or what seemed like a long time – Browne said nothing and I thought he must have gone. I stared at the hazy image, at the large eyes of Brenda. She was looking at the girl and she had a kind of dim, sad smile, like she was offering the girl encouragement, like she was saying, 'Don't worry, I'm here'. I thought I saw tears in her eyes, but the picture was too grainy and I could've imagined it. Maybe I just knew that she would've had tears in her eyes.

I heard the sound of rustling plastic bags, clinking bottles, shopping bags being put on the ground. Browne came forward and sat next to me on the sofa. The trembling had moved to my stomach and I felt a cold sweat seep out of my body.

Finally, Browne said, 'If you've got to look at this, I'll do it with you.'

I forced myself to clutch the remote control. My palm was wet. I pressed play. The image cut to another scene, this time from high up, in the corner of the room. This camera was static too, and fogged in the same way, by dark shadows. So, they'd set up hidden cameras. That meant that whoever was here, in this film, had no idea that they were being recorded.

I could hear Browne's raspy breathing. Every now and then he forced himself to swallow because his mouth had gone dry.

Another woman entered the picture then. She was slim and had long straight blonde hair. She had a long pale face, and her eyes were hooded, like she was on drugs. As soon as I saw her, I knew what a fucking idiot I'd been, and I knew why those children's toys had been there, planted for years in her front garden, small tombstones, reminders of dead childhoods.

Of course the fucking room looked familiar to me. I'd been there a couple of days before. And I'd met the woman, too. Christina Murray; Tina to her friends.

Brenda reached out to the girl, and took her free hand and squeezed it. Tina stood next to Brenda and started to peel off her clothes. She swayed as she did so and had to move a foot to keep her balance. They'd doped her up to the eyeballs.

I could see the man, then, more clearly, but it was only

a profile shot. He was in his fifties, with thinning dark hair and lard around his torso. He wore suit trousers, black patent leather shoes and a white shirt. He wore a wedding ring. His hand moved over the girl's hair and he said something to her. I felt useless, watching this thing. I wanted to take a hold of that man's arm and wrench it out of its socket. I found myself clenching my fists, like I'd done in the church at Kid's funeral when that dog-collared fuck had garbled about God and salvation and all that bollocks. My muscles were tight and my heart thumped at my chest and I had to breathe through my mouth. The man's hand wandered down the back of the girl's head and stroked her neck. She clenched her shoulders.

Browne said, 'Christ almighty.'

Brenda made an involuntary move forward, but stopped herself. She took a long deep drink of gin and hunched her shoulders as if she could feel those hands on her back, as if she was trying to put herself in the girl's place, trying to take it all onto herself. Tina had stripped now to her underwear, her clothes lying at her feet. Browne said, 'That is her, isn't it? Your woman? Barbara.'

'Brenda.'

'What was she doing there?'

'It doesn't matter.'

'Of course it matters. After what I'm looking at, it bloody well matters.'

'She knew about the cameras,' I said. 'She wanted evidence against them. She had to be there to try and get it. She did get it and she hid it and then they killed her before she could do anything with it.'

Browne was quiet for a long time. The pictures continued to move on the TV, a man, two women and a small girl going through some motions that, without the sound, seemed a pantomime, a mockery of life in living rooms in England.

I glanced at Browne and saw that he was no longer looking at the screen. I would've been surprised if he had been. Instead, he was glaring at the ground and there was a fury in his eyes that I hadn't seen since Kid had been alive. I could feel the tension coming from him, anger soaking through him and out into the air between us. He knew I was looking at him, but he wouldn't meet my eyes and I thought his anger was probably aimed at me for bringing this thing into his house, for involving him. I knew, too, that he'd liked Brenda, and the idea that she could be a part of what he was seeing was a shock. His silence was because he was having to square all his feelings and his memories, and that now he had to fit a sullied, dirty Brenda back into the picture. Before, she'd been one of the victims, a poor murdered prostitute who'd somehow hooked up with a thug like me who, at least, wouldn't hurt her. Now, her position was murkier.

I'd told him why Brenda was there. There was no point in me explaining things further. When he nodded, finally, it was to himself, and I knew that he'd managed to understand, and that he was relieved, at least, that Brenda wasn't a willing part of all this. I think that if he'd thought she was, his remaining faith in human nature, what little there was, would've dissolved and left him hollow, and he would've collapsed inside himself, taking his bottle and locking the world out.

'And she was there for the girl,' he said. 'To make sure.'

He wasn't talking to me. He was talking to himself, making himself understand.

The man on the screen looked around the room and I hit the pause button when his face was in view. I studied him. He looked successful. His hair, thinning on top, was neatly cut, and he was tanned – a real tan, not the orange kind. His shirt had cufflinks and an emblem on the breast pocket. What I'd thought was fat around his torso seemed now more evenly spread so that he looked like a man who'd been slim in youth but had since become used to a life of rich meals and money. Mostly, what gave him the air of success was the expression on his face. He wasn't feeling pleasure so much as satisfaction, like he was used to having anything he wanted and this was just another small perk, just another reminder of his strength and power. He wasn't enjoying himself; he was indulging himself.

'Who is he?' said Browne.

'Important.'

'You know him?'

'No.'

'How do you know he's important?'

'Because of this, because of the cameras, the set-up. They wanted him.'

'Who? Who wanted him? Who...' his voice cracked. 'Who would do that, Joe? Who in God's name could do something like that to that poor lass?'

I turned to him then, and when I spoke it was even and without emotion, because I wanted him to understand what I was going to do, and who I was going to do it to.

'It was Paget,' I said.

He looked at me and his face was white. He nodded slowly. It sickened him, but at least he understood it all. It was like I'd just told him he had terminal cancer; he would die, but at least now he understood why he had these pains. He stood up unsteadily and walked stiffly from the room. When he came back, he had two glasses, full to the brim of his cheap throat-burning Scotch. He held one out to me. I hated the stuff. I took it. I drank it in two gulps and it hit me like a brick and I had to grit my teeth to stop from throwing up. Browne took his drink and went and sat on the armchair, so that he could look at me. He took a moment before speaking and I thought he was trying to gather his thoughts, trying to keep from breaking up.

'This is what they did to Kid, isn't it? This is what traumatized her?'

'Yeah.'

'The same people? Paget?'

'Yeah.'

Neither of us said anything. The world stopped moving.

I thought again, as I had thought so often, how similar Kid and Brenda had been. So similar, in fact, that I had trouble separating them in my mind. They merged and became one. It was something to do with their characters, and their histories. They'd both suffered; they'd both had guts, refusing to let the cunts who hurt them win. But they'd both died, in spite of their courage.

'I was brought up a Christian,' Browne said, breaking the silence with his deafening whisper. 'I was told there was a reason for suffering, that it was part of God's plan, that he wouldn't abandon his children, that the innocent would be rewarded, one day. In heaven, I suppose.'

'Now you know better.'

'Do I? I don't know. I don't know anything any more. I try, Joe. I try not to hate. I don't want to end up like... like...'

'Like me.'

He put the glass to his lips. His hand trembled. It was an effort. He emptied the glass. He dropped his arm and let the glass slide out of his hand.

'Yes,' he said, watching the glass fall to the floor. 'Like you. Mechanical, like you. Cold.'

'You think I'm cold?'

'I think you try to be. Can't blame you, though. Not when I see that stuff. Can't blame you at all.'

Cold. Was I? The Machine. That's what they'd called me in the ring. The Killing Machine, as some had said.

'Maybe I should've been colder,' I said. 'Maybe they'd be alive then.'

'Perhaps, but then they wouldn't have felt what they did for you.'

Felt for me? What did that mean? What had they felt for me?

'They just wanted protection from me,' I said.

I suppose, if you looked at it, that was the thing they had most in common.

'They'd both needed me, and I'd failed them.'

I said that aloud for some reason. I hadn't meant to. I thought I was only thinking it. Or had I wanted to explain to someone? To Browne?

'Ah,' said Browne. 'So that's it.'

I looked at him.

'What?'

'That's why you do this; you're trying to redeem yourself, in the only way you know. You're still trying to save them.'

Maybe I was. I didn't care.

'I'm trying to avenge them,' I said, not knowing, really, if that was true.

'So you tell yourself.'

He didn't say anything for a while. He looked at the glass.

'But there's something else,' he said to the glass. 'You're punishing yourself. You're killing yourself to get your redemption, but you don't care, because that's all mixed up in it. It's redemption and punishment at the same time.'

'You sound like a vicar,' I said.

'Yes, well... once I would've said that wasn't such a bad thing. Now I'm not so sure. I don't know what to believe any more. I'll tell you one thing, though,' he looked up at me, and there was coldness in his eyes, as if he'd taken it away from me, soaked it up. 'If there is a god, he's a vicious bastard.'

THIRTY-TWO

It was the sound of a door closing that woke me. It took me a moment to remember where I was, and what had happened. I was still in the lounge, still facing the TV. The thing was dead now, but the images I'd seen haunted it still.

I got up to see where the noise had come from. I couldn't find Browne. His bedroom door was open, his bed had been slept in but he wasn't in there. The bathroom was empty, he wasn't anywhere downstairs.

I found him in the back garden, lit by the kitchen light; a dark shabby figure standing at the edge of the dark shabby lawn. He was wearing his pyjamas, dressing gown and slippers. He had a trowel in one hand and a mug in the other. I thought he must've been drunk, but when I got to him, I saw he was clear-eyed and sober. There was only steaming tea in his mug. I looked down at the ground and saw a patch of earth he'd dug up.

He glanced around at me, took a sip of tea.

'I've been gardening.'

I think he wanted me to congratulate him. He must've had a skinful, gone upstairs to sleep the booze off and then woken up with a brilliant idea; it's winter, the world is falling apart around me, I'll do some gardening.

'Right,' I said, not knowing what else to say.

He pointed to the ground with his trowel.

'I found it,' he said.

I looked and couldn't see anything.

'Right.'

'I think it's a violet, but I don't know.'

Then I saw what he was pointing at. In the shadows, surrounded by dirt was a small flower, barely the size of my thumbnail, on the end of a thin stem. He'd cleared most of the ground all around it so that the flower was by itself.

'Early for flowers, isn't it?' he said.

'Is it?'

'Must be the mild weather.'

He handed me the mug and trowel, bent over and grabbed a rock and heaved. The rock didn't move

'Need to give it some light,' he said. 'Need to give it some room.'

He nudged me. I handed his stuff back to him, bent over, lifted the rock and threw it away. When I did that, I saw some old geezer in the house next door peering at us from an upstairs window, his face lit by his bedroom lamp. All these houses were detached, so he was a long way off, but I thought I saw him saying something. Browne saw him too.

'What's he staring at?' he said.

'He's probably wondering why you're gardening in your pyjamas in the middle of the night.'

Browne looked down at what he was wearing.

'Yes, well, if I want to go into my own garden in my pyjamas, that's my affair.'

He waved at the bloke, smiled.

'Stupid old duffer,' he said. 'Probably thinks I've lost it properly this time.'

I was starting to think that myself.

'Do I water it?' he said, turning back to the flower.

'What for?'

He looked annoyed then, as if I'd insulted his plant. He threw the trowel into the grass, blade first.

'I don't know why I'm asking you, anyway. You're the opposite of a horticulturist. They bring things out of the earth. They touch things and make them live, a little like us of the medical profession. You… you're some kind of anti-horticulturalist. You put things in the earth, people mostly. You touch something and bring death.'

I had no idea what he was on about. I waited, though, until he was finished. I'd learned it was easier that way. But then he turned to me, laid a hand on my arm.

'Sorry, son,' he said. 'I know you cared for her.'

For a moment, I thought he'd really lost it. But then I clocked the way he was gazing at the flower, the pain in his face and I realized he wasn't talking about a plant at all, but about Kid. He must've come out here with a mug of tea for some fresh air, seen the plant and made some sort of connection with it, small and alone as it was, surrounded by weeds, rocks.

'We'll get some fertilizer,' I said, not knowing anything about gardening but figuring that that was the sort of thing gardeners did.

We stood there for a while, as if we were standing over her grave, which, I suppose, we were.

'I don't think I fully understood,' Browne said. 'Earlier, I mean. Watching that DVD with Barbara, I was shocked. I'm a bit stupid these days, I admit, and not always with it, but I'm not easily shocked.'

A breeze had picked up and Browne put a hand to his hair and tried to push it down.

'It must've been a terrible thing,' he was saying. 'For Barbara, I mean. To have to do that, to be brave enough to do that.'

'Yeah.'

He kept his hand on his head for a while, as if he'd forgotten about it, which he often seemed to do. Then he took it down and looked at me and there was some kind of fury in him.

'I understand, Joe,' he said. 'I understand you want to kill these men for her, for both of them, all of them. Part of me wants to do the same. But...'

He gave up on that thought and we went back to our vigil over the small flower.

Browne nodded.

'Yes,' he said. 'Fertilizer.'

Then we went inside.

THIRTY-THREE

'It's you,' she said. 'I thought you were a nightmare.'

She'd buffed herself up. She had more colour to her face and her hair was clean and a shining silver blonde. She looked ten years younger. There were dark rings under her eyes, though, and she was dressed in a loose T-shirt and jogging pants, which took away her shape, but when I'd last seen her she'd looked newly dead and now she looked newly awake with pale life in her pale blue eyes.

'What do you want?'

'I want to talk to you.'

'So talk.'

'Inside.'

She turned and walked away from me, letting the door drift open. I followed her into her lounge. She slumped onto the couch and drew her legs up.

'I suppose I should thank you.'

'Why?'

'For calling that doctor.'

'You already thanked me for that.'

'Did I? I can't remember. It didn't matter, anyway. I didn't need a doctor. I'd only taken a few pills.'

'I know.'

I looked down at her. She wouldn't meet my eyes, but stared instead at the carpet like a child pouting. It was gone four in the morning, but she didn't look like she'd been asleep.

I was knackered, but after Browne had woken me up with his gardening I couldn't get back to sleep. Things kept whirring in my head. It was a fine fucking time for my brain to be working for once.

'Do you want some coffee?' she said.

'Alright.'

She slumped off the couch with as much energy as she'd fallen onto it. I followed her into the kitchen. She filled the kettle and spooned coffee into a mug.

'Sugar?'

'No.'

We waited for the kettle to boil as if it we were waiting for someone else to leave the room. She chewed her lip and opened the cupboard and opened a pack of digestive biscuits and tipped them into the biscuit barrel. She did everything except look at me. When the kettle had boiled she poured the water into the mug and handed it to me.

'Milk's off.'

I followed her back into her lounge. She fell back onto the sofa. I stood and sipped the coffee, just for something to do. Neither of us wanted to talk. We both wanted to stop there, at the edge of things. If we stayed like that long enough, her staring at the floor, me sipping the coffee, maybe then we'd forget about Paget and Marriot and Glazer, and we could live happily ever after. Sometimes it was all I wanted to do; just stop.

I put the coffee down. I took the DVD out of my jacket pocket and tossed it onto her lap. She barely glanced at it.

'What's that?'

'A film. One of Marriot's.'

'I'm in it, I suppose.'

'Yes.'

She picked the DVD up and threw it back at me. It fell at my feet.

'I know what you did for Marriot and Paget,' I said.

'Congratulations. Have a prize. You gonna call the police?'

'No.'

'You should do. I would.'

'It wasn't your fault.'

'That's what I keep telling myself. But it was my fault I didn't go to the police.'

'Paget would've killed you.'

She laughed.

'So what.'

'Paget was your pimp, wasn't he? Not your boyfriend.'

'He was my boyfriend to begin with. I didn't know anything about him till later. By then, it was too late.'

I looked at the photos – the new ones of young children, the old, faded ones of other children, the picture of her as a bride.

'That's why your husband left you? Because he found out?'

'That's why.'

'And you have grandkids, but you don't get to see them.'

'Who told you?'

'Nobody. The toys out on your front lawn haven't moved in years, but the photos of the young children are new. Your kids send you photos, but they won't bring the kids round.'

'You're very clever, aren't you?'

'No.'

'What do you want?'

'I want you to watch the DVD.'

'Tough shit, then. I haven't got a DVD player.'

'It doesn't matter. You know what's on it.'

'Do I? There were lots of them.'

'This one was with a kid, a girl, eight, maybe ten. Long blonde hair.'

She laughed a small, bitter laugh.

'There were lots of those too.'

'There was a man, rich by the looks of it.'

She brought her knees up to her chest and hugged her legs.

'There's always a fucking man and they're always rich.'

'Would you know who he was?'

'I wouldn't know him if he came in here singing the national anthem. For all I know, you were one of them.'

'There was another woman.'

She looked at me then.

'Another woman? There were never other women.'

'There was on this one. Her name was Brenda.'

'Brenda.' Her eyes went filmy. 'Brenda. Yes. I remember her.'

'You remember the film?'

'I knew her. We both worked for Frank. What happened to her?'

'She died.'

'Died. Yeah.'

I watched for her reaction. I wanted to know if she'd had something to do with Brenda's death. She turned away from me, but not before I'd seen her eyes fill with tears. I pulled a chair opposite her and sat down. She swung round.

'What the fuck do you want from me? You want me to come clean, own up? You want me to pay for my crimes? Well, I've been paying. For years. So why don't you fuck off.'

The tears were coming now, but she wasn't crying. They were tears of anger.

'Tell me about her.'

She smeared the tears away with the back of her right hand.

'Is there something wrong with you? You don't get angry. You don't get sad. You don't get anything, do you? You just sit there and stare and ask questions like a fucking robot. You want to know about Brenda? Fine, I'll tell you. She was a fool. She thought she could outthink them, outsmart them. She was wrong. Then she died.'

'Why was she there?'

'Fuck off and leave me alone.'

'Why?'

'Fuck off,' she screamed.

She jammed her ears up with her hands and turned away from me and curled into a ball. Then she cried. I waited a while, then I got up and went looking for some booze. I found some vodka and poured it neat. When I took it back, she was still curled into a ball, but now she'd calmed down. I handed her the drink. She took it. I sat down. I said, 'I killed Frank Marriot. I'm going to kill Kenny Paget. I'm going to kill them all. Understand?'

Like a child, she nodded, sipping her drink, looking up at me with wide eyes, torn red from sobbing. It was like I was telling her she had to be careful of strangers.

'Why was Brenda there?'

'Bloke wanted it, I suppose. Frank gave them what they wanted. They paid and Frank gave it to them.'

'And the filming?'

'Frank. Liked to have secret films.'

'Blackmail?'

She shrugged.

'Suppose so.'

'And Brenda thought if she got a copy of the film she'd give it as evidence to finish Marriot and Paget?'

'Yeah. She thought. She was a brave woman, Brenda. Braver than me.'

'It was in your house. You must have known what Brenda wanted to do. You must have helped her.'

'I warned her. That was my help. I told her not to do it. She wouldn't listen. She thought she was safe.'

'Because she'd have the film?'

'No. Because of some bloke she was going out with, some hard man she thought would protect her.'

She tilted her head sideways and narrowed her eyes, like she was examining something odd.

I think I'd known it for a while. It was something Bowker had said to me. He'd said everyone had known about me and Brenda. He'd said it like it was an in-joke; like beauty and the beast, I suppose. He was right. It was a joke.

I sat down and reached over for the coffee and lifted it to my mouth. The coffee was bitter. It tasted like ashes. I drank it down. I felt that hollowness open up.

Maybe I'd known it all along, right from that moment in the casino, six years ago, when I'd been working security and she'd come up to me at the bar and started talking to me. I remembered that Paget had been in the casino that night.

I tried to think back over those days and weeks we were together, all those years ago. I'd thought then that she was what she'd said she was, a lonely person who needed someone, someone else who was lonely, someone like me.

But she'd known who I was, what I did. I suppose she'd known everything about me. I suppose I was the part she needed before she could carry out her plan. And, yes, she'd made sure we were seen together. I thought of the night in the pub when she'd smashed Paget on the head with the glass. Had we been there by accident? Or had she known Paget was going to be there too? How much had she used me?

What did it matter? What did anything matter?

Tina moved. I'd forgotten she was there. I looked up and saw her staring at me.

'It was you,' she said. 'You were the one she hooked up with, the one she thought would protect her.'

'Yes.'

'You and me. Her saviours.'

THIRTY-FOUR

I drove in a daze. I might have passed a hundred other cars. I can't remember. I remember staring ahead, the night closing in around the car's headlights.

When my phone rang, I had to pull over.

Green said, 'Bingo. Ever heard of a bloke called Laing?'

'No.'

'Gary Laing; not big time, but big enough. Bought a load of smack a few days ago.'

'From Paget?'

'No idea, mate. If I were a betting man, I'd say so, yes.'

'Where can I find Laing?'

'He's got a house in Hackney, but I wouldn't go there if I were you.'

'Tight?'

'As a fucking duck's arse.'

'Will he talk to me?'

'I wouldn't chance it. He'd probably shop you to Paget, or cut your head off and give it to him. He's a bastard, Joe.'

'They all are.'

'Yeah.'

'How do I get to him?'

'Can't help you there, old son.'

'Has he got anyone? A bird? Anything like that?'

'He's got a hundred birds. And I doubt he gives a shit about any of them.'

'Family?'

Green was quiet for a while.

'You sure you want to go there, Joe?'

'Yes.'

'If you use his family, he won't rest till you're dead.'

'He can join the queue.'

'If any of this gets back to me—'

'It won't.'

'Christ.'

There was another long pause.

I said, 'It won't get back to you.'

'Use his old man. He's got a dodgy ticker, though, so for fuck's sake don't overdo it.'

Green told me that Laing's dad lived in Wanstead, in a place called Ross Grove. It was a retirement court of a hundred or so brick flats set off from George Lane, a wide, long suburban cul-de-sac. Before I did anything, I'd driven over and scoped the place out. It was going to be too hard to do anything in the small space around the flats. There were too many overlooking windows, too little space, not enough cover. I'd seen a sign, though, for a Manager's Office, and that helped me. If I was lucky, I wouldn't need to use Laing's old man at all.

I drove back to the road. Access to the retirement flats was through a wide brick gateway. The wrought iron gates were open and probably never shut. At this point, the trees that lined the road made for good cover from witnesses, but the road itself was wide and straight and almost empty of parked cars, most of which were in the garages and long driveways of the detached houses spaced along the road. I didn't think I was going to be able to ram Laing's car as he drove up, like I wanted to do – there was too much chance he'd see it and even if he didn't, he could still manage to get away. I'd hoped I could smash the car side-on or maybe box it in. That was out. I had to think of something else.

Green had told me Laing drove a blue Lexus and he'd given me the number plate. I had his home phone number. I positioned myself and made the call. The voice that answered was foggy with sleep. I said, 'Can I speak to Mr Laing?'

'Fuck is this? You know what time it is?'

'I'm the manager from Ross Court.'

Immediately he was awake.

'What's wrong?'

'It's your father, Mr Laing. He's been taken ill.'

'What does that mean? Taken ill? Is he alright?'

'He felt faint, dizzy. He wants to see you.'

'Where is he?'

'Here, in his flat.'

'He should be in a fucking hospital.'

'The doctor doesn't think it necessary, but he is concerned that he's going to make himself worse by worry about seeing you.'

Laing sighed.

'I'll be there in half an hour.'

He hung up.

This was where my luck would show. If Laing decided to call the manager back or if he wanted to talk to his old man, I was fucked. If he got straight into his motor and drove over, I was alright.

Street lights glowed orange along the road, but there were pools of darkness between them, and the areas around the gate, where tall oaks stood, were dark with shadow. I fixed the gate then parked my car a few yards up. I got out of the car, walked back to the shadows and slipped into them, among the trees. There was only one way he could approach. I had to wait now and see if he was sending an army to meet me.

I pulled my coat tight, put my hands in my pockets, my right gripping the Makarov. The night was clear and a weak wind moved the coldness slowly into my limbs. I buried my face in the collar of the coat.

The branches moved and cracked. I thought of the girl, Kid, her body so thin, now nothing but ashes somewhere. She'd been used by Paget, trampled by him. But it had been me, probably, who'd killed her. I'd been firing blind and those walls were thin. I'd saved her and killed her at the same moment.

I tried to blank my mind, but the image of her kept coming to me out of the gloom. I saw her staring up at me, her eyes wide, her stick-thin body hunched against pain and fear.

Where I stood, in that darkness, I was only a couple of miles from the cemetery where we'd burned the girl. Were her ashes about me now? Were they on the wind or on the

ground where I stood or in the rattling branches? And
Brenda? Where was she now? What had her life come to?
And that boy, that Argentinean conscript who'd never had
a choice, whose life had taken him to me and the rounds
I'd fired on that foggy damp hill all those years ago? What
had become of him? I saw his face again, there in front of
me, frozen into a vile smile, as if he could see it all as a
lousy joke, and see me, too, as part of the same joke. Did
people think of him still, see his face, as I saw it?

I swayed and felt myself falling. I staggered into
branches. I caught myself and shook my head. I was
sweating, despite the freezing cold air. I shivered. My head
was empty and light and, for a moment, I didn't know
where I was or why I was there. All I saw was darkness.
I felt the Makarov in my grip. It was solid and heavy
and real. It was good. The feel of it brought me back. I
remembered where I was.

Then I heard a car's deep engine slow and I knew it was
Laing turning into the road. I flexed my gun hand and felt
anger surge through my blood. Murder was on my mind.

I watched the car's headlamps throw light onto the road.
Then the car was slowing down again and I heard the tyres
grind grit as it passed me and made to turn into the entrance
for Ross Court. It was the blue Lexus, just like Green had
said. It braked sharply. There was one man in the front,
none in the back. Laing had come alone, then, and now he
was staring at the gates and wondering why they were shut.
That was when he could have realized something was wrong,
but I was hoping he'd never been here this late at night
and that he didn't think there was anything strange about

the gates being closed. I heard the handbrake go on. He opened the door and got out and went over to the gates. I moved. He turned when he heard my feet crunch the dead leaves. I saw it in his face. He knew he was fucked. There was desperation in the way he grappled in his jacket for a weapon. I brought the Makarov down on the side of his head. He grunted and fell to his knees, his hands flat on the ground. When he tried to get up, I smacked him again at the base of his skull and he hit the floor face first. I checked him for weapons and found a lock knife with a three-inch blade. I removed his trainers, took out the laces and used them to tie his wrists together behind his back. Then I grabbed the back of his jacket and hoisted him up and carried him to my car. I stuffed him into the boot and drove off.

We were a couple of miles away, in the park, near the Eagle Pond. I'd stashed the car in the middle of a group of trees. I took a recce, found no sign of anyone. I unlocked the boot and let it glide open. Laing was conscious, curled up as much as he could be. He stared out at me with eyes wide, part angry, part scared. I told him to get out. He struggled onto his knees, using his shoulders to lever himself, and then climbed out slowly, looking at me all the time.

He was a small man, no more than five and a half feet and slim, but he was wiry, his muscles ropey and tight. On his left wrist he wore a Rolex watch. On his right a thick gold bracelet. He had a deep suntan. He had money alright, and he looked like he'd gotten used to the easy life. I wanted to rip that tan from his body.

I smacked him, a short jab to the mouth. My fist was

half the size of his head. His lip split and he staggered backwards, doubling over and dribbling blood. When he straightened up he backed further away from me so that he was almost back in the boot of the car.

'I haven't got much money. Take it.'

'Where's Paget?'

'What? Who the fuck's Paget?'

'Where is he?'

'I don't know what you're on about. I don't know anyone called Paget. You've got the wrong fucking man. My dad's ill. I was on my way to see him. That's all.'

He could see what was coming. He pulled at the binds around his wrists. He looked for a way out. I gave him a quick combination to the body. His legs buckled and he swayed and fell, doubling up and vomiting. I waited. When he'd finished retching, he fell over onto his side, took deep breaths. I hoisted him back to his feet and gave him some more body shots, finishing off with his kidney.

'Where is he?'

'Don't know.'

I slammed my fist into the side of his face. He flew sideways and hit the ground four feet away. His face was in mud and he didn't move. I thought I might have hit him too hard. I didn't much care.

I realized I hadn't found a mobile phone on him. I should've checked his car. I wasn't thinking right. I was being stupid, making mistakes. If I didn't calm down I'd go too far and fuck myself up. I wanted Paget. I had to remember that.

After a few minutes, Laing came round and tried to get

to his knees. I waited. He gave up and stayed where he was.

'I don't know what you want,' he said into the mud.

'Where's Paget?'

I walked over to him. He tried to crawl away but with his hands tied behind him, he had no leverage and as he rose he fell again. I lifted him up and held him under his shoulders so that his feet dangled above the ground. He was limp, his head rolling backwards and forwards. I set him on his feet but held him up with my left.

'You've got the wrong man.'

'Where's Paget?'

'Paget who?'

'Kenny Paget. You bought some heroin from him.'

There was a flicker in his eyes. He knew something. I brought my right back.

'Where is he?'

'Honestly, I swear, I never heard of him, I don't know what this is about. I don't know who you are, I don't know anything.'

I lowered my hand. Maybe Green had wrong info. Or maybe Paget had got someone else to sell the drugs for him. One thing, though; Laing wasn't denying that he'd bought the junk.

I let go and he crumpled to the ground and stayed down there.

'You bought some heroin a couple days ago. A lot of it.'

He lifted himself up onto his knees. He stood slowly.

'I don't know anyone called Paget. There's been some

mistake here. I was going to see my dad, that's all. He's – fuck. He's not ill, is he? That was you on the blower.' He spat blood. 'That was stupid of me. I exposed myself.'

He used his shoulder to wipe away some of the blood from his mouth.

He was tough, and he was successful in a dangerous trade, which meant he was smart enough to know that he wouldn't be in business long if he grassed his suppliers every time he got slapped. He could go on telling me he didn't know Paget and I could go on beating him until he stopped saying anything. Maybe he'd eventually spill it all, but I didn't have time to make sure he was telling me the truth; I wouldn't get a second chance to question him. I'd have to try something else.

I took the lock knife from my pocket. I flicked open the blade. He watched it.

'You think that's going to make me know who Paget is? You start slicing me up and I'll just give you a load of bollocks.'

I grabbed him and spun him round and cut the laces that bound his arms. He turned slowly, rubbing his wrists. He was looking up at me, no anger or fear in his face, just a kind of bafflement. He ran his tongue round the inside of his mouth.

'I think I swallowed a tooth.'

'Buy another one.'

'You're not the police. You're not trying to rob me. You don't work for my rivals. Who do you work for?'

'Myself.'

'Oh? You're pretty good. Not many people can control

violence like that. You were a fighter, right? Boxer? I could give you a job. More money than you earn now.'

'You don't know how much I earn.'

'No, but I'd give you more. I always need people like you.'

'Not interested.'

'Who told you about me?'

'It doesn't matter.'

'It matters to me.'

'If I think you'll go hunting for a grass, I'll have to kill you now.'

He nodded.

'Okay,' he said. 'I'll leave it. So what do you want?'

'I told you. I want Paget.'

'Yeah, well, I never heard of any Paget.'

He spat some more blood and rubbed his stomach. He patted his pockets and pulled out a crumpled pack of cigarettes.

'Got a light?'

'No.'

'There's a cigarette lighter in the car.'

He must've thought I was stupid.

'You made a big buy recently.'

He smiled and put the pack of cigarettes away.

'Who says?'

'Know whose stuff it was?'

He looked at me suspiciously. I said, 'Ever heard of Bobby Cole?'

'What's Cole got to do with it?'

'Kenny Paget worked for Cole. He nicked a million quid's worth of heroin.'

'I keep telling you; I never heard of Paget.'

'Maybe. But that's Cole's stuff you've got and he won't care if you've never heard of Paget.'

'Bollocks. How do I know that's Cole's stuff?'

'You've heard about Cole, right?'

'I've heard something, sure. Trouble with some East Europeans. So?'

'They're Albanians. Cole owes them money. It was them Cole got the heroin from.'

He moved over to the car and slammed shut the boot and sat on top of it.

'Say I believe you—'

'It doesn't matter if you believe me or not. That stuff's going back to Cole. If you tell me where you got it, I'll let you take it back to Cole yourself.'

'Or?'

'Or I'll put you in the boot of this car and deliver you to him.'

'You're lying.'

'You know I'm not.'

'So you work for Cole?'

'I told you, I work for myself.'

'So, suppose I give you some money to forget what you know?'

'No.'

'If I have to give that stuff to Cole, I'm gonna be out a lot of money.'

'You can get it back from whoever you bought it from.'

He smiled.

'Fuck,' he said. 'I don't seem to have much choice, do I?'

'You can choose to live.'

He spat more blood.

'Bloke called Whelan. Doug Whelan.'

Whelan. I knew that name. Where had I heard it? No, not heard it. Read it. It had been on the list kept by Harry Siddons.

THIRTY-FIVE

I couldn't reach Cole on the phone. When I got to his place, there was a single light on downstairs. I hammered on the door. The door opened and Cole's wife stared out at me.

'Yes?'

'Remember me?'

It took her a couple of seconds to focus her eyes. Without her make-up, she looked just like any old woman. She scrunched her face up for a moment, then it cleared and she said, 'You were here before.'

'Where's your husband?'

'Out.'

'Where?'

She shrugged.

'Just out.'

I went into the house. The woman watched me and then wandered off, back to her bed or her glass of gin or whatever. I searched the place. Downstairs, in a study out back, I found the small bald bloke with the bad leg. He was in a chair with his eyes closed. I nudged him. He opened his eyes and looked up.

'I wasn't asleep.'

'Where's Cole?'

'He's found them.'

'The Albanians?'

'Yeah. He said you might come by.'

'You need to stop him.'

He sat up.

'Can't.'

'Call him.'

He looked at me a moment then got up and limped over to a desk. He lifted the phone and dialled a number. After a while, he looked at me and shrugged.

'Phone's off.'

'Try someone else.'

He tried. Nothing. He put the phone down.

'All off.'

'Where is he?'

'The Albanians have got a warehouse in Barking.'

'You know where?'

'Yeah.'

'Let's go.'

It took us twenty minutes. As I drove, I watched the thin grey line grow on the horizon. A new day crept in, people started moving about, trucks and busses chugged away.

The little bloke told me his name was Gibson. He told me Cole had waited for me to come up with something, but when he got the information that the Albanians had this place they were working out of, he decided to try and take them out in one knockout blow.

He gave me directions from a piece of paper he had in his hand. We were on some large industrial site closer to Dagenham than Barking. It seemed like mile after mile of large warehouses and workshops and lock-ups, spiked metal fences and breeze-block walls separating the places from the cracked concrete road. We passed a scrap-metal yard and Gibson told me Cole would be down the next right.

As I turned at the end of a concreted road, I slowed the car to a crawl, moving between two rows of garages. I killed the lights and peered ahead. I could see an iron gate a hundred yards away, and beyond that an empty forecourt leading to a large prefab warehouse. Ahead of us were four cars. A group of shadows moved about, ten or so men. Many were probably the same ones I'd seen at Cole's a few days earlier.

I stopped a dozen yards short. There wasn't much room to turn the car around, so I left it facing the other cars. We got out and walked towards the shadows. A dark, squat shape pulled itself away from the others and came towards us.

'They're in that building over there,' Cole said, pointing to the large warehouse at the end of the row. 'It's gonna be hard getting in. The roll door is well secured. There's a couple of windows high up, so we're gonna chuck some petrol bombs in and wait for them to come out. You tooled up?'

I peered through the gloom at the large square shape. The windows were small. Whoever had to throw those petrol bombs would be exposed.

'Call it off,' I said. 'It's what Dunham wants. He's playing you.'

'Fuck Dunham.'

'He's putting you lot against each other. He stands back and sweeps up what's left.'

'Fuck him and fuck you. I'm taking these cunts out.'

262

'It wasn't the Albanians who shot your place up.'

He looked uncertain, but he was in front of his men.

'You don't know what you're talking about.'

I looked back where we'd come. That road, more a narrow track, pitted with potholes, a corridor of lock-up garages, quarter of a mile long. Ahead of us, the large building, all corrugated steel and aluminium, no way round, no way through, just a block of metal and a large open forecourt and an eight-foot-high spiked metal fence. The hair on the back of my neck stood up. Cole was walking away from me. I grabbed him.

'We've got to get out of here.'

His men were looking at us. Cole's voice was low, hard.

'Fuck off, Joe. I mean it. If you ain't helping, you're in my fucking way.'

'Listen to me, this is wrong. Look at it. You're blocked in. It's a bottle-neck.'

He snatched his arm away from my grasp.

'You've got Dunham on the brain.'

'It's a fucking trap.'

'You fucking mad? We've got the cunts. We've got them.'

'It's wrong.'

'Get out of my way, Joe.'

'I found your drugs.'

That stopped him.

'Where?'

'Bloke called Laing. He bought them from someone called Doug Whelan. Does that name mean anything to you?'

'No.'

'It should. Your nephew used to work with him.'

'Carl? What are you on about?'

'Yes, Carl. Think about it; that shoot-up on your house was an amateur job. You think the Albanians would fuck about like that? They'd torch the place. They'd make sure you were home. It was Carl.'

'Why would he do that?'

'How do I know? He's ambitious. He got a better offer from Dunham.'

The men heard us. They looked at Cole. They were getting nervous and closing up, into a tighter group, moving closer to the cars. Gibson turned and looked up the way we'd come.

'He might be right,' he said.

Cole looked down the track and back to the warehouse.

I said, 'Who told you the Albanians were here? It was Carl, wasn't it? It was your nephew.'

'He wouldn't fucking dare.'

'So where is he?'

'Christ, when you decide to talk, you don't fuck about.'

'Tell me it wasn't Carl who told you about the Albanians and I'll help you now.'

Cole's face was grim. He said, 'Tell me about it.'

'We haven't got time.'

'Tell me about it.'

I needed Cole. If it wasn't for that, I would've dumped him. I said, 'I got someone looking for a large amount of heroin that might've hit the streets. Your heroin. Paget had to cash it in and I think he gave it to Dunham in return for protection. Dunham gave it to Carl, or some of it, as a pay-off. Carl used Whelan to unload the dope.'

Cole thought about what I'd told him. He said, 'This Laing character will confirm this?'

'Yes. He doesn't want you on his arse.'

'We've been here twenty minutes. If this was a trap, why haven't they sprung it?'

'I don't know.'

Gibson said, 'Maybe they're waiting.'

'For what?' Cole said.

Gibson looked at me. Cole's men looked at me. Cole said, 'Fuck.'

The first rounds hit the cars, pocking the windscreens, shattering them, thudding into the metal bodies. We scattered for cover and I saw one man crash to the ground. The shots were coming in from high and Cole's men started returning fire towards the small windows in the warehouse where the blaze of automatic rifles flashed in the night. I had the Makarov in my hand, but from this distance and without being able to sight properly, it was useless.

But there was something wrong with this. Those two, high up, were easy to avoid, easy to outmanoeuvre. Then I heard a sound and turned and knew we were fucked. Two garage doors behind us burst open and men poured out. They were waiting alright.

'Behind,' I shouted.

Cole's men swung round as one and let off bursts. I picked off one man and hit the ground as a half dozen bullets hammered into the concrete at my feet. Rounds hailed down on us from ahead and behind. Cole had grabbed a Heckler-Koch MP5 from a bunch in the boot of his car. Now he was standing madly in the middle of the carnage, screaming murder, his knuckles white as he emptied one magazine and dumped it and rammed another home. Gibson was yelling at him to get down. Cole's men returned fire as best they could, but they had no cover aside from the cars, which were getting torn to bits. They were getting pummelled: two dead; another two or three wounded. I looked around for cover.

'The garages,' I called to Cole.

He looked at me. I pointed to the garages. I was crouched down between the cars, keeping my head down as best I could. The others were spread out between the other cars. I could hear rounds zipping through the air all around, deep droning wasp sounds. I felt the car judder when another burst of automatic fire rocked its frame. They were getting closer. I peered around the car I was behind and saw them, ten, twelve of them, moving forwards slowly, all with autos on full, spare clips taped to the ones they were emptying. When they got thirty yards away, their firepower would be enough to tear us apart. The garage nearest me had two wooden doors, locked by a bar and padlock across the middle. I aimed from five feet away and emptied my magazine at the wood around the lock. The wood broke, but still held. Cole saw what I was doing.

'The doors,' he shouted.

Gibson got the idea and nudged another man near him. One of Cole's men made a wild bolt for the door and bounced into it and got cut in half. I reloaded. Cole scrambled over to me and levelled his Heckler at the wood around the lock and let go with a burst that cleaned out his magazine and shattered the wood to splinters.

Gibson and the other man did the same over their side, breaking through into another garage. Shattered concrete erupted from the ground and hit me in the face. I heard a tyre explode. I looked around the car and saw that the men behind us were closing in, forty yards, thirty-eight. One of the men stopped now and pulled a bag from his back. He fished around inside and when his hand came out it was holding a small dark object. Gibson saw me looking. He looked too.

'Grenade,' he yelled.

The man pulled the pin. Gibson stood first. I stood. Cole stood. We unleashed everything we had at that man. He jigged as the rounds smacked into him. He fell and the grenade trickled out of his hand. One of the others with him dived for it, grabbed it and chucked it towards us. We threw ourselves down. The blast was short of us, but not short enough. It rocked the ground. Debris rained down on us. The car I was behind took the shock and jumped in the air. My ears rang. I crawled around the car and peered through the dust and saw that the attackers had also been staggered by the explosion. They'd hit the dirt and were exposed, but they were too far away to charge. If we'd tried, they would have cut us down. I scrambled over to Gibson and Cole.

'Now,' I said. 'Get cover.'

Gibson shouted the order. I grabbed a bag of ammo from the boot of Cole's car and tossed in a couple of Heckler and Kochs. Then I saw the bottles he was going to use as petrol bombs. I gave the bag to Gibson and snatched up the bottles. To Cole, I said, 'Where's the petrol?'

'Huh?'

'You were going to throw petrol bombs at the ware-house. Where's the petrol?'

He shook his head.

'We were gonna get it from the cars.'

'No time now.'

We rushed to the garages either side, Gibson and Cole and another man with me, the rest over the other side. Gibson's bad leg slowed him up, but he managed okay. The enemy had regained their feet now and were figuring out what we were up to.

It was black inside the garage, and we were crowded by something covered in a tarpaulin. Gibson flared up a lighter. The shadows danced around, but we could see the place. It was big enough to house a single car with space to move around it. The walls and ceiling were all made of the same concrete slabs. The object covered with the tarp was smaller than a car.

'We've trapped ourselves,' Cole's man said, panic rising in his voice.

'It's cover at least,' Gibson said. He looked at the mass in the middle of the garage. 'What is this? Can we use it?'

The other bloke lifted the tarp and peered underneath.

'It's a boat.'

'Shit.'

Cole was on his mobile, calling up reinforcements.

'Everything you got,' he said. He dropped the phone into his pocket. 'They won't get here in time.'

He was right.

'What kind of boat?' I said to the bloke.

'You know, speedboat.'

'Outboard motor?'

'Yeah.'

I looked at Cole.

'Petrol,' he said.

I gave the bottles to Gibson to fill up. Then I went up front to the gap in the doors. Outside, the enemy were spread out along the fronts of both rows of garages, moving slowly forward. They were cagey, not sure how to finish us off now that we'd got some cover. One of them opposite saw me and let off a burst that battered the wooden doors. I ducked back. They were all firing now, their rounds ripping up the wood but not getting much further. The wood was thick.

Cole and his other man were at the back of the boat. They'd got the cap off the tank, but they couldn't get the petrol out.

'We need a tube, something to siphon it out.'

I looked up at the ceiling, five feet above our heads.

'How much ammo we got?' I said to Gibson.

He looked through the bag and pulled out a dozen magazines.

'Few minutes' worth.'

'Think we can blast a hole in the roof?'

He followed my gaze.

'Maybe. This concrete isn't reinforced. Yeah. Take a lot of fire.'

I turned to Cole. Outside, the sound of gunfire had erupted again. Through the gap in the doors, I could see that some of Cole's other men were trying to make a break for it. They'd gone back to the cars and were in a firefight. I saw something sail through the air.

'Grenade.'

I dived backwards. The blast smashed the doors back, but they took much of the impact. There wasn't much time.

'Is there a fuel line, hydraulics, something like that?' I said.

Cole pulled the tarp back and rooted around.

'Got something.'

'Get that petrol out. Gibson, with me.' To the other bloke, I said, 'Hold them off as long as you can.'

I left Cole to do what he could with the petrol. The other bloke went up front and peeked out through the gap in the doors. He brought his pistol up and started to fire, aiming carefully. Gibson came over to me and we stood and loaded Hecklers with new mags. We aimed at a spot above and let off a burst. The bullets smacked into the concrete ceiling, dust and chippings fell down onto us, dust filled the garage.

'It's not enough,' Gibson said. 'We're not getting through.'

'We use everything,' I said.

Gibson turned to Cole who was ripping tubing from the boat.

'If we can't get through, that'll be our ammo gone,' Gibson said. 'We'll be sitting ducks.'

Cole looked from Gibson to me. He looked to the bloke at the front of the garage who was taking single aimed shots and ducking for cover.

'Almost out,' he called over his shoulder.

'We can't outlast them,' I said. 'One grenade through that door and we're dead.'

'Do it,' Cole said. 'Keep a few rounds in your pistols. Use everything else.'

We loaded new magazines.

'One spot,' I said.

We took aim and fired, letting the magazines empty, holding the Hecklers tight to our shoulders. The gunfire became a constant deafening roar. Debris rained down on us, chips of concrete first, then shards, then lumps. The garage filled with a cloud of dust that filled our throats and noses and eyes. We fitted new magazines into the guns and emptied them, then more magazines. There were only a few left. My ears rang. I was firing blind. Gibson was choking on dust.

'Hold it,' I said.

We let the air clear a bit. Cole had a hose to his mouth and was sucking petrol out of the fuel tank. He spat a mouthful of fuel out and stuck the hose into one of the bottles. When the air had cleared some, I looked up. Over us, a small jagged hole gaped in the concrete slab.

'Short bursts,' I said.

I took aim, targeting the sides of the hole. I fired a small burst, breaking away more of the concrete. I emptied the magazine and loaded one more and fired at a point a few inches away from the hole. Gibson saw what I was doing and followed. The Heckler kicked in my hands and I thought I was wasting our ammo, and I didn't care. I kept firing and a foot-square lump of concrete fell and crashed into the boat. My magazine emptied. Gibson was out too. He picked up the ammo bag and threw it aside.

'We're out,' he said.

We looked up at the hole. It was rough, about two foot by one.

'I'm the only one can fit,' Gibson said. 'Get me up.'

'Once you're up there, those machine guns in the warehouse will be able to spot you. You'll have to move fast. Light the petrol bombs, chuck them and then jump down.' I glanced at his dodgy leg.

'Don't worry about me,' he said.

I gave him a boost up and he reached into the gap and pulled himself in. It was tight and he had to scramble to get his upper body through. And then he stopped. He was stuck just above the waist, his legs dangling. I got underneath him and put my hands under both his feet and pushed. I could hear him yell in pain. I pushed, sweat dripping down my forehead and mixing with the concrete dust and running into my eyes, my mouth. There was the sound of a muffled groan. Gibson was stifling his pain as much as he could. If he made too much noise, the men in the warehouse would turn on him and he wouldn't be able to run. I looked up as I strained and saw a corner of broken concrete jabbing into his gut, blood staining his shirt. I heaved and watched the concrete scrape his stomach as he slowly, slowly squeezed through. Finally he was out. I chucked his pistol up to him.

Cole had tossed his jacket and pulled his shirt off, ripping it into strips and trebling up the strips which he now jammed into the bottles, tipping the bottles up to let the petrol soak the cotton cloth. He handed the bottles up to Gibson. We watched Gibson kneeling over the hole. He vanished and we waited. I had my Makarov, still with a few rounds. Cole had a small revolver which I hadn't seen him holding, probably an ankle piece. The other bloke had his pistol, but he was out of rounds. Still, he pointed it towards the garage doors, too scared, maybe, to remember that it was useless.

The gunfire had died down. They were getting ready to storm us. We moved to the back of the boat and crouched. There must have been ten rounds between the three of us. We waited.

'What's keeping him?' Cole said.

A hand reached out and touched the edge of the garage door.

'They're going to toss a grenade in,' I said. 'When they do—'

There was a whoosh and a smashing of glass. The front of the garage lit up bright orange and yellow. We heard men shout, others scream. Gunfire opened up again, near this time, some of it hitting the garage doors. We ducked down, behind the boat. There was an explosion and a crash that shook the whole building. I felt a rush of air that pushed me into the ground. Dust filled my mouth, my nose. The noise was like a wall of pressure squeezing my head. I thought we were probably dead.

Then it went quiet. I tried to move. As far as I could tell, I wasn't injured. I looked over at Cole and saw that his face was white from dust, blood trickled from his nose. He moved his head and looked my way, but his eyes wouldn't focus. He raised his pistol in a kind of reflex action, but it was slow and I thought he was concussed.

The other bloke was dead, his face full of wooden splinters. He hadn't ducked in time.

I slapped Cole on the face a couple of times. He shook his head, put an arm up and pushed me away.

'I'm alright,' he said.

When we pulled ourselves out of the mess, I saw that the garage doors had blown inwards. One was twisted on a hinge, the other had landed on the boat just above our heads. We climbed of the debris and came out of the front with our pistols in our hands.

Some men were standing around and it took me a moment to realize they weren't firing at us. Then I saw Gibson, bent over, his pistol in his hand. I looked up at the windows in the warehouse. Gibson saw me.

'Scarpered,' he said. 'All of them. All that ain't dead.'

And there were plenty who were dead, from both sides. They lay like piles of rubbish. The ones who'd survived were scattered all over, some on the ground, some staring at nothing, some lighting cigarettes with shaking hands.

Cole looked over at the motors. They'd been torn apart by bullet holes, scorched and scraped. He looked at the men lying on the ground, some still burning. He coughed a lung up, spat and bent over, hands on his knees, catching his breath. He stood up straight.

'Fuck,' he said. 'I'm too old and fat for this shit. I thought we'd had it then. Close thing.'

He was right. This hadn't been a fight, it had been a battle. We hadn't won, we'd survived.

I had dust, bits of concrete in my hair, stuck to the sweat on my face. Dust clung to my clothes.

In the distance, headlights came towards us. Cole's phone rang and he answered it. Gibson got down on one knee, ready to fire at the newcomers.

'They're ours,' Cole said, putting the phone in his pocket.

Gibson stood. Cole wiped a hand over his face and spat again. He looked over at me. His look was fierce.

'Wherever you go,' he said darkly, 'wreckage. Shit. They wanted you, they were after you.'

I brushed the concrete from my hair, took my jacket off and knocked the dust out.

'You're here, aren't you? They wanted both of us.'

'How did they know you were coming here?'

'Laing must've called Whelan about his money. Whelan must've called your nephew.'

'My nephew. And he would've guessed you'd come to stop me.'

'Something like that.'

'My nephew. A curse.'

'You know who did this,' I said. 'And it wasn't your nephew alone. And it wasn't fucking Albanians.'

THIRTY-SIX

The bouncers eyed me up as I neared, but they didn't look spooked. They didn't know I was the enemy. One of asked me if I was a member. I pushed him aside. The other thought he'd better try and do his job and stepped forward and put a hand on my chest. I grabbed his wrist with my right hand, bent it inwards and locked his arm at the elbow with my left. He cried out in surprise as much as pain. When he was on his knees, I kicked him in the face and heard something crunch. The first bouncer didn't like the look of things and backed away from me, pulling a radio handset from his jacket. As he was trying to get the thing to work, I smacked him with a right hook and he crumpled to the ground. I stepped over them and passed a gaping city-type who'd gone outside for a smoke.

It must've been near to closing time and there was only a scattering of people inside the club. The music throbbed and a few fat men watched a few thin girls move back and forth to a different tune. The lights were black.

I didn't think they'd want a fuss in front of the punters, no matter how drunk they were. I was right. By the time I was up the stairs and into the casino, the word was out and a dozen pairs of eyes were on me, but nobody came near. Men in monkey-suits shadowed me. They had a plan. They were steering me towards the back offices. That was fine with me.

When I got to the back, they were waiting. There were three of them between me and Dunham's office. They were tooled up, but they were unsure.

It was busier up here than in the club downstairs. Getting pissed and gawking at half-naked women wasn't as popular as getting pissed and throwing your money away.

The punters out on the casino floor couldn't see us, but they'd hear. This bunch knew that, and they knew too that Dunham wouldn't like a fuss, not in the West End, not in his flagship establishment, his guise of respectability, not with the place full of rich tossers who were pissed and handing over their money.

The one in the middle was the red-haired bloke I'd met before. He held an automatic by his side, gripping it tightly. He didn't know what to do. The other two kept their guns holstered. They looked at each other. I wasn't going to stop and wait for them to make their minds up. Red Hair raised his gun.

'Stay right there,' he said.

I kept walking.

'Stay fucking there.'

The other two had their weapons drawn now, but they were backing away, caught in uncertainty. That was good. Red Hair thumbed the safety off and pulled back the hammer, but he was backing away too. When I was six feet away I charged and he panicked and turned side on, forgetting he even had a gun. I slammed my shoulder into his midriff and lifted him off his feet. His gun clattered somewhere behind me. I kept on charging, carrying the man as I went. The other two were fumbling with their guns now, but it was too late. I hit them and the whole lot of us crashed into the wall at the end of the corridor, smashing the plaster into bits. One of them was unconscious, his gun a few feet away, another scuttered towards it. I pulled my Makarov out. Red Hair lunged at me and grabbed my arm. I dropped the gun. I lifted him up and slammed him into the wall. He grunted. I kicked out at the other bloke and caught him on the shoulder. He rolled over and tried to stand and I kicked him again, this time putting the flat of my boot in his chest. Red Hair was pounding me in the face. With my left, I pulled him close. With my right, I whacked him on the jaw. His head snapped back and he went limp in my hand.

A voice behind me said, 'Don't break them, Joe. They're not insured.'

I dropped Red Hair, picked up my Makarov and turned to see Eddie standing there, an amused look on his handsome face. I managed to hold off from smacking him one. I wondered if he knew what was in my mind. He would probably have dodged it anyway. He'd always been a good mover in the ring, and out of it.

'You might as well come in,' he said, holding the door open.

He was armed, but he wasn't in a hurry to pull his piece. There was something wrong with that. He should've wanted me dead. He should've been scared of what I might do. He should've been fucking terrified.

Other men had turned up now, but they stopped short when Eddie held up his hand. He waved them away. I went into the office, the Makarov at my side. Dunham was seated behind his desk, papers in front of him, a burning cigarette in one hand, a pen in the other. He looked at me coldly, but he didn't seem surprised to see me. He didn't even bother with the gun in my hand. They didn't seem to know I was supposed to be dead. I thought that maybe Carl had set me up off his own back, scared of what I'd do to him when I knew the truth of his involvement. I stowed my gun. I'd used it to get into Dunham's office. I wanted to be able to get out again.

Dunham put his pen down and flicked ash into the ashtray. He glanced at Eddie. Eddie shrugged. When they'd finished that performance, Dunham sat back in his seat and said, 'Your instructions not clear enough? Didn't understand what I told you to do?'

'I understood.'

'So why are you here?'

'I want to know what you're up to.'

Eddie looked amused.

'Up to?' he said.

'You've been fucking me from the start.'

'Take it easy, Joe. What are you talking about?'

'All that about the Albanians being our problem. You wanted Cole going after them. You wanted me to push him that way.'

Dunham took a drag of his cigarette and blew smoke out and said, 'The Albanians are a threat.'

'No, they're not. You knew they weren't. You lied.'

'Did we? Why would we do that?'

'Distraction.'

'Start making sense.'

'You knew me and Cole wanted Paget, and you knew I'd kill him when I found him. You had to try and throw us off the train, me especially. But if you told me outright not to go for him, I'd be suspicious, so you gave me that bollocks about the Albanians and about the pact you had with Cole.'

'Like I say, why would we do that?'

'Because you wanted Paget for yourself. Alive. So you had to buy some time while you found him, have me and Cole running around fighting the Albanians. Then when you got him, all you had to do was make me think you were still looking for him. Thinking like that took someone who would know I wouldn't give up on Paget.'

I looked at Eddie. He was leaning with his back to the wall and his hands in his pockets. He was trying to look relaxed. The more he tried, the more I knew he was churning up inside. It wasn't because of fucking me over. That wouldn't have bothered him.

He'd known exactly how to get to me. I almost admired him for it. Haul him in, he must've told Dunham, haul him in and make like the law. Tell him he's got to hand Paget over. Make him think you want Paget for something. Then turn him loose and watch what happens. The last place he'll come looking for Paget is here. The last people he'll suspect will have him is us. If you play him right.

It was only business. I knew that.

I turned back to Dunham. He smiled and raised his glass to Eddie.

'You're right. Eddie told me you'd go after Paget and you'd track him down sooner or later. He said that you might tell Cole where he was. Then we'd have a lot of bother.'

'Why didn't you warn me off?'

'Eddie said you wouldn't listen.'

'What else did he say?'

'He said you were a stubborn, bloody-minded bastard. He said if we warned you off, you'd suspect something. He said you'd go at it twice as hard. He said to stop you, we'd have to kill you.'

'He said a lot of things.'

'He was right, wasn't he? I could use someone like you. Come onto my payroll.'

'Now the bribe. I wouldn't work for you. I should kill you.'

Eddie inched away from the wall.

'Watch it, Joe.'

'If I'd had my way,' Dunham was saying, 'I'd have wiped you out before you even got started. You're a fucking nuisance. I could have stamped on you whenever I wanted.'

'Why didn't you?'

'Eddie.'

'Out of the goodness of his heart?'

I was watching Eddie as I said that. He smiled, but the smile didn't reach his eyes like it usually did.

'There was no goodness in it, Joe,' Eddie said, relaxing his body back against the wall. 'Just logic.'

'Right. You knew if you killed me Cole would suspect something. You should've killed me anyway,' I told Dunham. 'Eddie made a mistake.'

'You're making one. You don't know what you're talking about.'

'I know you saw an opportunity. Paget was on the run. He knew Cole was after him. He knew I'd find him and kill him. He needed protection. So he came to you, or you found him and made him an offer. But you wouldn't take him in unless he had something to bargain with.'

'Oh? What would that be?'

'I thought it was Cole's drugs. He gave them up, I know, because they went back onto the street a few days ago. Sold to a dealer called Laing by a small timer called Doug Whelan. Whelan used to run with Carl Kohl.'

'You're pretty fucking good. I'll give you that.'

'You needed time to set something up. The Albanians are finished and if you could get Cole out of the way too, you'd step into the gap. Cole's nephew would take over his firm, but you'd be boss.'

'You could be a part of it,' Eddie said. 'Be smart.'

'Smart like you, Eddie?'

'Yeah, Joe. Like me.'

His mouth was working alright, but there was nothing in the words. I knew it, and he knew I knew it. I turned back to Dunham.

'You did a deal with Carl Kohl. He was your informant inside Cole's firm. When he told you Cole wasn't going after the Albanians, you got Carl to set up that pantomime at Cole's house. Then Carl gives his uncle dodgy information putting it down to the Albanians, tells Cole where to find them and Cole falls right into your trap.'

Dunham's face had changed now, and there was a glint of fear in the way his mouth had thinned, and I knew he'd ordered my death along with Cole's and that his coolness was a front and the front was crumbling. Not only was I alive, I knew more than he thought I would. He moved his hand, flicking us all away.

'What do you care about Cole? He's fallen, finished. So what?'

'Didn't you hear? Cole didn't fall.'

Dunham half-rose from his seat. His face became a bit redder.

'What?'

I saw Eddie glance at him quickly, and then, just as quickly, he looked away, as if he didn't want to see it.

'The trap you set for Cole,' I said. 'He got out alive. And he knows you set him up.'

'You told him?' Dunham said.

'I told him.'

'Why would he believe you?'

'He doesn't have to. Soon as he finds his nephew, he'll know the truth.'

Dunham's lips drew back over his teeth.

'You don't know what you've done.'

'I hope I've started a war. I hope you all die.'

'Why, Joe?' Eddie said. 'Why would you do that? I know you. You don't care about anyone. Why do you care about Cole? And Paget? Why destroy yourself like that for them?'

I shrugged.

'Why not? At least if I go down, you go down with me.'

'Jesus, that doesn't make sense.'

'Doesn't it? Did you know Dunham ordered my death?'

Eddie's eyes had narrowed now, and I could see a throbbing in his throat.

I said, 'They were waiting, your men. They had Cole in their sights, but they were waiting for me. Only then did they hit us.'

Eddie's hand flexed and tightened into a fist. He tried to smile through it, but he couldn't quite get his mouth to work. He didn't look at his boss. Instead, he shrugged.

'You were in the wrong place. Simple as that.'

'Yeah. It's all so simple.'

'Joe...'

I turned back to Dunham.

'Paget was buying your protection. But there was only one way you could give him protection: kill Cole, and kill me. That was the deal, wasn't it?'

'You're in over your thick fucking head,' Dunham said, the words coming slowly, darkly, sounding like echoes from a deep pit.

'I wondered what your price was. When I realized Glazer was a copper, I thought it must be him that Paget was giving you. He's a good contact, valuable. But he works vice, and you're into bigger things. Glazer wouldn't be anything to you. So, you were after something more. Couldn't have been the drugs because they went to Carl. If not Glazer, if not the drugs, then something else.'

Eddie pushed himself away from the wall.

'Christ, Joe. Leave it, before it's too late.'

'It was too late a long time ago.'

His hand clenched and unclenched. I looked at Dunham, straight into his cold flinty eyes.

'I've seen the DVD.'

His face froze.

'What DVD?' Eddie said, trying to sound casual.

'You know what DVD. The bloke. Who is he?'

Dunham looked like he'd stopped breathing.

'Kill him, Eddie.'

There was something here I wasn't getting. Dunham was scared. That didn't make sense. He shot a glance at Eddie. I looked at Eddie. His eyes were flicking from Dunham to me and back again. He didn't understand it either. Then I knew.

'You haven't seen it, have you?'

'Pack it in, Joe.'

'You don't have it. You can't have. Sure. Paget would need something to hold back, otherwise you'd have killed him. So all of this shit – wiping me out, wiping Cole out, dealing with Cole's nephew – all because you haven't got that DVD, and you want it.'

Eddie's face was flat, his eyes cold. Here it was, the professional, pushing everything else out of his mind because a killer can't afford to feel guilt, can't afford to care. He was forcing it, though. We all knew it.

'Do you know what's on there?' I said to him. 'Did you know there's a girl in the film? Huh? Do you know what he does to her?' I pointed to Dunham. 'He knows. Look at him.'

'And you care?' Dunham said to me.

I glanced at the photo of Dunham's daughter, smiling with Eddie in that sunny country garden.

'Eddie might. Right, Eddie?'

Eddie followed my gaze and quickly looked away. I saw it in his eyes then. He and Dunham were dealing with a cunt who destroyed children, and Eddie hated it. And that was what Dunham feared; that Eddie might not go along on this one, that he might draw a line, that he might, after all, care.

I'd seen that look in Eddie's eyes once before – only once. It was enough. I knew then where Paget was. I should have known before.

'It's just business, Joe,' Eddie said, his voice tight. 'You know that.'

'Well, your fucking business is all a waste of time. I've got a copy. I can fuck you up if I give that copy to the law. Whoever that bloke is will go down and your power over him will go with it.'

Dunham was standing now. His face was red.

'Give us that fucking disc.'

'You'd better give it to us, Joe,' Eddie said.

His voice was low and weary now. He was resigned to it. He sounded to me like he was damned, and knew it.

'Can't do it.'

Eddie shook his head slowly.

'We go back, Joe. Don't do this. You don't want to make an enemy of Vic.'

'Fuck him and fuck you. You want to make a deal with Paget? With that cunt? Do you, Eddie?'

'Joe, don't do this.'

'Shoot him,' Dunham said. 'Shoot him. He's got a gun in a casino. Shoot him. The law won't touch you.'

'Vic—'

There was sweat on Eddie's brow.

'Shoot him.'

'You know what Paget is,' I told Eddie. 'You know what he's done.'

Dunham was breathing heavily through his mouth; his chest heaved. I wanted to rip his lungs out.

'Shoot him.'

'You know what he did to Brenda.'

'Don't.'

Eddie looked at me, held me in his eyes.

'Shoot him, Eddie. Now.'

The room crackled.

'Joe...'

Dunham's face was a mass of fury. I'd stopped breathing. Eddie was frozen, watching.

We hung there, silent, waiting.

Then Dunham blinked and I knew that he was going to murder me. He made a lunge for his desk drawer. I went for my Makarov but Eddie's gun was in his hand before I made it.

'Don't do it, Joe. Wouldn't want to use this.'

My hand hovered. Every muscle in me, every sinew and pulse and throb was shouting at me, screaming to unleash the gun. I wanted Dunham gushing blood. I wanted him to suffer. But, behind all that, my mind told me to hold off. I knew that Eddie would drop me before I fired a shot. They had the advantage: we were in Dunham's casino and

Eddie had a licence for his piece and they knew people on the force. And I was in Dunham's office with an unlicensed Makarov. Eddie could have unloaded into me and they would've claimed I was trying to rob the place. Nobody would have believed them, but that wouldn't have mattered, they would still have got away with it. People like Dunham always got away with it.

But.

I pulled the Makarov from my waistband, and held it by my side. It was a stupid thing to do. Eddie's finger was a millimetre from depressing the trigger. I felt like I was fighting my own body. The strain of holding back shook me. Eddie was steady, his feet firmly planted, properly spaced. He was in the marksman's position, his left hand supporting the grip of his Beretta. I focused on his eyes. They were steady, and dangerous, but there was something else there, something I'd never seen from him, something I would never have expected. There was pain. It was a long way off, deep inside, but it was there.

'Shoot him,' Dunham shouted. 'Fucking shoot him.'

I tightened my grip on the gun. It felt a part of me, cold and hard like the hatred inside, itching to be let go, begging for freedom.

'Don't,' Eddie said quietly.

I heard him, but it was like my mind wasn't working. Don't, it said. Fuck you, my gun said.

Don't.

Finally, my mind broke through, forced apart the hatred. I wanted Paget more than I wanted Dunham. If I was dead now, I couldn't wipe Paget out. Dunham could wait. I let my muscles relax. I eased the Makarov back to my waistband.

I turned to Dunham.

'Cole's outside. I don't come out, he comes in.'

'Bollocks.'

'How do you think I got here? Half an hour ago I was in Barking dodging bullets. I got out. Cole got out. His men got out. We all got out and came here.'

'Fuck Cole. Shoot him.'

'You're short-manned, Dunham, you've spread yourself too thin. You've put your men in Barking, here, your house in the country. Cole's got you outgunned.'

'Shoot him.'

Eddie hadn't holstered his gun. He was still aiming it at me. Still a millimetre from putting a half dozen holes in me.

'Shoot him. Or I'll take your fucking gun and do it myself.'

'Back off, Vic. I'll handle this.'

'Go on, Eddie. Shoot me.'

'Shut up, Joe. Will you for God's sake shut up.'

Dunham slammed his fist on the desk.

'We should have killed him from the word go, instead of trying to deflect him. Don't fuck it up now. Shoot him.'

'You can't, Eddie. You can't because if you do you'll be as guilty as Paget, and that's not in you.'

Dunham said something, but I didn't hear it. I don't think Eddie did either. It wasn't about Dunham now. It wasn't really about Paget. Eddie's gun was steady, but his insides were wavering, screaming at him.

I said, 'You can't do it. There are people who care about you, Eddie. What would they think of you if they knew?'

'Nobody cares about me, Joe.'

'There's someone you care about, though, isn't there?'

Sweat was running down his face. His eyes were scared.

'Nobody cares about me,' he said through gritted teeth.

I could've said something, then, I suppose. I could've told Dunham what I'd seen on Eddie's face when we'd passed Dunham's wife. And what I'd seen on hers: the coldness, aimed at Eddie. Only a woman who knew a man was in love with her would do that.

Instead, I nodded to the photo of Eddie and the girl.

'That man can't do it,' I said.

'And you, Joe?'

'Me? I want Paget to pay.'

'Why?'

Why?

Revenge? Was that it? And for what? For a woman who'd used me, clung to me because I was a monster in a monstrous world, because I had a reputation that could scare the people she was scared of, because I was violent and deadly, because I was useful? Was it for her, the woman I'd seen smile at me like a child smiling at its parent? Was it for Browne? Because he always had hope for me? Because he always had his lousy dying fucking hope for the world, sour as it was and mixed up with his hatred and burning Scotch? Or was it for Kid? Was it for that small thin girl, used and thrown out like something broken, as she had been?

Was it for all of them? For any of them? Or was it,

somehow, for me? For this lumpen thing, this battered and torn wall of muscle?

I heard Dunham slump back in his seat. We'd forgotten about him. He didn't matter.

'I don't know why,' I said.

'Not good enough. I know you, Joe. I know you. You don't care about anyone. You always need a reason to risk your neck. What's the reason, Joe? Why does this matter to you? Why the fuck would you stick your neck out for a dead woman?'

It didn't matter what I said. Eddie wasn't asking me why I'd stick my neck out. He was asking me why he should. I didn't have to answer him. The question was enough.

Before I left, I turned to look at Dunham. I hadn't known before how much he needed Eddie, how much he relied on him. Dunham looked then like what he was: an old man, hollow at the centre with a shell cracking under the weight; an old man whose fear of losing his power was the only thing that kept him desperately clinging to it.

He sagged at the desk and stared at his cigarette, resting in the ashtray and burning away to nothing.

I went out the back way and into the side street. At the end of the street were three cars. I got in the back of the front car. Next to me was Gibson. Cole was in the front passenger seat. I told him where Paget was. We pulled out.

THIRTY-SEVEN

The weak sunlight seeped through the grey cloud cover and gave everything a dull light that was more night than day.

We drove in silence. Cole looked lost in grim thoughts of betrayal and revenge. He stared out the window and barely seemed to care what we were up to.

For men like Cole and Dunham power was their blood; it crawled around their bodies, filled their guts, their muscles. But it was a force that fed on itself – the more power they had, the more they wanted, the more they needed to keep down the others who wanted it. But, when it came down to it, it was all front; they died like anyone else. They had only as much power as people believed they had, and when, in moments like these, the mask slipped, the power slipped too. Cole's nephew had betrayed him, he'd been stupid, had been set up like a mug and almost wiped out. His mask was falling off. Now, staring out the window, he looked old, like Dunham.

When we went through the village, we drove more slowly until I could work out where we were. After a few minutes, I saw the high long brick wall with its iron spikes like teeth. I told the driver to stop. We were still a few hundred yards from the security gate.

Cole turned to me.

'What do we do?' he said. 'Can we rush the place?'

'No. His men'll be looking for us. There's a security gate up ahead. Even if we get past that, there's a hundred yards of clear ground before we get to the house. We'd be out in the open for too long.'

Gibson said, 'How do we get in?'

'We don't. I do.'

I expected Cole to put up a fight about that. He'd wanted Paget for himself and I was taking that away from him. But he didn't argue. He didn't seem to care. He said, 'Tell me what to do.'

'Over the far side the wall is close to trees. I'll get over that way. You hit the front gate with everything. They'll send men to reinforce it and I'll slip in the back. I'll need a car to take me there, round the back way.'

'Why the car?' Gibson said. 'We don't want to split our forces.'

'The wall's too high for me to climb. I'll need to stand on the top of the car and jump over. When I'm over, the car can come back to you. Then you attack.' Cole stared ahead. 'You hear me?'

'When the car comes back, we attack.'

'Right. When I hear you, I'll head for the house.'

I got out of Cole's car and into the rear one. I told the driver what to do and he turned around and followed the wall for a few minutes. When I could see trees overhanging the top of the wall, I told him to get as close to the wall as he could. He parked and I got out and climbed onto the roof. I was still short of the top of the wall, and those spikes were going to make it difficult to get over. I got the two men out of the car and onto the roof. I told them to boost me up higher. They muttered and sweated and cursed my weight, but they got me up high enough so that I could reach the branches of the oaks overhanging the wall. There was a squeak, then, from behind us and we turned to see a teenager on a bike, paper bag over his shoulder. He slowed and gaped up at us. One of the men underneath me said, 'We're pruning the trees.'

The kid cycled away from us fast. I reached up and took hold of the thickest oak limb. It was damp and slippery with some kind of slime. I couldn't get a hold. I tried a thinner branch. It bent under my weight but it was strong enough. I moved along, hand over hand, lifting my legs over the metal spikes. I dropped down and tried to do a parachute landing that I hadn't done in over thirty years. I hit the firm ground hard and it knocked the wind out of me. I rolled over onto my back and lay there, knowing I was too old for this stuff, knowing that I was on a fool's errand, knowing I was dumb, wondering why the fuck I was bothering.

I heard the car start up and drive off. After that it was quiet. Above me, the bare branches rattled in a slight wind and looked like cracks in the sky. Crows, silent, sat and watched me, waiting to feed on my guts.

The sky slid slowly along like a slick of oil on filthy water, like the wasted hours of a wasted life, like Browne's hopeless hope, like the smile in Brenda's face when she remembered something she'd seen, like my chances to help her, like the world, a mass of people caught in that oil, like me, crawling somewhere, anywhere.

Fuck.

My head was clear for once, like the icy air that stung my eyes; clear, now that I wanted it to be dull and far off; clear, now that I wanted to murder and hide the deed in murk. My bastard head, clear, setting it all before me, crisp and cold: my failures; my debts unpaid. Yes, it was all clear.

Then I heard a far-off crash. Cole had rammed the gate. There was another crash. The world had slid on.

I got up and moved forward through the trees, stopping short of the open grass. From where I stood, I could see the back of the house. There was fifty yards of open ground. There was a swimming pool there that I hadn't known about, tables and chairs around it. Beyond that, French windows that opened onto a patio.

There was another crash at the front gate. Lights came on in the house and the front door opened. Two men ran from the house, weapons at the ready. There were shouts from somewhere. The crackle of automatic fire carried on the thin cold air.

I pulled my Makarov. I looked around once more. There was nobody my side of the house. I moved, running straight for the patio.

The French windows were locked. I moved along the wall, trying other windows as I went. It was the kitchen door that let me in. Someone had left the key in the lock on the inside.

I used the butt of my gun to break the glass, my jacket muffling the sound. I opened the door slowly and stepped in, crunching glass. I closed the door and stood a moment, listening. I heard nothing except clatter of gunfire that sounded far off now. I moved through the kitchen and into the gloomy, curtained dining room. Light came from somewhere beyond the open doorway. I neared the light and stopped again. I'd heard something. The stairway was to my right. A creak had sounded there. I stayed in the dim doorway.

A ghost passed me and I caught a smell of creamy flowers, like the kind of smell Brenda's face lotions had. It was Dunham's wife. She wore a thin white nightdress that flowed around her like mist. She stopped a couple of feet from me, as if she'd sensed something. I held my breath. She turned slowly. For a moment, she saw me and did nothing, didn't even breathe, and I thought she was going to turn away and walk off into the night, disappear like that mist surrounding her. And then her eyes widened and her neck muscles tightened and I knew she was going to scream her head off. I flung out my hand and grabbed her by the throat and pulled her into the dining room. She thrust her hands up to mine, trying to claw them off. Her nails dug in deep, and she scraped, and all the while she was doing this I was lifting her off the ground and her feet were kicking my legs, scrambling for a hold. I pulled her close to me.

'I'm going to put you down. If you scream, I'll hurt you.'

She nodded as much as she could, her eyes wide in terror, her mouth trying to work, trying to say something. I let her down and loosened my hand but kept it on her neck. With my other hand, I pocketed the gun and took a handful of her nightdress and turned it tight and pulled her towards me. She staggered and threw her hands around my arm to hold herself steady.

She held on like that for a few seconds, letting her breathing become regular, letting her heartbeat slow. Her face was white, her lips pale. She shivered and squeezed my arm again, trying, I thought, to stop herself fainting. We were in a kind of dance, locked together by our arms, and by powerful and murderous men.

After a while, the colour came back to her face. It came with a vengeance. Her lips flamed, her cheeks burned red, her eyes flashed fire. She had guts, this one.

I couldn't hear the gunfire any more. If Dunham's men had got the upper hand, I didn't have much time.

I still had a hold of the woman's nightdress. She trembled, but she stood straight and looked me directly in the eyes.

'Who are you?'

'It doesn't matter.'

'Yes. It does. It matters a lot. This is my home.'

'My name wouldn't mean anything to you.'

'I see. One of them. You want my husband, I suppose.'

'No.'

'I could scream.'

I tightened my hand around her slim neck. 'No, you couldn't.'

My middle finger touched my thumb. Her eyes went big. I loosened my grip as her hands started to pull at my arm. She staggered back a step, rubbed her throat.

'I suppose you enjoyed that.'

'No.'

I took my hand away. The noise of gunfire picked up again.

'What do you want? What's all that noise out there?'

'That noise is Bobby Cole.'

She caught her breath.

'That's shooting? What's he doing? What does he want with us? My husband's not here.'

'He doesn't want your husband. He wants the same as me: a man.'

'I don't understand.'

'Yes, you do. Where is he?'

'The police—'

'They won't save you. Now I can tear the place apart, or you can tell me where he is.'

'My daughter's here.'

'I know. You don't want her caught up in the crossfire, do you?'

She shook her head.

'Where is he?'

'Please, just go.'

'Where is he?'

'Why do you think anyone's here?'

'Eddie told me.'

That stopped her. I let go of her nightdress. If she noticed, she didn't do anything about it. She could have run. Instead, she said, 'That's a lie. Eddie wouldn't tell you anything.'

'I came here before.'

'I remember. So?'

'Today I saw something in Eddie; I saw pain. I only ever saw that once before; here, with you.'

'Me?'

'I saw the way you ignored him, the way you were cold to him. You wanted to hurt him. And he was hurt.'

'So?'

'You knew who Eddie and your husband were dealing with, what kind of man, what monster. And you hated them for it. But your husband is a ruthless man and I don't think you'd expect anything else from him. But Eddie... your anger was targeted at Eddie. And it hurt him, as you knew it would.'

'You don't know that.'

Her hand went back to her throat. I don't think she knew she'd done it.

'I know it,' I said. 'I know it like I know my own face. It fits. It makes sense in a mad way. I would never have thought it until today. But now I know. He's in love with you.'

Her lips were closed tightly. Her eyes blazed. She breathed heavily. Her heart must've been racing. Her hand stroked her throat. I could see her vein pulsing there.

'You're guessing,' she said. 'You don't know anything about me.'

'There's something else. They brought me here.'

'You're talking in riddles.'

'There was no reason for them to do that. When they got me here, they didn't tell me anything new. If they'd wanted to give me a message, they could've done it any time. So I had to think why they would bring me here.'

'And now you have the answer.'

'It was misdirection. They brought me right to where they were hiding the man I was after and made me think they were after him too. For a while it worked. This was the last place I thought he was stashed. It was twisted thinking, a joke. Your husband doesn't think like that. He's a club, a hammer.'

'And Eddie...?'

'He's a blade.'

'Even if that was the case—'

'It was the case. It is.'

'You're so sure.'

'Yes.'

'And now you want me to point him out to you. You're going to kill him, aren't you? You want me to condemn a man to his death.'

'He's already dead. The question is, do you take me to him or do you wait until Cole arrives with his army and rips the place apart, you with it, your daughter maybe. Is he worth it?'

I wasn't touching her now. She looked up into my face, her eyes wide, her chest heaving. Her hand left her throat, glided down, stroked her nightdress.

'Why do you want him? Why do you want to kill him?'

'I knew a woman once, a bit older than you, and a girl, a bit older than your daughter. That's why.'

She looked into my eyes for a long time. The sounds outside didn't matter. Finally, she nodded and her arm lifted and her hand pointed towards the side of the house.

'There's an extension. He's in there.'

'Describe the room.'

'It's about twenty foot by fifteen. There's a single bed along the connecting wall and a table and chairs around the place. There's a bathroom at one end. Two windows are in the far wall. The door has a lock. I don't have a key.'

'Right. Now go and get your daughter and lock your-selves up somewhere. Don't come out.'

She went, but at the bottom of the stairs she stopped and turned.

'It should have been my husband,' she said. 'Or Eddie. Not you.'

I watched her go, then went and found the extension. The door was shut. There was no light coming through the cracks around the edges. It was a heavy door, probably locked. I knew he'd be in there, listening, armed, waiting. If I tried to open the door, I'd alert him. I took a step forward and put my ear to the wood. I couldn't hear a thing except the distant rattle of the gunfight and my own heart pounding in my throat. But I knew he was there. I knew it.

The door was solid and if I went for the windows, I'd be an easy target. That didn't matter so much, just as long as I got to him. I didn't have time to work at this slowly, Dunham would have men on the way and who knew when the law would turn up.

I pulled the Makarov from my pocket, moved away from the door and took a breath and aimed. The gun bucked in my hand. The shots were explosions in the small space. The lock tore apart. I threw myself at the door. It crashed open, smashed into furniture. I fell and half-rolled and got back to my feet and brought the gun up and aimed into the darkness. And froze. A face was there, small and white, something glinting below it. Above it, something else hovered; a mask, long and thin, a scar of a mouth, razor-blade eyes.

The scream came from behind me. It was wretched, savage. I half turned to see who it was, but, as I turned, I knew who it must have been and why. I lifted my gun as I spun back around. It was too late. The flashes lit up the room and blinded me. The roar of gunfire split the air and deafened me. The screaming started again, and it didn't stop. Something slammed into my left arm and threw me back. I fired blind, the gun rocking in my hand, the rounds slamming all over the place. My arm split with pain. I fired until my gun was dry. The flashing lit the room and left after-images on my eyes; a man with a girl, a knife. Something ripped through my side. My mind screamed at me to fill the gun. 'You're naked,' my mind said. 'You're dead,' it said. I had to get another magazine from my jacket pocket but my free arm was useless now, a lump of meat. I tried to find the faces again. I saw them. The girl had her eyes shut. Above her, the mask gleamed sickly, the mouth twisted now, mangled with pain.

The woman was in the doorway. Light came through her nightdress and surrounded her with a silver mist. She was still screaming, her hands at her mouth, staring at her daughter. Blood had spattered her. My blood. I turned back to Paget. I should've charged him, not given him time to aim. All he had to do was squeeze. He was good at squeezing. I couldn't do anything. I was lead. I was dumb. I was a carcass waiting to drop. I was dead and I knew it and I didn't much care, except my mocking mind was clear and I knew I'd failed her, and that hurt.

The woman's hands were still at her mouth, but she'd stopped screaming. I waited. She waited. Time waited.

Nothing happened.

The gun pointed straight at me. And then I saw that the slide was all the way back. It hadn't recoiled. His gun was empty. Still I couldn't move. I knew he'd slice the girl's throat. I felt coldness creep down my right side. Then I felt stabbing pain in my ribs. The room tilted and my head went light. I was leaking blood fast. The pain disappeared. I saw Brenda. I saw Kid. I lived with the dead.

We stood there, the four of us. I saw Dunham's daughter, and the blade Paget held to her throat. It was a kind of joke; both of us standing like actors on a stage, waiting for the cue, both surging with the need to destroy the other, both scared, both impotent, both unable to reload and finish the job; me with a fucked-up arm, him with a blade in his free hand. I should have charged anyway. Fuck the girl.

The blade moved across the girl's throat. He was going to cut her. I knew it, knew how his mind worked. I lunged forward. And knew I'd made a mistake. I'd done what he wanted me to do. He sneered and turned the blade towards me. At the last instant, I turned side on. The blade sliced through my left arm, my fucked-up arm. Someone screamed. It might've been me. I hit Paget and the girl like a bag of cement. We crashed to the ground. Something broke under us. My gun fell from my grip. The girl was there, somewhere. I didn't care any more. I wanted Paget. Everything was a mass of bodies, seething limbs, seeping blood, pain, darkness. I saw him. His face was screwed into a fury of agony. His fists pounded my face, but he had no room to move and there was no power in the punches. His eyes were wide, he breathed frantically.

'Cunt,' he said. 'Cunt.'

My left was fucked; it had a gaping bullet wound, the knife was stuck in the muscle. I threw a punch with my right that missed and hit the floor. Paget laughed hysterically. I grabbed for his throat. I saw the woman near. She kicked us, shouted madly. The girl was on the floor, crying, her leg trapped beneath us. Paget saw them. He saw the knife in my arm and seized it and pulled it out. The pain was electric. He tried to plunge the blade in my throat, but he kept missing. He reached over and tried to skewer the girl. I tugged him and he missed her. The woman pulled the girl free. I threw another punch, landed it on his jaw, but there was no weight behind it. I needed leverage. I got to my knees. The room spun. I hauled him up with my right. He laughed. The knife arced towards me. I put all my energy into my torso and shoulders and legs. I stood and wrenched him up. The knife flew from his hand. He laughed harder. He collapsed and I saw that he was crying. His right leg was pumping blood. His knee was shattered. One round had hit home. Christ knows what had kept him up. I lifted him by his throat. His hands reached up and took hold of my jacket, pulling himself up, keeping the weight off his knee.

'All this,' he said through blood and spit. 'Insane.'

He saw the punch coming. I hit the top of his skull. It felt like I'd broken bones in my hand.

'Cunt,' he said. 'Dumb fucking cunt. All this, for what?'

I reached down and took a hold of his face and turned it up so that I could see his eyes. Pain was coming at me all over, my arm, my side, my hand. It didn't matter. It was important that he hear me, that he understood. It was the most important thing in the world.

'I want to remember her alive,' I said. 'I want to remember her alive, not in a fucking alley with a face of blood.'

'All this? For a fucking whore? Why?'

'I want to remember her smile,' I told him, snarling. 'But I can't see it, not without the blood.'

'She used you, you dumb cunt. She knew who you were.'

'You took that from me. You took her smile and her shining eyes.'

'She was grassing us to the law. She was only with you because she thought you'd protect her.'

'I know.'

I smashed his face. Pain shot through my fist, through my arm. Some bone was cracked. It didn't matter. He coughed blood.

'It doesn't make any sense,' he said, to himself, I thought. 'It doesn't make any fucking sense.'

'I know.'

He pulled at me, his hands grappled for a hold.

'Dunham needs me. I'm valuable to him. I can't die. He'll gut you. He needs me.'

'I know.'

I hit him again but I couldn't ball my fist. He shook it off. I hit him again, but it was weaker. I staggered. He pulled. I was losing strength. He pulled harder.

'Cunt,' he said. His voice rasped.

I tried to hit him again, but my body was weak, my hand busted, my punches useless. He clawed at me. I thought I'd failed.

Something tugged at my elbow. The woman was there. There was something in her hand. She held it out to me. I took it. I held it. Paget saw it. He flailed. I smashed him on the head with the butt of my Makarov. I heard his skull crack. He held onto my jacket, his fingers, like daggers, tried to pull me down with him, tried to tear at me. His face was the colour of porridge. He wanted to rip my throat out. I could feel the life draining from me. I could see blood pooling at my feet. I didn't know if it was mine. We grappled with each other, each trying to tug the other down to some hell.

'She wanted to be a beautician,' I said. 'That's why you cut her face off.'

He laughed madly, and blood fell from his mouth.

'She died screaming.'

'As you should.'

His face curdled in pain.

'Cunt,' he said.

His head swayed and his fingers loosened. I swayed with him and felt cold. The Makarov fell from my hand. My arm was heavy. I was losing strength and he knew it. He lunged and fell on his broken knee and screamed. His hands were on me, pulling me down, down, and I was afraid. I reached for the gun. The room moved. I got hold of the gun, I lost it, I got it and tried with all my strength to hold onto it.

'Madness,' he said.

I clubbed him with the gun, pounding his face, mashing it to pulp, but still he held on, still he looked up, his mouth a wrecked smile.

'Madness.'

'I know.'

I kicked him off. He sprawled backwards and rolled over onto his front and crawled to my feet in some kind of final act, a death throe. I raised the gun and smashed it into his skull, again and again, crushing the bone and pulping the thing that had been a head until it was nothing but a kind of clot of flesh and bone and brain and blood. I wanted to enjoy it. I didn't. I felt sick. Madness.

THIRTY-EIGHT

The woman and girl had gone. I walked out on shaking legs. Blood was running down my shirt, down my trouser leg. I was cold all over.

Cole stood at the top of the steps, his men around him, Dunham's men face down on the ground, lined up, arms behind their heads. I saw bodies in the distance, by the gate. One of Cole's men was being propped up by comrades, another held his shoulder. Cars were coming up the driveway. Cole looked at me. They all looked at me.

'Jesus Christ.'

When the cars got there, Cole's men got in. Cole helped me get into one of the cars. He got in beside me.

'Will you make it?' he said.

'Dunno.'

We took a long route back because Cole didn't want his car tagged on some CCTV camera, returning from a crime scene. We didn't say anything. There'd be comeback for this, we both knew that. It didn't matter.

As soon as we got back, Browne got to work on me.

'Happy now?' he said as he cut my shirt away.

He didn't touch the booze while he was looking after me. It was all too much for him, though, and Cole sent his doctor round. Browne didn't complain this time. I passed in and out of consciousness for a couple of days. Browne told me there'd been nothing on the news about Paget, which meant Dunham must have cleaned it up. I didn't think he'd come for us straight away, but Cole had a couple of men at Browne's place just the same. There'd been a lot of stuff on the news about the fight in Barking, but Cole had been lucky about the location and had managed to cover his involvement. The news said something about a turf war and Dunham had had to fend off the law. But he had contacts and the thing had died down after a few days, blamed on rival East European gangs, who nobody particularly cared about. As long as they were killing each other and not some local upstanding citizen, everyone could pretend it didn't happen.

After a few days, Compton and Bradley and Hayward came round. There was a bit of fuss outside when they came face to face with Cole's men, who wouldn't let them through, but Browne settled things and they came traipsing in like they'd come to pay their respects to the dear departed.

I was propped up in Browne's favourite chair, bandaged around my arm and torso. It only hurt if I breathed. There was a break in the clouds and sunlight bounced around the room and lit up the specks of dust floating in the air.

'Had some kind of accident, Joe?' Bradley said.

'Sure.'

'Must've been a bad one.'

'Yeah.'

I didn't want them there, but Browne told them all to sit down. He went and made them tea. He was up to something but I was too fucked-up to argue. So, we all sat around and drank Browne's tea and they asked me how I was feeling and that kind of thing. When they ran out of small talk, there was silence. Then Compton said, 'We've heard a few things. Interesting things. Seems Dunham's had something of a dispute.'

'Uh-huh.'

'Paget's disappeared,' Hayward said.

'So?'

'Disappeared for good,' Bradley said. 'From what we hear.'

'Yeah?'

Compton smiled wryly.

'Unbelievable,' he said.

Browne cleared his throat.

'Joe,' he said.

He made eyes at me and I wondered what the fuck he was on about. And then I realized. I shook my head.

He stared at me, furious. But he didn't say anything to the coppers.

Compton saw it, but he didn't know what it was about.

'Well…' Browne said. 'I think Joe needs some rest.'

Compton got up. The others followed and they all started to file out.

'You knew, didn't you?' I said.

They stopped. Compton turned.

'Knew? Knew what?'

'You knew who I was. You knew about Brenda before I told you. You knew what I'd do.'

Compton smiled.

'Did we?'

'You knew she was the one who'd sent the evidence against Paget to Glazer. You knew who I was. And you knew I'd go after Hayward. He was bait.'

'We thought you might. But, Christ, we didn't think you'd get to him that quickly. His wife wasn't supposed to be there.'

'She's about ready to divorce me,' Hayward said.

'He ain't kidding,' Bradley said. 'And you thought Dunham was tough.'

They laughed. It was funny now. They had what they wanted, they were all alive, Paget was dead. Everything was funny.

But...

Still I had the feeling about these blokes. They were law, after all. And there was something phony about this act of theirs. They were making too much of an effort to be friendly.

'When did you know about me?' I asked Compton.

'The hospital. The first time I saw you. I recognized you. There were photographs of you from the Elena file. And, yes, we knew about you and Brenda. We thought she might've kept some evidence of what happened. We thought she might've given it to you, but then you didn't seem to know Glazer's role in things and we thought we must've been wrong.'

That was a cue. I ignored it.

'But you wound me up and let me loose anyway. Just to see.'

'We gave you enough rope,' Bradley said.

'What you did, you did yourself,' Compton said. 'You

worked things out. You wanted vengeance. Like I told you before, we're the law. We can't be involved in the planning of a crime.'

'You didn't want to get your hands dirty.'

'If you like. You have to see it from our point of view.'

'Yeah.'

With that, they walked out, Browne following them to the door. Then they were gone.

'Why didn't you give them the DVD?' Browne said, coming back into the room. 'That was evidence. They could use it to get these people.'

'I don't trust them.'

'You don't trust anybody. So, you want it for yourself, I suppose. The DVD. You're going to use it to find the people left. You want it for your so-called revenge.'

'Yeah. My revenge.'

I slept for a while. When I woke up, Browne was sitting on the sofa staring at me. It was dusk, or maybe dawn He got up and closed the curtains and turned on the light.

I said, 'What's wrong?'

He reached down and picked up Brenda's box and handed it to me.

'You never looked properly,' he said. 'I'll go make some tea.'

I opened the box. There were Brenda's bottles of lotions and tubes of creams all laid out in their cardboard slots. Underneath was a cotton dress and, beneath that, an envelope. On the front, in Brenda's handwriting, was written, 'Joe'. I ripped the envelope open. My hands shook. 'Dear Joe', the letter said, and something cracked inside me.

Dear Joe,

I suppose if you've found this box it means I'm dead. I thought I would be. I'm glad, though, in a way. I know you'll know what to do with this, what it means.

We've just got back from the Winston Churchill. I'm a little drunk, but I keep thinking of the day we had today, up London, looking in all them fine shops. You brought me this gift set in Liberty's. Thank you.

I suppose you'll know by now that I used you. You asked me what I wanted, remember? You didn't believe that I could just want to be with you. Well, you were right. To begin with. I was scared, because of what I was doing and who I was doing it to. I was scared and I needed someone strong. I needed you.

Like I say, that was to begin with. The truth is, I did love you, Joe. I do love you. And I'm using you and it tears me up inside. But I do love you.

Don't hate me, Joe. Please. What I did, I did for the children. Someone had to and I was in the best position to do it. I took my chances, I knew what I was doing. Don't hate me.

There's one more thing I want to say, Joe. Don't destroy yourself for me. Whenever I think of you, I think of that old ship, that warhorse, The Fighting Temeraire. Remember you told me about it? About how, in that picture, it was being tugged in to be broken up? I don't want to think of you like that. I

PHILLIP HUNTER

don't want you to go seeking revenge for what's happened to me. Please don't.

Well, that's about all I've got to say.

Goodbye, Joe.

Love, always,

Brenda.

I heard a noise and looked up. Browne was at the doorway, a mug in each hand. He looked at me and nodded, once.

'Tea's up,' he said.

I folded the letter in half and put it down.

'I thought you were leaving,' I said. 'Going to your sister's.'

He came in, handed me the mug of tea.

'Eh? Oh, well, I'll have to stay awhile. I've got the violet in the garden,' he said. 'Have to make sure that's alright. Can't leave it to you, can I? You'd probably kill it.'